Praise for Alvaro Zinos-Amaro's Traveler of Worlds:

"Silverberg is as brilliant as you expect him to be, and Alvaro Zinos-Amaro knows how to bring that brilliance out of him. An excellent and important book."
　　　—Mike Resnick, author of *Santiago*

"Reading Alvaro Zinos-Amaro's interviews with Robert Silverberg is a lot like parasailing: an exhilarating rush through atmosphere higher and richer than one usually inhabits, with sweeping views of everything below. Zinos-Amaro is a skilled interviewer and Silverberg a brilliant polymath looking back at a long life well spent. Writing, reading, travel, art, opera, archeology, food—he talks wittily and interestingly about them all. I learned something on every page."
　　　—Nancy Kress, author of *Yesterday's Kin*

"Robert Silverberg is always interesting to talk to, as he is a brilliant writer and a well-read and well-traveled man, as well as a long-time participant, observer, and historian of the science fiction community. Within that community he tends to be a fairly cool and deflective character, who talks about many other things before himself. That habit means this book is distinctly more than a sequence of ordinary conversations with him, because the well-prepared and congenial Zinos-Amaro has taken the time, and Silverberg has given the time, to talk at some length, and coherently, about many of his central interests, including his own life. It makes for a typically indirect but ultimately fascinating portrait of the artist, and a very nice supplement to his wonderful novels and stories."
　　　—Kim Stanley Robinson, author of *Aurora*

"Bob Silverberg seems to have been born with delight in the sense of 'enwonderment.' As he says in his insightful conversations with Alvaro Zinos-Amaro, '[familiarity] leads to a lack of strangeness. And wonder requires a certain amount of strangeness.' Pursuing that wonder, following a curiosity about archaeology and anthropology, history and modern cultures, and, of course, the future, led to a career illuminating such concepts in exquisite fiction and nonfiction. Readers have long shared in Bob's joy of discovery. Now, Bob and Alvaro's perceptive dialog allows us to discover the brilliant man behind the writing."
    —Shelia Williams, editor of *Asimov's Science Fiction*

"*Traveler Of Worlds* is a fascinating and erudite conversation that invites the reader to become a mesmerized fly on the wall. This is your best chance to peer into the life and mind of the legendary Robert Silverberg—take it."
    —Jack Skillingstead, author of *Life on the Preservation*

TRAVELER OF WORLDS

CONVERSATIONS WITH

Robert Silverberg

TRAVELER OF WORLDS

CONVERSATIONS WITH

Robert Silverberg

ALVARO ZINOS-AMARO

FAIRWOOD PRESS
Bonney Lake, WA

TRAVELER OF WORLDS

A Fairwood Press Book
August 2016
Copyright © 2016 Alvaro Zinos-Amaro & Robert Silverberg

Fairwood Press
21528 104th Street Court East
Bonney Lake, WA   98391
www.fairwoodpress.com

Cover and Book design by Patrick Swenson

ISBN: 978-1-933846-63-7
First Fairwood Press Edition: August 2016
Printed in the United States of America

For Rebecca

Contents

Preface   10

Introduction   12

The Vividness of Landscape   15

Aesthetics   45

In the Continuum   98

Enwonderment   127

Libraries   167

Potpourri   195

After the Myths Went Home   226

Afterword: Travels With Bob   271

PREFACE
Alvaro Zinos-Amaro

This book was composed in eight days but took two decades to write.

In 1996, when I was seventeen years old, I discovered Robert Silverberg's work with *Nightwings*. The subtle melancholy of its three lyrical novellas moved me deeply. Beyond this, I was thrilled to realize that I had made first contact with a vast and cool intelligence, one that had spent decades producing enthralling stories now awaiting my discovery. I immediately hunted down as many Silverberg books as I could find, reading perhaps fifty over the next two years. It was a bibliophilic infatuation of the first order.

But I wasn't just hooked on the work itself.

With each book, I was struck by a growing number of questions regarding the author. How could one person have written so much, and at such a high level? His characters seemed to express every possible view and opinion—what did *he* think, and why? Where had his travels taken him? What kind of music and films did he enjoy? What were his eccentricities and foibles and hobbies? What about the mysterious breakdown through overwork in the 1960s, and the mid-career retirement in the '70s? Above all, wherefrom sprang the creative well that had thrust up so many works of visionary wonder? The mysterious "aloofness" that other writers ascribed to Silverberg, the seeming impenetrability of his persona, only made these questions more tantalizing.

So I did research, starting with the backlog of whatever interviews I could find, moving on to *Starmont Reader's Guide 18*, then lengthier academic studies. Correspondence seemed the next logical step, and in 1998, at the age of nineteen, I wrote Robert-soon-to-be-Bob Silverberg a fan letter. Over the next six years our exchanges engendered a long-distance friendship, cemented when we finally met in person in 2004. Eight years later, we published a book called *When the Blue Shift Comes*. For me it grew, at least in part, out of that same desire to *understand* I had experienced, fever-like, at seventeen.

The book you're holding in your hands right now—or perhaps reading on a screen—stems even more explicitly from that aspiration to peel back layers, to decipher, and ultimately to connect.

Thus, while it is true in a literal sense that the conversations comprising *Traveler of Worlds* unfolded over four weekends in 2015, they were informed and shaped by years of deep, abiding curiosity about Silverberg's art and life, his experiences, his attitudes and beliefs. "It is my craft and my science to Watch," says a character in *Nightwings*. I'm delighted to share with you this investigation, the result of my own budding craft and science.

INTRODUCTION
Gardner Dozois

Science fiction is a field that has been graced by many very smart people, many of whom I've had the privilege of knowing: Gene Wolfe, Samuel R. Delany, the late Joanna Russ and Alice Sheldon, Brian W. Aldiss, the late Tom Disch, Isaac Asimov, Avram Davidson, and Fred Pohl, and many others.

Robert Silverberg could without hesitation be added to the list of SF's smartest practitioners, and even amongst this brainy bunch, his intelligence stands out as impressive, as is the depth and breadth of his erudition, and the *range* of topics that interest his restless intellect. (It's not widely realized by SF readers today, who mostly know only his huge body of novels and short fiction, but in his time Silverberg has written over thirty acclaimed non-fiction books, on topics that range from El Dorado to the Mound Builders of the American West to Mesopotamia to the Seven Wonders of the Ancient World, and from ghost towns to Sequoias to mammoths to atomic scientists to the tribesmen of prehistoric Europe.) Silverberg is also one of the most-traveled of SF writers, having followed his interests to exotic destinations all over the world.

Perhaps all this helps to explain the air of sophistication that Silverberg generates, for although there are other smart and well-educated people in the genre, Silverberg has always struck me as the most *urbane* of all the field's practitioners. It's his effortless urbanity, sophistication, and charm that has made him the best Toastmaster ever to work a Hugo or Nebula Award ceremony (and believe me, in more than forty years in the field, I've seen dozens of Toastmasters, some embarrassingly inept or lame, most of whom were so boring that even the flies fell asleep and dropped from the ceiling). That and his wit, which is dry as a bone and sharp as a razor, so that you can be cut by it and not realize it until you walk away and your head falls off.

That wit and urbanity, as well his deep knowledge of the history of the field and his understanding of how writing works, have enriched and enlivened the many discussions I've had with Silverberg over the decades, at innumerable dinners and lunches, sitting around in bars at science fiction conventions, as a participant in convention panel discussions, even snowbound in a car on the Massachusetts Turnpike during an unseasonable Spring blizzard.

You may never get the chance to have a meal with Silverberg or chat with him in a bar, but here in *Traveler of Worlds: Conversations with Robert Silverberg*, Alvaro Zinos-Amaro has given you the next best thing, transcripts of interviews with Silverberg that give you a taste of his wit and erudition and incisiveness of intellect, and at least a feeling for what it would be like to sit across the dinner table from him.

Until you can track him down at a science fiction convention and invite him to dinner or buy him a drink, this will have to do.

CHAPTER 1
The Vividness of Landscape

Alvaro Zinos-Amaro: In your essay "Starting Too Soon" you wrote that you coped with the problems of early success as a full-time writer by traveling a lot, reading a lot, getting out into the world of events and conflicts as much as you dared. What were some of those experiences? How did you participate in events and conflicts?

Robert Silverberg: When I wrote that I didn't mean events in the sense that I would join the Foreign Legion. I meant getting involved with other human beings, instead of—as some writers do—sitting behind my typewriter all day long.

Zinos-Amaro: Did you attend marches or protests?

Silverberg: No. I've never been an activist. I believe in the futility of marches. I don't think we can cure AIDS by marching, or cancer by marching. The only time I have seen that kind of activism cause any real kind of change was during the Vietnam War. We had constant demonstrations against the war by the large baby boom population that was at risk of being sent *to* that war, and had every motive for trying to halt the hostilities. The Vietnam War caused such uproar in the country that it became necessary for us to extract ourselves from it, and we did, even though we failed there. It's a war we lost, even though we pretend we've never lost a war.

Zinos-Amaro: What about the march at Selma, for instance?

Silverberg: Yes, the civil rights marches changed things too. Though what really brought forth the change in civil rights was, of all things, the ascension to the presidency of Lyndon Johnson—not one of my favorite politicians—who showed great force in changing the legal existence of segregation.

When I wrote the column you mentioned, I pointed out that if a writer stays home all the time, the writer has no knowledge of what's happening around him. We didn't have the Internet then, we didn't have all the wonderful media that are now available. And so you spiral inward on yourself. What I meant was that I got out of the house as much as I could without deviating from my working schedule.

For example, one day a week I went down to the New York editorial offices and moved around visiting editors, chatting, having lunch with them, being very social. I thought, "Otherwise, I will lose touch with the real world." And if you lose touch with the real world you cannot write about invented worlds.

After I moved to California, of course, it became impossible to go down to the editorial offices, and I withdrew more and more from interaction with the world as I got older. I preferred to be in my own house and read.

Zinos-Amaro: You also wrote less.

Silverberg: I wrote a great deal less. These were two linked processes. I was now doing the spiraling inward, quite aware of what I was doing, and preferring the reclusive life of an elderly writer. When I wrote that column for *Galileo* I was in my forties and I was writing about the way I had lived in my twenties. Well, in my seventies it was an entirely different attitude.

Zinos-Amaro: You've observed that most science-fiction writers are great world travelers, and that the greater the scope of one's travels, the richer one's science fiction tends to be.

Silverberg: Heinlein went everywhere. Jack Williamson, at eighty-five, after having had colon cancer, went to China. I've been to a great deal of the world. On the other hand we have the case of Isaac Asimov, who rarely left his own apartment, not because he had any psychoses that nailed him indoors, but he just didn't like to fly or go anywhere. Isaac was a very inventive writer, but if you look at the worlds he invented for the Foundation series, they all look like Manhattan, and there are no aliens in them, either.

I felt very early as a writer that the more I saw of the world, the more I could transform the differences from New York's life into invented ones. You have to start from a base, and if the only base I had was Manhattan, I could make the buildings shorter or taller, but if I hadn't seen France, or California, or the West Indies, or you name it, then I didn't have a broad enough base.

When I was a boy, during World War II, it was impossible to go anywhere. There were travel limitations because of the war. I lived in New York then, and one couldn't get more than fifty miles without extreme logistic difficulties. When I was, I believe, eight years old, a friend of my father's gave me a subscription to the *National Geographic* magazine and opened the world to me. I looked at these photographs and thought, "There's Shanghai here, there's Timbuktu, there's Nepal. I'll go to them someday."

Zinos-Amaro: Your desire to travel was born that early?

Silverberg: Yes. I looked at the pictures and thought, "I want to see these," just as when I looked at the dinosaurs in the museum it stirred a great romantic fervor in me for the distant past and the distant future, neither of which I could visit except through science fiction. But I knew I *could* visit these countries once I grew up and could make my own choices, and once this annoying war got out of the way.

Well, as it happens, though I've traveled widely I've never been to Shanghai, or Timbuktu, or Nepal, and I never will. But I *have* been to a lot of places.

Zinos-Amaro: Have you been to Tibet?

Silverberg: No, not to Tibet. I haven't traveled widely in Asia. I've been to Japan, once. I've not been to China, not been to India, and I've gotten too old now for these very challenging countries, and I'm not going to go there. But so far as Europe and the Middle East, even Africa, I've been around quite a lot.

The first real trip I took was an expedition to Philadelphia. Philadelphia is ninety miles from New York City. But when you grow up in a world where you can't go *anywhere*, going to Philadelphia is an overwhelming experience the first time, especially if you do it as I did it, when you're fifteen. I went with a friend, another science fiction fan of about my age. We took the bus down from the terminal in Manhattan, got off the bus in Philadelphia, and I was astounded to see they had a different kind of lamppost there. "Look," I said to him, "those lampposts aren't like the ones in New York!" Which he thought was a preposterous observation. But to me it held great significance. Cities differ. And Philadelphia didn't look much like Manhattan in any way. Well, I got beyond Philadelphia. By the time I was twenty-one I had been to England and France, and I've gone on from there. It's been an essential part of my writing artillery, to be able to draw on these alien landscapes.

Zinos-Amaro: But maybe there's a counterargument to be made here. I once read a profile in *USA Today* of a very famous writer who hadn't flown or had any interest in world travel in thirty years. "You can see everything you need to know about life in one square mile of the Earth, no matter where it is," the writer said. "Everything you need to know, everything you need to think about and work your way through is going to happen in life, anyway, no matter where you are."

Silverberg: The writer you mentioned, a man I know and like, is not a *science fiction* writer. I haven't read very much of what he's written, but I understand it has to do with intense crime, horror and suspense. I imagine it's possible for him to set every book on the same street and, so long as he has an exciting plot and someone in terrible jeopardy, he will tell a story of the kind he's known for telling. His books sell by the billions, and justify themselves on that basis.

Zinos-Amaro: But the idea that "you can see everything you need to know about life in one square mile of the Earth" sounds stronger to me.

Silverberg: Everything you need to know about life *to write the kinds of books he writes*. He started as a science fiction writer. His science fiction books weren't terribly well received by the public or by the critics. So he tried doing something else, and the rest is history. We discussed it at a convention once. Cromwell, listening to the debate in the English parliament, said to the people whose opinions he didn't care for, "I beseech you in the bowels of Christ, consider that you may be wrong!" I essentially said, "I beseech you, writer X, consider that you may not be a science fiction writer."

I am—or was—a science fiction writer, and one of the things my science fiction is noted for is the vividness of landscape, the descriptive sweep. I don't think I could have done that had I seen only one square mile of Brooklyn in my entire life. Though Isaac made a pretty good stab at it.

Zinos-Amaro: What are some of the places you've visited out of archaeological curiosity?

Silverberg: Everything stems from boyhood reading for me. My parents saw to it that I was well stocked with books, and wherever they sensed an interest of mine, they followed it up with the right book. I was given a book by Anne Terry White, called *Lost Worlds*, which talked about Assyria, Egypt, Sumer, places like that. I was nine or ten when I read it. When I began to travel, I thought, "I'd like to see some of these places." Travel was much more difficult than it is now. The planes were smaller and slower and much more dangerous, so I moved gradually across the world. One of the first places I went to was Pompeii. I visited Italy when I was twenty-five and made a point to visit Pompeii. When I got back, I talked to my agent at that time, and he asked me what the most interesting place I'd seen was. I'd been to Rome, I'd been to Naples, I'd been to Capri—and I'd been to Pompeii. "Why don't you write a book about it?" he said. I wrote a book called *Lost Cities and Vanished Civilizations*, which was something of a retread of the books of my childhood. Now I'm doing my own version of it, but some of it is at least first hand.

Zinos-Amaro: How many of the other places in that book had you been to?

Silverberg: I never went to Cambodia to see Angkor Wat.

Zinos-Amaro: Reading that chapter I could have sworn you had been there! You fooled me.

Silverberg: I used to write travel articles for the Diners Club magazine, about places I'd never been to. And then I would use my own articles as references when I went to those places.

Zinos-Amaro: [laughs]

Silverberg: I did go to Chichen Itza. I've not been to any part of Mesopotamia and I won't be doing it now.

Zinos-Amaro: What about Troy? You'd read a lot about it.

Silverberg: Curiously enough, though I did go to Turkey on four different occasions, I missed Troy each time. But there's nothing there basically but the hole in the ground and the foundations. In Turkey, though, I went to all the other sites. I saw Ephesus and Halicarnassus and Cappadocia—wherever there was a ruin, I visited it.

Zinos-Amaro: How about Crete, Knossos?

Silverberg: I did go to Crete, I went to Knossos, toured the labyrinth.

Zinos-Amaro: You mentioned Egypt before. Did that inform *Thebes of the Hundred Gates* by any chance?

Silverberg: Oh, of course. I wrote that as soon as I got back. Egypt was tingling in my head. I didn't climb the big Pyramid but I looked up at it. I have made the archaeological tour.

Zinos-Amaro: South America?

Silverberg: I haven't gotten very deep into South America. I went to Guyana, which had just barely emerged from being British Guiana, and Dutch Guiana, now called Suriname. There were really no ruins there, but there was a lot of anthropology. Interesting cultural clashes between the East Indians who lived there and the blacks, who jockeyed for power in a very troubled way. And then when you go inland in Guyana you encounter the American Indians. The descendants are still living the fairly primitive life of the natives. And also in Suriname, deep in, there are the descendants of runaway slaves, who have been back there since the eighteenth century. *Bosch-Negers* they're called, "negers" not being a pejorative in Dutch. They're living an African tribal life, deep in the jungles of Suriname. I visited them, and at one point I veered too close to a small hut that was in a plaza, and my guide said, "Don't go any closer to that. It's a holy building."

Zinos-Amaro: You also mentioned Africa before.

Silverberg: A fairly extensive visiting of North Africa, the Maghreb, Tunisia and Morocco, where they had remarkable Roman ruins. The Romans just popped across the Mediterranean and settled there, and in that dry climate their cities are in remarkably good condition. Earlier I visited Kenya, Tanganyika, as it was called then, and Zanzibar. Zanzibar had recently had a revolution and was now a black republic. A taxi driver drove us down a street of interesting-looking stone buildings, and he said, "That was where the Arabs used to live. One day we killed them all." Zanzibar had been slave trading under Arab domination and somewhere around 1964 the blacks slaughtered twenty-thousand people in one day and took the island over. You learn about the world as you move around in it. "One day we killed them all."

Zinos-Amaro: Wow. What destinations have you traveled to because of your long-standing interest in botany?

Silverberg: It's a funny thing. We live in California. We have a very forgiving climate here and I have filled my garden with plants most of which are native to similar climates around the world, Mediterranean climates: from the actual Mediterranean region, or South Africa, or certain parts of Australia, or certain parts of America, that have the dry summer and the wet winter. As I travel around the world I tend to gravitate towards the botanic gardens that specialize in the *same* plants that I have at home. Karen has occasionally nudged me about this, that I travel all over the world, looking to see the same plants. I want to see them where they've been growing for several hundred years, as they have in some of these gardens. Or where they're native and have reached full size.

One of my favorite gardens is in Southern California, the Huntington, near Pasadena. I found in Spain, along the Catalan coast, some very fine botanic gardens. Again, a Californian climate. Italy, along the Riviera. In Nice there's some lovely gardens. In the Côte d'Azur. Wherever the sun shines a lot, there are splendid gardens. I'm getting a little tired, actually, of looking at aloes and prickly plants!

Zinos-Amaro: [laughs] Very well. I'm curious if you had experiences, while traveling, that have changed your mind about certain things, redefined your opinion in some way.

Silverberg: We were recently in France and Karen's iPhone got us out of trouble. We were lost and the phone's GPS got us back on track. That's a recent example, and very explicit. I don't like smartphones, but I was forced to eat crow.

Of course when you talk to people abroad you learn about other attitudes. In Egypt a taxi driver asked me how many children I had. I have, by choice, no children. When I said that he was shocked! He had seven, or nine, or whatever number, and he believed it was his duty to fill the world with new Egyptians. I heard the same from a Mexican taxi driver, in almost the same words. So I know that in some countries there's a reproductive imperative that I don't share, and they're shocked that I don't share it.

Zinos-Amaro: But clearly that didn't change your mind—you didn't come back home and start having children.

Silverberg: Well, my perspectives aren't that easy to redefine. But the perspectives *of my characters* can be redefined. I myself don't change a lot, but I take in information and use it in my writing. Otherwise I would just be writing about a lot of people who are just like me, and though I would think that's wonderful, the readers may not.

Zinos-Amaro: What are perhaps the four or five most memorable trips from the last five decades?

Silverberg: The most memorable ones. Hmmm. I suppose those would be the first ones to come to mind!

The safari to east Africa in 1968 was quite memorable. Seeing lions and cheetahs and elephants—I'm particularly fond of elephants, as any reader of *Downward to the Earth* might remember—at close range. In those parks you can't travel on your own, you have to take a driver and a park ranger with you. We got caught once between a mother elephant and her calf. Seeing the park ranger staring uneasily in the car and moving his rifle around, and wondering what he was going to do if this elephant decided to step on our car, that was educational.

Another time my first wife, who liked to take pictures, unrolled the car window and leaned out to take a picture of a lion sleeping under a bush. The driver, in some anguish, said, "Madam, that is a lion!" She backed up and closed the window. We'd had the case just two or three weeks before of two women on consecutive days being killed by lions because they leaned out of their cars. I didn't get a cheap divorce that way, but I remember that driver after fifty years saying, "Madam, that is a lion!" Seeing that other world—that was an important trip.

Going to Israel in December of 1967, right after the June war of 1967, was another memorable trip. I wrote a book about Zionism, *If I Forget Thee O Jerusalem*. I've never been an observant Jew, but I am Jewish. And though I would hesitate to call myself a Zionist, I think that what they have achieved in Israel is something worthwhile and worth supporting. This, of course, gets me into political trouble with some of my left-wing friends now. That was not the case back then. I had never been in the Middle Eastern environment until I crossed over into the old city of Jerusalem. And suddenly, narrow streets, sacks of spices on the ground, donkey carts, Arabs in hooded Arab costumes—it was the old *National Geographic* emotion in me twenty years after my childhood. I saw the two great mosques, the al-Aqsa Mosque and the Dome of the Rock, one gold and one silver. I was able to go anywhere I wanted then, on both sides of the border. There was no fear. The war was over, the Palestinians were in shock. At Jericho I saw ruins of the Neolithic city there. It was a very exciting trip.

Zinos-Amaro: I seem to remember Philip Roth had an intense experience in Israel.

Silverberg: He met another Philip Roth there who claimed to be him. I didn't have that experience.

In one of my earliest trips, 1958, I left New York behind and came out to the western United States. When all you've seen is New York and Philadelphia, suddenly to find yourself in Yosemite or Yellowstone or the Grand Canyon ... and the trip finished in Los Angeles, which was quite alien to my New York eyes. A strange, wonderful place. I had no idea that in another thirteen years or so I'd actually be living in California. But that trip was a revelation.

Zinos-Amaro: Any trips to Eastern Europe that have left a mark?

Silverberg: Well, I didn't go to Eastern Europe until fairly late in life, because I don't relish discomfort and the Communist regimes specialized in that. I didn't want to have to deal with secret police, bad hotels, terrible food. But after the Soviet Union fell apart I traveled quite extensively in Eastern Europe.

My first taste of it was East Germany, Berlin, in the early nineties. The dark city of my childhood—this was Hitler's capital. With that overlain by all the Communist stuff—the wall, all the people that tried to escape and were shot—Berlin carries dark, dark vibes. I thought, "Here I am, in Berlin. I'm strolling around as though I'm in any normal city." Then I took a train from Berlin to Leipzig and then to Dresden. To see the emptiness of East Germany was to have all of my prejudices about Communism confirmed. Miles and miles of it was just nothing. Then we'd come to an empty factory, where they hadn't been able to produce anything anyone wanted to buy, and so the factory was just left to fall down. And then a little town where nothing was happening. And then miles of emptiness again. This, in the middle of Europe!

And then of course to see Leipzig and Dresden, which in part had been rebuilt, stone for stone, with the pre-War buildings, the museums and the palaces, and the rest Soviet-style barracks—quite an education.

I've been to Hungary, what used to be Czechoslovakia, Poland, East Germany, and briefly to St. Petersburg. I've been to Budapest several times, and the first time was not long after the liberation, and it was filthy. You could see that there was a beautiful city under all the grime, but they had not been able to do anything about it, and their Communist masters were certainly not interested in doing anything about it. But the next time Budapest looked a great deal better to me.

I've been to Croatia, and I spent ten minutes in Bosnia. I went to Croatia in 1998, the year the Kosovo War was going on. And there had been, of course, a terrible war between Serbia and Croatia a few years before. When we flew to Croatia we had to come in at four thousand feet, because above that was the military zone. We stayed entirely in Croatia but we drove up the coast from Dubrovnik, where we started, to Zagreb, where the convention where I was a guest of honor was being held. Bosnia, which is an inland, largely Muslim country, smack in the middle of what had been Yugoslavia, has a tiny corridor that runs westward through a bit of Croatia, to give them an opening to the sea. The highway that runs along the Croatian coast crosses Bosnia, where culturally things are quite different. There is a Muslim-style toilet, which is essentially just a hole in the ground. This is not found in Croatia. But at the service station where we filled the tanks, we found it was Muslim territory. Wherever you go, you make little anthropological discoveries.

I've also been to Estonia and Latvia. We went to the local museums. One aspect of going to the local museums in *any* country is that you see the provincial artists that you've never heard of. If you go to Germany you'll see the work of a lot of German artists whose work doesn't travel. The same in Latvia, the same in Estonia. That's interesting, because many of these are very capable artists, but they're known only in their own countries. I'm not sure what drew me to Latvia and Estonia other than the fact that we were going to be in St. Petersburg and these were the countries next door . . . . They were friendly, charming places.

Tallinn was very cute, though the Soviet texture had been totally eradicated. All of the signs that were posted on the streets—the street signs themselves, and the various plaques posted on historic buildings—were in Western script. They were in the local language and usually also in English. Anything that had been in Cyrillic had been removed. But there was still a substantial Russian population. The Communists had moved Russians into these countries, and a lot of them were still stranded there, but they were not allowed to use their own languages. We went to one shop where we bought a little amber jewelry, and the shop-girl, who was twenty-two years old maybe, spoke very good English, and of course she spoke Latvian, and I heard her speaking German too. She also spoke Russian because she was in fact ethnically Russian. She had to speak Russian to her parents, who had never learned Latvian. But once you speak three or four languages, adding a few more is nothing!

Zinos-Amaro: You also travel for culinary experiences, is that right?

Silverberg: I've just come back from France, and you can't get more culinary than that. Let me enlarge on this topic.

I grew up during wartime. This was a shaping experience. I grew up in a middle-class Jewish culture that didn't regard food as particularly important except as a source of nourishment. There were the basic middle European foodstuffs—the pot-roast and so on—that we ate, and it wasn't until I got off to college when I was seventeen and started eating at restaurants of my choice that I discovered the aesthetics of food. It can taste really good; it isn't entirely a matter of basic nourishment! I even learned about pizza. Of course, you're

European, so pizza may not have the same meaning to you. For an American today, pizza is just the basic junk food of every day, but pizza had just *happened* in the United States when I reached college, and it was startling that so many flavors could be packed onto one piece of crust! I learned about wine. Here I am, living as an adult in Manhattan. I didn't live in the dormitories, I had my own little apartment. The world was there to be discovered, and so I went from the Italian restaurant to the Japanese restaurant to the French restaurant—I was just a kid. It was a revelation similar to that of seeing Yosemite or the redwood trees of California, to know that food can be prepared in so many different ways, and can have such a sensory impact. It's not simply a matter of not starving.

So I've continued my researches everywhere. Sometimes my travel has been keyed to culinary discoveries. In San Francisco there's a Sardinian restaurant. Sardinian food is a subset of Italian food, pasta- and sauce- and seafood-based. The owner and chef of this Sardinian restaurant is an extremely gifted cook, and I've had some wonderful meals there. Finally I said to Karen, "Why don't we go to Sardinia?" We did. And discovered that yes, you eat very well in Sardinia, but we get just as good in that one place.

My archaeological interests converged on the Sardinian trip and nearly brought me to an early grave. (I regard getting to the grave at *any* age as an early grave.) This was just a few years ago. There are in Sardinia prehistoric structures called *nuraghe*, which are built of massive chunks of stone, building up to several stories. They're quite strange, and they're not found anywhere else. They're all over the Sardinian landscape, and they're two or three thousand years old. We toured the *nuraghe* in between dining at Sardinian restaurants and one day as we were climbing one of the greatest of the *nuraghe* in southern Sardinia it began to drizzle. And then to rain. And then to deliver lightning. We're out in the open, clinging to metal railings, as this electrical storm begins, and we're at the highest point in this field. We looked at each other and thought, "What a way to go."

Of course, there are different great cuisines. I suppose the French have made more of a science out of it than anyone else, and I have never encountered a cuisine more complex or challenging than the French cuisine. I'm just back from yet another trip where I succeeded in upsetting my stomach by continuing my researches beyond a plausible point.

I went to Morocco in 1975 to find out if the food in Morocco was as good as the Moroccan food in San Francisco—and yes, it was! Besides which, Morocco is a stunningly beautiful, alien place, with Roman ruins and mosques that we were allowed to enter back in those innocent days. Deserts, marketplaces. A good deal of *Lord Valentine's Castle*, in fact, is drawn from my trip to Morocco. Anyone who's been to Morocco would probably recognize the scenery.

So food, travel and writing are completely interrelated for me. I don't do much writing any more, but I still travel and eat every night, and still move around looking for new culinary experiences, because that sense of novelty and the search for beauty still drive me. I was talking with my wife this morning about what we would do for dinner tonight. Shall we go to that Indonesian restaurant? No, it turns out we're going to be in a different part of the city, so let's go to the Peruvian instead. Luckily we have these choices here.

Zinos-Amaro: On the dust jacket of your 1965 biography of Niels Bohr it mentions that that you liked to spend several weeks each winter exploring the coral reefs in the Caribbean. When did that phase start, how long did it last, and what did you discover there?

Silverberg: It started as soon as I could buy a plane ticket there! I graduated from college in 1956. In 1957 we were off to Europe; England and France. In 1958 we did the big Western trip. And my first Caribbean trip was in 1959. Maybe earlier. Certainly in 1959 I was in Puerto Rico. It's only a three-hour flight from New York to the near Caribbean islands, and even with a two-hop trip you can get almost anywhere in four hours. We would go to one or two islands each February, because I don't like cold weather, and I lived in a place that had it. I never managed to get to scuba diving, but I learned how to snorkel. I would get out on the reefs—alien world. It's the world next door, and has a different population. Every winter we would go to Jamaica, Dominica, Antigua, you name it, until I moved to California. It's a very big trip from here to the West Indies. You've got to go essentially to Miami, cope with the dreadful Miami airport, and get a second flight out to one of the islands, and I just haven't been doing it. Also, I'm not the athlete that I was fifty years ago, though I have done some snorkeling in my later years. We were in Hawaii seven or eight or ten years ago, and I went out on the reefs there, which I found did not compare with those of the West Indies. And after one of the Australian science fiction conventions, Karen and I went out to the Great Barrier Reef, which was one of those places I had always wanted to see, and so we saw it. A lovely hotel, actually out *on* the reef, that George R. R. Martin had recommended. We stayed there for four or five days. So even at the age of seventy-five or so, I've been looking at coral reefs, though I don't think I will any more.

Zinos-Amaro: You don't like the cold. What about travel to Nordic countries then?

Silverberg: Well, I just don't go there in the winter! I don't like extremes of weather, which is why living in the San Francisco Bay Area is so satisfactory. It's almost never hotter than eighty degrees, or colder than forty-five. We have a few deviations, but it's basically like springtime all year round. I won't go any place that has real winter. The Nordic countries have terrible winters, yes, but I don't have to go there in February.

I've been to Norway, Sweden, Denmark, Finland, St. Petersburg. I like the midnight sun. I like being there during the late bright nights. I like the food.

Zinos-Amaro: Do you have any favorite travel writers?

Silverberg: Patrick Leigh Fermor is fun to read, though I don't think he qualifies as a travel writer. The Polish writer Ryszard Kapuściński does qualify. He was a great journalist, and would go to places like Ethiopia and the Congo and do remarkable reports on them, making those places come alive for you. (Though you wouldn't want to go there). Lawrence Durrell did a splendid book on the Greek islands. But I don't read a lot of travel writers.

Zinos-Amaro: In six decades of globe-trotting, what are some of the more interesting souvenirs and artifacts you've picked up?

Silverberg: We have a collection of medieval Islamic ceramics, mostly from Iran. I used to admire them in museums and then I went to London in 1982 and across the street from my hotel was a gallery that had very similar Islamic ceramics in the window. Almost in a joking fashion, I went to find out what they cost. I was quite surprised to find out that they were within my budget of 1982, and so we began collecting them. We have at least thirty of them by now, bought at London and Paris and Tehran. That's one set of what I suppose you might call souvenirs, though I'm not sure that's the right word.

Zinos-Amaro: What about them fascinates you?

Silverberg: The color. The abstract patterns. The Islamic artists don't favor representational art, though they did some. There was trade, apparently, between Persia and China during the time of the great T'ang Dynasty artistic efflorescence, and the Persian potters, one of whom was a poet named Omar Khayyám, imitated the Chinese porcelains but in a distinctly Middle Eastern style. They created something quite interesting that the Chinese wanted to buy, and sold it back to them!

Back when I was writing books on archaeological and anthropological subjects, I proposed writing one about the Pueblo Indians. That required me to take a trip to Arizona and New Mexico. This was perhaps 1964. I was quite taken by Pueblo ceramics, particularly the Hopi, and began buying them at roadside stands for forty and fifty dollars, which seemed like a great deal of money then. Now, of course, they go for thousands of dollars. So we have a large collection of Pueblo ceramics also.

Zinos-Amaro: We'll talk later about your responses to visual art in a narrative context. I wonder, with these ceramics, is your response a narrative one or are they too abstract?

Silverberg: They're abstract, yes. Particularly the Pueblo ones, which *can* be deciphered: there are birds and animals on them, but they are quite deconstructed. The Islamic pieces no, they have no narrative appeal for me, it's strictly visual.

On the African trip I took in '68, at one of the game parks, a young Maasai boy, maybe fourteen, came up to me and wanted to sell me his spear. I thought that would be a cute souvenir, but the spear was about six feet long. I said, "Can't buy it, no way to transport it." At which point a second Maasai boy came out of the underbrush, said, "You can buy mine," and he proceeded to disassemble it. He's probably now the President of Tanzania! He took it apart into three pieces in about ten seconds, and it's now leaning against a wall by one of the doors to our living room.

Somewhere in Mexico, maybe Yucatán, at one of the ancient sites, a little boy, seven perhaps, had what he said was an Olmec statue, and he offered it to me for five pesos. The Olmec culture dates back to three thousand BC, and is the earliest known in Mexico. Five pesos was seventy-five cents. I couldn't resist it, so I bought it, and here it is. I'm aware that the Olmec statue is not genuine, but it was fun buying it.

In Turkey we went to one of the towns along the Mediterranean coast where there is a three- or four-story arena, a coliseum. I climbed up to the top level of the arena and discovered that a Turk was climbing up *on the outside* of the coliseum, course by course. He looked through the open place and said, "I have Roman coins." He put his hand through with some coins, which I was of course free to take, put in my pocket, and push him off, but I'm not that kind of fellow. I looked at the coins. They were of course fakes. One had one emperor on one side, and the inscription of a different emperor on the other: Hadrian and Trajan. One of the coins might have been Roman on one side and Greek on the other. I bought them, and they're right over there. I was so impressed with the Turk's intensity, like the kid in Africa.

We don't *only* buy fakes. But when it's an amusing enough fake we do. In Egypt we did the same thing. We went to the home of a grave-robber. Now, it is strictly forbidden to take antiquities out of Egypt. He knew it and I knew it. But I also knew they were phonies. You have to bargain for everything in Egypt. It's essentially the law. He began by quoting a price that might have been five dollars, and I was required by custom to reply, "I'll give you a dollar fifty," and then we'd have to haggle for a while between settling on what we knew would be the middle price.

There was a botanic garden on the other side of the Nile, at Aswan. I hired a boat, as you do, to take me across. Well, the wind was blowing against him, and he could not cross the river. Just couldn't get there. Finally he told us as much and took us back to the shore we had departed from. I think the price of the passage was fifty cents. But he didn't want to charge me at all! "That's too much," he said. "I'll take twenty five cents." I had to haggle him up. There was no way for me to communicate the fact that no matter what I paid him it was really nothing—not an insult to their culture, but a comment on their currency.

Here in the living room we have some reproductions, but also some originals. We have two Italian majolica ceramics, pretty good copies of sixteenth-century ware, but they aren't sixteenth-century. I think we bought them in the same town where they were originally manufactured, but four hundred years later. There's one in between that we bought at an antique shop and I do hope, in fact, that it is of its period, seventeenth-century perhaps, maybe a little earlier.

There's a big bug above it that came from a period when I was collecting Mexican masks.

Zinos-Amaro: Tell me more about that.

Silverberg: It's a Mexican dance mask. You put it on your head and jiggle around in the plaza during some festival. It's a transformational piece. I did write a horror story about collecting Mexican dance masks, called "Not Our Brother," and that was around the time I bought this, 1981. The strangeness of them is what attracted me to them. A lot of the things we keep here are *strange*. I remember some repairman came in here and said, "It's like walking into the History Channel."

One of the only artifacts here that has ever frightened me is a statue we have near an archway, a four-foot figure of a goat-like creature. It's a sculpture by a contemporary Californian artist named Peter Winter that I bought in 1980. I was living alone in that period and one morning I came out of the bedroom, early in the morning as I always do, and dawn light was striking the statue in a strange way and it frightened me. I thought, "Who is that standing there? What kind of creature is that?" It took me about ten seconds or so to get my perspective and realize it was my statue. It is pretty weird looking. But you can de-terrify it by going close and discovering that the white stripes are newspaper clippings of stock market quotations.

Hanging on the wall we have a wooden object called a baku, which is not the oil-producing town in Azerbaijan but a Japanese artifact. It's an eater of bad dreams, which as far as I know may function part of the time, but certainly plenty of bad dreams do slip through, especially now that I'm not writing. My imagination still generates a lot of imaginaries, and not all of them are pretty ones. The baku has been up there twenty or twenty-five years, and I don't remember where it came from. It's a funny looking thing, elephantine. Perhaps the trunk is pointing in the wrong direction.

We have a large, bright cross painted by a local science fiction fan named Lou Goldstone, who did some illustrations in the '40s for small-press science fiction publishers. I got to know him after I moved here. He and his wife are dead now but they lived in San Francisco. I was quite taken by the piece. The thing I remember most clearly about the transaction was that he charged me sales tax. I bought a painting from him in his house, after having dinner as his guest. I said, "Would you sell me that?" And he said, "Yes, it's X hundred dollars." It was 1973 or thereabouts. He added sales tax, as though I'd bought it at a gallery.

Zinos-Amaro: Someone seeing the painting today might interpret it as the clashing of two lightsabers.

Silverberg: Jack Vance didn't like this piece. Back when he could see, he said to me, "Silverberg, that doesn't belong where you've got it!" Well, sorry Jack.

Zinos-Amaro: Where did he think it should go?

Silverberg: I don't know. I thought it fit very nicely in that angle up there.

Zinos-Amaro: Have you collected other paintings?

Silverberg: We visited Australia several times and bought Aboriginal paintings, of which there are four or five scattered around the house, one visible from the living room. The Aboriginal art was abstract to us until it was explained to us that these are not abstractions, they're telling mythological stories that they have boiled down into patterns. That didn't matter—we bought them because they were pretty patterns.

But I'm particularly fond of ceramic pieces, which is of course a silly thing to do in earthquake country. A lot of this stuff is archaeological. Whenever I can find something that's connected to an ancient site that we've visited, or one that in the olden days I wrote about, I will try to get it. There's a quite elderly Persian vase here, of the period that I wrote about when I was writing books about Mesopotamia. There's a cuneiform tablet here and there, a hieroglyphic inscription, a piece of *The Book of the Dead*.

We have an African bronze guardian figure from a tribe called the Kota, or Bakota. It's actually a decoration for a reliquary. The bones would be below it. We used to see them in museums. There's an artist name Arman who collected them by the droves, and we ran into the Arman collection of reliquaries at an airport, a dozen or twenty of them. We thought, "We should have one of these. They're interesting, alien faces." We have a beautiful owl mask that came from the same dealer.

Zinos-Amaro: In your travels do you ever have a moment where you feel like you've entered a science fiction world?

Silverberg: I'm *always* in a science fiction world [chuckles]. No, we can tell the difference between a gallery in Paris and, say, Betelgeuse 9.

Zinos-Amaro: Speaking of travels and your writing, in an introduction to one of your short stories, you talk about how Alice Turner from *Playboy* referred to some of them as your "IRS stories."

Silverberg: That's right. We had a very close editorial relationship. There was no nonsense. We spoke our minds. She was a great editor with deep knowledge of story structure. I loved working with her. But now and then, we would really disagree. I would write a story set in some place I had recently visited. Why not write about what you know? Write about Turkey, rather than Persia, because I've actually been to Turkey. She turned down a couple of them, saying, "This is another one of your IRS stories," meaning, "You have turned it into a tax deduction. By writing about a place you've just visited now you can deduct your airfare." I resented this because anything I did—anyplace I went—was a legitimate tax deduction, because you never know when you're doing research for a future story. I wasn't writing these stories for tax purposes, I wasn't playing a game. I couldn't shake this off, couldn't get through to Alice there. At least two or three times she told me they were IRS stories. So I sold them to *Omni*. Writer's travel is a form of research, like taking a course would be: I've taken a course in what the streets of Istanbul look like, and I've set a lot of stories there.

Zinos-Amaro: "A Tip on a Turtle" is one of many stories that come to mind that had a strong sense of place.

Silverberg: Yes, a Caribbean story. I've been at that hotel. I've seen turtle races. Is it an *IRS* story? No, it's a story! And because I've had the advantage over, say Isaac Asimov, of actually having been to that island and seen a turtle race, which he couldn't imagine having done, I could write that. I could have set the story in New Jersey just as easily: a hotel in Hoboken that has turtle races. But that would have been fantasy, not science fiction.

Zinos-Amaro: With all the travel you've done, have you ever found yourself in unlikely situations? Have you ever worried about missing connecting flights and being stranded somewhere?

Silverberg: I *always* think that I'm going to miss connecting flights. On our most recent trip to the Catalan coast of France we were due to land in Toulouse on May 2nd, coming one hop from London. The French air controllers, an easily aggrieved group, decided to call three strikes, of two to three days' duration, right around that time. When they actually called the first of the strikes, which is when we learned about it, all European air travel was thrown into chaos. The second strike would be ten days later, and the third strike would conclude on the day of our landing in Toulouse. So our flight would be canceled, we'd be stranded in London, and the trip would be undermined. We might lose days. Karen came up with an alternative plan that would get us to Toulouse. Because we were flying non-stop from California to London on our first leg, we could take the Eurostar from London to Paris, and get a train from Paris to Toulouse. But here's what it would entail in real-world experience: a ten hour overnight flight, getting as much sleep as we can, then landing at Heathrow, getting our luggage through the clearance process, going through customs, getting a cab, zooming down in London to the Eurostar terminal, getting there in time for the 1:30 or 2:00 pm train to Paris, getting to Paris, crossing Paris from the Eurostar terminal on the north side of Paris to the train terminal on the south side of Paris, and then taking a five or six hour train ride to Toulouse and arriving there at midnight on the second day of our trip after having had no sleep. That would get us to Toulouse on May 2nd. Well, the strike was canceled, and none of this happened. We got our flight and arrived in Toulouse on the afternoon of May 2nd. But there was a little travel anxiety dangled just when we didn't need it.

Zinos-Amaro: Any anecdotes that are not anxiety-related?

Silverberg: There are none.

Zinos-Amaro: [laughs] Encounters with interesting characters? Ever end up at an unplanned destination? Bump into people you know unexpectedly in strange places?

Silverberg: I went to New York on a business trip sometime in the eighties, and crossing Third Avenue I ran into Sandy Mendlesohn, who lived here in California but was also in New York on a business trip. We pointed at each other and laughed. A little while later I ran into Ellen Datlow on the same street. This is a city of eight million people, and here are two people I know within hours of one another. On a separate trip I ran into the boyfriend of my agent Ralph

Vicinanza, Jimmy, at almost the same place.

Saul Diskin, a close friend of mine who died recently, was a member of a pair of twins. His twin brother was a professor of anthropology at MIT. We were traveling with the Diskins in Sicily somewhere in the late nineteen-nineties. In a remote corner of Sicily, in some dinghy little *trattoria* where we had stopped for lunch, a person from another table came over, stared for a moment, and said, "Are you Dr. Diskin?" Without batting an eye, he said, "That's my brother."

When I went to Chichen Itza in Yucatán, and stayed at the hotel right near one of the great Mayan constructs, there was a very annoying German tourist staying at the same hotel. He was loud and bumptious and ordered the staff around as though he were the head of a concentration camp and they were the prisoners. He infuriated everybody. Time comes to leave. We're going to fly from Mérida, Yucatán to New Orleans. It turns out he's leaving the same day, and we ride together on the hotel bus to the airport. He's got a box with him. As we check in to the airport desk, the clerk says, "Open that box." He pulls out a pre-Columbian artifact, a clay animal of some kind. You can't, of course, export artifacts from Mexico. The clerk says, "You can't take that." It was a souvenir from a gift shop, a ten-dollar piece of trash, and he knew it, and the clerk knew it. But somebody at the hotel had reported it: "Herr So-and-So is going to try to smuggle a valuable artifact out." It wasn't the clerk's job to determine whether it was legitimate or not. So the German was told to go into a room and discuss it with the manager, while his plane took off. He missed his flight, and those days they didn't have flights every hour. That's the price you pay for being a very annoying tourist.

On that same trip, I went wandering around the ruins at Chichen Itza. They cover acres and acres. There are vast temples and fortresses and whatnot, a huge place. I'd been there three or four days by that time. I wandered into a far corner of the area where I discovered some Mexican workmen carving Mayan sculpture. A particular one, with a sort of elephant nose. They were carving them out of the local stone, a row of them. I looked and I looked and thought, "That's how they've done this. They've built the whole thing in the last ten years or so! And here they are, constructing the next temple." One of the workmen saw me staring and I could speak a little Spanish then, and said, "¿Qué pasa aquí?" He explained it to me. They were building the Mexican pavilion for the Montreal World's Fair. They were *copying* one of the Chichen Itza temples. Later in the year, when I went up to the Montreal World's Fair, there it was! But it was a disturbing moment, when I thought they were constructing the ruins right there.

One time I was at the Frankfurt book fair, in 1985, as guest of my German publisher of the time, who also published the *Perry Rhodan* series. I had several German publishers, but this one had imported me, paid my way. I was hanging out with them, to the bewilderment of the editor Wolfgang Jeschke, one of my other editors, who said, "What are you doing with these people?" I explained to him that they had brought me here. Anyway, I was having breakfast with a little group of the Moewig people, the editor-in-chief and one of their translators, a man who is just as bilingual as you are. No accent whatsoever, could move from one language to the other with no hesitation. As we're having breakfast, suddenly the editor-in-chief turned to the bilingual fellow and said, "What's the German word for pineapple?" He'd so completely shifted over into English he'd lost his own language!

During our first trip to Budapest, when things weren't terribly Westernized yet, we had chosen a restaurant which turned out to be one of three of the same name, not necessarily related. But whatever the name was, there were three of them in central Budapest. We took a cab from our nice Intercontinental Hotel and had the hotel people tell the cab driver where we were going. He took us to the restaurant, we went in—and they had no reservation for us. This is immediately post-Soviet Hungary: no reservation, goodbye. So we came back out and the taxi was still there. "Not that restaurant, they don't know us," we said, somehow communicated this fact. "Ah," he said, "I know. Different one." He took us to the second one, way across town. They'd never heard of us either. As well they shouldn't, since we had no reservation there. The taxi driver and the restaurateur now had a conference, since clearly there's a developing problem. It's getting quite late, it's a spread-out kind of city. We had an eight o'clock reservation, it's now eight forty five and we're still nowhere. The restaurateur told him, "Take them to the third restaurant." He explained this to us, sort of. I asked, "Do you understand where you're going?" He smiled and said, "*No!*" We think *he* thought he was saying "yes." It was a very confident "*No!*" He took us to the third restaurant, which was indeed the place where we had our booking. And it was four blocks from our hotel!

In Istanbul there was a restaurant called the Vitamin Restaurant, very close to all the great monuments, right around the corner from the Haghia Sophia. As we walked past it there was a huge, brawny Turkish cook with a big moustache in the window, assembling dishes and crying out to passersby, "Yes! Yes! Yes!"

Zinos-Amaro: The Vitamin Restaurant: what an odd name.

Silverberg: It sounded good to them.

Zinos-Amaro: "Yes!"

Silverberg: Coming back to the anxiety level, I told you that we flew to Croatia during the Kosovo War. We were flying from Paris to Dubrovnik. It's four or five in the afternoon and we were about to land in Dubrovnik when the airport lights went out. Power failure. No landing. They took us from Dubrovnik up to the coast to Split. It's very scary when you're landing and the landing is aborted and you feel the jets come back in, especially when there's a war going on. So they explained we were going to Split. It's a small country, so that would be like going to Monterey from here, the San Francisco Bay Area. However, we discovered that they're going to get us to Dubrovnik that night, by bus—a school bus. Not so quick. By the time they got it all organized it was eight or nine in the evening and cold, miserably cold. Here we are, aboard this rickety bus, on a cobblestone highway, freezing. And there are two Germans sitting in the seats right in front of us, being rowdy and smoking. We got to Dubrovnik at four in the morning. At least the hotel was expecting us.

You put up with this sort of stuff, and then eventually you're in the trip, caught up with the jetlag, but it makes you wonder, "Why am I doing this to myself?" Then you get the answer: "You're in beautiful Zagreb. Or Dubrovnik." It's a typical Silverbergian position. While I'm having an unpleasant time abroad, as I did recently, I think to myself, "Maybe it's time to stop." And hardly am I home—in fact, while I was on the plane headed home—I'm already thinking about the next trip.

Zinos-Amaro: Being a creature of habit, do these experiences leave a mark when you're back home?

Silverberg: I have anxiety-related dreams all the time. *Not* having them is perhaps more notable.

Zinos-Amaro: Wonderful!

Silverberg: The worst part of traveling for me is the dawn. Here, I get up, I'm in my house, I get the newspaper, feed the cat, read on the couch, and eventually it's not dawn any more. Over there, there's nothing you can do at six in the morning. You can't go out for a stroll before dawn, though I used to do that occasionally—not fun. You can't make breakfast, because you have to wait for your wife, and breakfast is hours away. The newspaper, which I've asked the hotel to deliver, hasn't yet come. It's pretty bleak. I'd like to sleep until seven thirty or eight instead of waking up so early.

Zinos-Amaro: How quickly do you reset your clock?

Silverberg: As soon as I'm past a day or two, the clock has been reset and I'm back on the same preposterous dawn time.

Zinos-Amaro: When you travel, are you recognized? Mistaken for other people, perhaps?

Silverberg: At conventions I've been mistaken for other bearded writers: L. Sprague de Camp, who was maybe six feet two, Timothy Zahn, who's around five feet seven, and Terry Carr, who was also six two and wore glasses. For a while George Alec Effinger and I were greatly confused, and there was a certain justification because we were more or less the same height and we both then had dark hair and dark goatees.

I've been encountered in the strangest places. In Budapest there's a huge structure overlooking the river called the Fisherman's Bastion, and we had walked out on it to look at the river view. A voice next to me said, "Hello, Mr. Silverberg." A Hungarian fan.

When we were in Westminster Abbey, before the World Fantasy Con I never got to, I was recognized. I've been recognized in bookstores, particularly. In Toulouse we found a science fiction bookstore. I don't get my French editions shipped to me by the French publishers: I have to ask for them. So I went up to the bookstore and bought five Silverberg books. It was reasonable for them to conclude that I just loved his work, but instead the clerk said, "It's an honor to have you here, Mr. Silverberg," which surprised me—and I got a discount too.

The Budapest underground is *really* underground. The subway is very nice, clean, slick, but you take an escalator about a mile down. One time we rode slowly down this immense escalator to the bottom, where there was a table of books laid out, including two of mine. Which I bought. Didn't have them.

Zinos-Amaro: How often do you use public transportation?

Silverberg: We'll take public transportation in Paris, because getting a cab is a real headache, and then communicating with the taxi driver is not so easy either. In London we used to take the underground a lot. We take taxis more commonly now. In Budapest we had been told something about the trains, and we wanted to try them, so we did.

Zinos-Amaro: Germany has nice trains.

Silverberg: We took a train in Berlin last year, couldn't figure out how to pay for it and wound up cheating. There was some machine, we didn't know how to deal with it, the train came, we got on it, came to our station, and got off again.

Zinos-Amaro: When this book is released they'll find out about your crime and hunt you down. There's probably security footage somewhere of you fumbling with the machine and not paying your three euros.

Silverberg: I tried, I really did. As I often tell people when there's some such situation, "When I begin stealing, it won't be three euros."

CHAPTER 2
Aesthetics

Alvaro Zinos-Amaro: In your non-fiction, particularly your essay collections *Reflections and Refractions* and *Musings and Meditations*, you often talk about catharsis when discussing art. Catharsis can be traced back to Aristotle's *Poetics* and suggests that art can offer some kind of cleansing or purification. What are your thoughts on theories of art that perhaps move away from that classical Greek notion?

Robert Silverberg: Most of my theorizing about the art of fiction, which is the only art I'm directly concerned with, is internalized to the point where it's not an explicit formula. It's what I've been doing all my life. It's things that I've abstracted from my reading and from my thinking. The Aristotelian part of my aesthetic is derived from the *Poetics*, largely, yes, but also derived from reading pulp fiction, and all other kinds of fiction.

There's a basic structural element to fiction. I wrote about this in three columns for *Asimov's*, called "Toward a Theory of Story," in which I said that story involves a protagonist struggling with a problem and breaking through to a perception, which may involve his destruction or his triumph—that makes no difference, it's still a perception. That's the cathartic effect a story has. The rest of what I regard as my aesthetic has to do with using this structural plan in the most effective way.

That involves a sensory appeal. I try in each page to provide some color, some sound, taste, olfactory perception, and tactile sensation in order to make the work more vivid for the reader and to have more impact, as I'm leading the reader through the stages of the road to catharsis. There is a stylistic element having to do with prose rhythm, punctuation even: I want to maintain the reader's interest by writing in such a way that the prose itself—the sound of it, the rhythm of it—engages his interest.

One of the problems I have with reading modern science fiction is that much of the prose deflects me. Either I can't follow the narrative because I'm so bothered by the typing-with-the-elbows-effect of the prose or I start rewriting it in my head and that creates a problem between me and the narrative also.

And the language has changed. Remember, I've been writing now for sixty years, and words are squirreling around, as they do. Back in Thucydides' account of the Peloponnesian War he talks about how the Corinthians invade Corcyra right at the beginning of the war. Under the pressures of war, words lose their meaning. They take on new propagandistic meanings. In that very sinister chronicle of the war, Thucydides' masterpiece, that's the most sinister part of all: words losing their meaning. I find it frightening.

The word "edgy," for example, doesn't mean what it did when I began writing. "Multiple" is vastly misused; "fortuitous" is totally misused; and so on through a long, dreary list. And so when I read, my sense of the language is constantly being attacked the way that Chaucer might find Shakespeare's language bothersome or Shakespeare find Henry James' or Henry James' mine. This is a natural evolutionary process.

Anyway, I've gotten a long way off from your question, but you see that my theory of writing fiction starts with a structural sense. My stories are carefully plotted to create a certain effect. And then I enhance these effects through the use of sensory appeal and prose rhythm.

Zinos-Amaro: Are there any other formal elements that you consider in the planning stages that are not structural? Specific character manipulations or other prose effects?

Silverberg: Well, the prose effects *are* structural to me. There was a period in my work when I was very fond of the catalog. I would build lists, sometimes of a page or page-and-a-half. I would want to pile on a series of effects, particularly between '67 and '74, when I was writing with great rapidity and a kind of manic joy. There's one of them in *The Man in the Maze*, I think, that goes on and on and on. It was a matter of incantation, for effect. I did it less and less as time went along, but it certainly was a technique of mine in many of the books. The use of sound effects, sensory effects, is all part of the carpentry.

The character manipulation falls in a different category. It's not structural. It is one of the things the structure is designed to hold up. In planning a story I select characters, a science fictional situation, a certain texture. I used to think of novels as having certain color for me. "This novel is going to be kind of purple." Try to explain that to anybody else.

Zinos-Amaro: I've heard composers talk about color in relation to their music. The film composer James Horner, for example, would talk about starting with the colors of his composition, the palette of orchestral instruments.

Silverberg: Well, it's different for composers, because theirs is a non-verbal art. I can make a book sound purple just by writing "purple" on every third page.

Zinos-Amaro: You could also write purple prose . . .

Silverberg: [laughs] None of this is what I mean by "purple," and I'd be hard-pressed to explain what I *did* mean by "purple" or "blue" as part of my conceptual process. But I don't have to explain it.

Zinos-Amaro: Could the colors be stand-ins for moods or textures?

Silverberg: Possibly. But as I said, I don't have to explain it. It's just one of those non-conceptual concepts that I would have in my mind as I began writing a novel. But the range of emotions that I want a scene to evoke, the behavior of the characters, these things are chosen to permit me to go through the structural path that I want the story or novel to achieve.

Zinos-Amaro: Those elements are chosen to allow you to go through that structural path, rather than the structural path being chosen to get to those elements?

Silverberg: Yes, I guess that's the case. I start always with the notion that *somebody* is going to be put through changes and come out somewhat different at the end. I think if you look at most of my work you see that that is ordinarily the case. So I have to choose someone who is in need of going through changes. And that involves having the structural imperative first, and then fitting the world, the narrative style—which changes for me from book to book—the character interaction, the texture, the ratio of exposition versus dialog, and a lot of other things that go into making up the writing of the book. I say book, but I regard books and short stories as interchangeable in that sense.

Zinos-Amaro: I'd like to take us in a slightly different direction now. It's clear that after decades of exercising the art of fiction through the aesthetic model you've been talking about, all of those ideas live somewhere in your brain. But as a consumer of art, how do you think about the domain of art, where it starts and where it stops?

Silverberg: A lot of what I see in museums now is outside my domain. I'm eighty years old and have grown considerably more conservative in my view of the universe over that course of time, which is a natural and standard progression.

Zinos-Amaro: What is that domain for you now?

Silverberg: I do spend a lot of time looking at paintings. I travel overseas widely and my first stop is always the museum of the city. What I need to do when I look at a painting is understand the aesthetic of the artist. Or, as we say here in California, where he's coming from.

What Titian or Veronese are doing is rather different from what Diebenkorn or even Picasso are doing. The classical masters are, among many other things, telling me a story. When I see a painting of Perseus rescuing Andromeda—and those are generally four hundred year old paintings—what I see is a hero, a dragon, a woman chained to a rock at the edge of the ocean, and this creates certain responses in me that are narrative rather than painterly. The first thing that I look at in Perseus and Andromeda is not the artist's use of color or use of perspective, it's his use of story. "Oh look, that's a mighty fearsome dragon. Andromeda, she's a cute chick. Perseus, I hope he gets the dragon!" This has nothing to do with the art of painting, this is myth.

On the other hand, when I look at a Matisse let's say, I see that he rarely bothers with perspective. A lot of his work is flat. He knows how to do perspective, he's just not interested in doing that. Frequently the first thing that will attract my attention in a Matisse is the color. "What a wonderful thing he's done with red there. Look down at the corner, he's clashing with the red. What a brave artist he is." That's discussing the aesthetic, not the content. So one's response to paintings shifts according to the context.

To some degree that's true when reading fiction, or listening to music. My response to a Beethoven symphony is going to be quite different from my response to a Bach prelude and fugue or to a John Cage work for prepared piano.

Zinos-Amaro: In order to have the kind of response we're talking about to a specific piece of art, you need, going in, some idea of the artist's aesthetic. Otherwise you can't get very far, is that right?

Silverberg: I don't think you need a notion of what that artist's specific aesthetic is, but you need to be able to react to the aesthetic you're being presented with.

Zinos-Amaro: But what if you don't know what it is?

Silverberg: Then you're bewildered, as I am when I walk into a museum and I see large boulders scattered on the floor of the gallery. I look at them and think, to put it in modern terms, "What am I supposed to be feeling here?" The answer for me becomes, "I don't care." I am no longer willing, at my age, and after a lifetime of absorbing artistic impressions, to meet that artist halfway. I dismiss the piece in the way that the academic critics of Paris in the 1870s would dismiss Monet and later would dismiss Cezanne and van Gogh. They were wrong, and probably I'm wrong too, but I'm not obliged to bend myself out of shape for every little movement that comes along in the course of ninety years. In fact, I would rather look at Picasso, who certainly upset a lot of people before I was born, or Monet, or Turner. There's an example—Turner was regarded as insane in his later period. I'd rather look at their work than the work of the sculptors who are scattering objects on the floor of the gallery. I've drawn the line. I've said, "Thus far and no farther." This is perhaps a definition of age.

Zinos-Amaro: In terms of art history, where is that line for you? Is it surrealism, abstract expressionism, primevalism . . .?

Silverberg: For me it's somewhere on the far side of abstract expressionism, by which I mean that my painting aesthetic was formed in the New York Museum of Modern Art in the 1950s and '60s. Picasso, Miro and the surrealists—that's modern art to me. What they call contemporary art is perhaps beyond the effort that I'm willing to make.

How we can apply this to science fiction requires a little bit of stretching. Reading H. G. Wells, reading Robert Heinlein, reading Ray Bradbury or Cordwainer Smith; in each of these cases they're coming from very different stylistic places, but their narrative intent is pretty much the same. We don't have the range in science fiction that I just elicited in my tour of the art museums. This is partly because science fiction is a commercial medium and if somebody writing science fiction attempted to do what, let's say, Diebenkorn did in painting, he wouldn't get published, because it's non-representational. Fiction *can* be non-representational, but it's going to have a very small readership in that case.

Zinos-Amaro: John Updike, whom you've referenced throughout your essays, was a connoisseur of art and wrote about it at length, but you haven't really discussed the subject in print. As an avid gallery-goer, who are some of the artists and pieces that quicken your metabolism?

Silverberg: I should distinguish my connoisseurship from Updike's to the degree that Updike himself could draw and perhaps even could paint. I don't have those skills. I'm strictly a consumer, although an educated consumer.

The artists I look for in museums begin with the Romans, but of course the great Roman paintings can only be seen in a few places. You can see them in Pompeii and in the museum of Naples and a few places in Rome. I jump from there to the early Medievals, the almost Byzantine paintings of the Gothic period, the Flemish paintings— Rogier van der Weyden, van Eyck, astounding craftsmen. I admire the way they could represent convincing tactile objects through paint on a two-dimensional canvas. For the Renaissance itself I have something of a blind spot. Certainly I admire Michelangelo, Leonardo, Raphael and all those people, but I tend to jump very quickly from there to the northern painters: Vermeer, Hals, and so on. I then move quickly over the 18th century completely into Impressionism and then to what I think of as modern art, running from Cezanne to Picasso and Miro. There it stops for me, pretty much.

Zinos-Amaro: No one from the 18th century?

Silverberg: Watteau, Chardin.

Zinos-Amaro: What about Goya or maybe John Constable?

Silverberg: Goya I think is very powerful. Constable I have not paid much attention to, though I know Turner did, and I pay great attention to Turner. Whenever I'm in London, which is usually about every other year, I'm out at the Tate staring at the same old paintings with the same old astonishment. Some of my favorites by Turner would be "Rain, Steam and Speed—The Great Western Railway," showing the railway bridge with the frightened rabbit running; "The Fighting Temeraire" in the National Gallery; and at the Tate he's got some wonderful, almost totally abstract paintings of the world newly created. Some of his unfinished paintings, the names of which don't come to my mind now, are just as splendid as the finished ones.

Zinos-Amaro: What specifically keeps bringing you back to these paintings?

Silverberg: His dissolution of form. He was an academically trained artist—as was Picasso. If you look at early Turner, from say 1799 or thereabouts, you'll see that he can do the landscape just as precisely as Claude Lorrain. In fact, at the National Gallery in London there's a little octagonal room that by Turner's wish has two Claude Lorrains and two Turners. He left them those two under the stipulation that the four always be hung together and you can see that he has the same kind of flawless craftsmanship that Claude had.

But then, forty years down the line, he's disappearing into a kind of abstraction fifty years ahead of the time. So his dissolution of form, I believe, must be based on an intimate knowledge of how to handle form. And then his color—the brilliant colors, the explosion of light. In the recent Turner movie, which I saw with great pleasure, his alleged last words—"The sun is God"—would indicate his reverence for light. Of course, those weren't his real last words. They were put in his mouth by Ruskin, who wasn't present at the deathbed. The real last words, said to his doctor, were "Go downstairs and have a glass of sherry." Much more in keeping with the man.

Zinos-Amaro: One thing I found striking in that movie was his way of communicating with others primarily by grunting.

Silverberg: He was, at least late in life, a difficult kind of man. The grunting, who knows? He communicated with the brush.

Zinos-Amaro: I want to talk for a moment about science fiction art—book covers, magazine covers, etc. Has your relationship with art in science fiction affected your relationship with art in general?

Silverberg: I admire craftsmanship wherever I find it. I admired the craftsmanship of Sandy Koufax when he was pitching for the Dodgers. And the craftsmanship of a Kelly Freas or a Michael Whelan or a Jim Burns or an Ed Emshwiller also—and the intellectual capacity of these artists, these four in particular, I know there were others. They were able to think in science fictional terms, and their covers were frequently not based on somebody else's story, but an idea of their own that *could* have been a story but became a painting instead. Quite frequently those paintings were then handed to me to write a story around. This was particularly true with Emshwiller, with whom I did a kind of collaboration on a number of paintings.

But science fiction art is after-the-fact to me. When I write a story I don't think about the kind of cover it's going to have. And just as well, because usually the kind of cover it has—unless Jim Burns is doing it—is not what I would have wanted. It also has very little to do with what I experience in a museum. Except when I look at a van Eyck or a van der Weyden and I think, "He's even better than Kelly Freas!"

Zinos-Amaro: In the same way that in writing you've had non-SF influences that have directly inspired or motivated your work—Joseph Conrad for example—have you ever had a similar response to visual art, an experience that's motivated you or compelled you to write an SF story?

Silverberg: The Conrad was explicit. Those were quotations in the same way Bruckner would take a piece of Wagner and mortar it right into a symphony. To answer your question, I haven't had that experience in the sense that a piece of art *initiated* a story. But they've contributed to my work frequently.

I remember circa 1983 or 1984—I know it was around that time because it was before I married Karen—I was working on the novel *Tom O'Bedlam*. I went to the San Francisco Museum of Modern Art and wherever I looked there was some image on the wall that inserted itself into what I was writing. Of course, by the time it got filtered through my memory and my technique and the needs of the story it wasn't recognizable any more. There was no one-to-one correlation. But I remember walking from room to room that night at the museum and thinking, "Oh, I could use this," and "Look at that!" and "Yes, yes!" So it does happen. I remember that particular evening but I'm sure it's happened many a time.

Zinos-Amaro: I know there are some artists to whom you've consistently responded strongly. Wagner, for instance. What is your response to Wagner's aesthetic?

Silverberg: It's very complex, because it keys into my childhood fascination with the Norse myths. From the age of seven on, when I encountered Padraic Colum's retelling of the Prose Edda, the tales of Odin and Loki and Thor gripped me. Very soon thereafter I discovered that there was a thing called opera, and that there were four long operas based in part on the Germanic version of those myths.

Zinos-Amaro: How old were you when you discovered opera?

Silverberg: Eight or nine. Of course, I didn't go to the opera at the time! But there was a lovely series of little books, maybe sixty-four pages, retelling, with illustrations, the tales of the operas. I have those books to this day: the four Ring operas in the four little books in a boxed set, and also an opera called *The Three-Cornered Hat* by Manuel de Falla that is unknown now but which caught me then.

Anyway, my entry into Wagner was by way of the Norse myths. Though Wagner's libretti, as I later learned through much study, are interwoven with the Germanic Nibelungenlied, which is a much different secular proposition. When I came to the opera house to see Wagner, here were those towering figures of those myths—which helped me, incidentally, to disassociate myself from the religion I was born into and from any other religion, because I realized, "They're all stories. And this is a better story than some." There is of course the greatness of Wagner's music. The sound of Wagner is like no sound that had previously been heard on Earth, though there have been many imitators since. And then, in the days when Wagner was done by traditional opera directors, there was the look of it, the visualization of those myths.

So the operas attacked me on a number of levels. I came to the mythological one from almost the time I began to read. Sigfried slaying the dragon and having blood poured all over him and being rendered almost invulnerable but not quite. As a child I didn't understand the tragedy of Wotan, a god who ultimately is broken throughout the course of the first three operas, through his own hubris. Then there was the visual level of the scenery. And the musical level: a wonderful method of telling the story through interweaving motifs and of course the grandeur of the motifs themselves.

I don't go to see Wagner any more because the current directors—again, I'm getting very crusty and curmudgeonly—know better than Wagner. The last time I saw the Ring at the San Francisco Opera House it opened with Wotan on the telephone.

Zinos-Amaro: Was he texting by any chance?

Silverberg: He wasn't texting—that hadn't been invented yet. But it was an anti-capitalist screed in which Wotan was a Texas oilman. Yes, Wotan gets into trouble through his own arrogance: he doesn't want to pay the contractor who builds his palace. But he wasn't on the telephone, he wasn't sitting on a desk. It spoiled it for me, because it broke the connection I had.

Zinos-Amaro: Some commentators refer to the more dissonant elements of Wagner's music as somehow capturing the Dionysian life-force; you discussed the importance of Dionysian rites in your "Toward a Theory of Story" essays. Does Wagner hearken back to the Greek ideas of art for you in some way, as well?

Silverberg: Associating the Dionysian life-force with the Ring operas is a stretch, but of course you could do it. What the Ring is about for me is the overreaching of the head god, who determines to cheat the two giants who build Valhalla for him, and as a result brings into the world the powerful ring—the "one ring to rule them all," as the later and lesser creator said. The ring is made up of gold that had previously been stolen by another bad man, Alberich the dwarf, who steals it from the Rhinemaidens by foreswearing love, which makes him invulnerable to their charms. He grabs the gold, and then Wotan takes it from *him*. The ring is forged and there's a curse on the ring, and so on and so forth. The series of interlocking events show the tragic results of overreaching—sinning, to use a Christian term—and ultimately, sixteen hours later, we see Valhalla burning and the gods within it dying. The implication there, which Wagner never dealt with openly, was that a subsequent god was going to come along and take over. I don't think Wagner was any more a Christian than I am, but indeed in them—the Norse and Teutonic worlds—the supremacy of Odin and Wotan was swept away by the new creed of Jesus. And that's implicit in the Ring, that when Valhalla burns and the old gods die, *something* is going to take their place and you know what it is.

Structurally, the four Ring operas fit into that great formula we were talking about—a narrative that results in a cleansing of the commonwealth, a climactic and cathartic event—that I think everything from the Gilgamesh legend and the *Odyssey* do.

Zinos-Amaro: Nietzsche, who it seems liked Wagner's operas in general, offers a critique of *Parsifal*, which came after the Ring, as being too Christian or too decayed in some fashion. What's your take?

Silverberg: I don't respond to *Parsifal* in the same way I respond to the Ring, but in part that's because of my childhood conditioning to that set of myths. *Parsifal* is indeed rather Christian, as well as Wagner could be Christian. After all, in the opening of Act Two the Grail Knights essentially perform mass on stage. They are passing around the blood and singing, "This is the blood, this is the body." And what is the Grail, but the vessel in which Christ's blood was collected? But Wagner was a miserable pagan, and he came up with some confusions in Parsifal, but it's basically a Christian concept. Nietzsche—he didn't end well, you know?

Zinos-Amaro: [laughs]

Silverberg: I've read Nietzsche's essays on Wagner but I don't remember them very well, so I don't know exactly what his problem with *Parsifal* was, but he may have just preferred the *Ring*. We haven't mentioned *Tristan and Isolde* for that matter, which is not in any way

Christian. But we see there the classic structural formula. Through no fault of his own, Tristan is led into a tragic situation. He's handed a love potion and doesn't know what he's drinking. He's eventually destroyed but redeemed in a ten-minute climactic aria, the marvelous *Liebestod*.

Zinos-Amaro: Shifting gears for a moment to another famous philosopher who developed a theory of art, Kant, I had a question about another of your lifelong interests, gardening. Kant wrote that "[L]andscape gardening [. . .] consists in no more than decking out the ground with the same manifold variety (grasses, flowers, shrubs, and trees, and even water, hills, and dales) as that with which nature presents it to our view, only arranged differently and in obedience to certain ideas." Is gardening a type of painting with forms and color for you?

Silverberg: Eighteenth-century landscaping was very explicitly painterly. The laying out of the trees, the flowers, and the lakes of the great estates of the eighteenth century; I'm sure they saw paintings when they were planning them.

In my case it's not so much color, because of the idiosyncratic nature of my favorite plants. Shape is more important to me than color. I've not been ignorant of the color effects but my garden has lent itself so much towards succulents, which are not famous for their color. An aloe has a beautiful red flower—there are some going outside in the garden right now. I have tried within the limits of the available space I have to observe my sense of form, to lay things out agreeably. I began here with a garden that was already established, and I've changed it drastically in the course of the last forty-five years.

Landscape gardening, particularly on a large scale, certainly evokes an aesthetic response. I'm thinking, for example, of the botanic gardens of Melbourne and Sydney, both of which are enormous pastoral tracts within major cities, where everything was laid out in the nineteenth century with a wonderful eye for form. Of course many other botanical gardens too. The landscape artist is indeed painting with plants, choosing the color of the bloom, the shape of the tree, the color of the leaf. Just today I was working outside on this lovely warm winter day and I came upon a plant out there that I had neglected for some years—

Zinos-Amaro: Years?

Silverberg: Yeah, it's a big garden [chuckles]. The plant had just gone its way without any maintenance from me, and it needs maintenance. I had forgotten its name, as can happen at a certain age. I traced it back by looking through a book that listed plants not by their species but by the color of their foliage. I went to the trusty Internet and got some expert advice on how I can bring this plant back to its proper form, which requires drastic pruning.

Zinos-Amaro: In thinking about art in traditional cultures from ancient times, it seems to me that there wasn't as much recognition of individual artists as there is today. Ancient artists didn't always sign their name, or maybe regard themselves as artists in the same way we do. What do you think of this change?

Silverberg: I don't think there's been much of a change. Remember that the classical civilizations are alien cultures to us, far away. Periclean Greece is twenty-five hundred years ago. We're looking through a glass darkly, and we're lucky to know as much about them as we do. We certainly know a great deal about the Greek individual artists. There was Phidias the sculptor, Zeuxis the painter—and those are just two whose names that have come down to us.

Zinos-Amaro: Well yes, there is a record. We know of the Pioneer group, for instance, which I looked up for this conversation: Euphronios, Euthymides, Smikros, Hypsias, the Dikaios Painter and Phintias.

Silverberg: The Greek coins are miniature works of art and were designed by great artists. Not so the Roman coins, but the Greek ones. We know because they signed the dies. We know who did the great coins of Syracuse; we know that Kimon did that one, and Euainetos did that one. They have survived. We don't know anything about them, but we know their work. Artists in these times probably had a similar standing to artists in the Renaissance: hired hands supported by patrons.

Since we know so much about individual Roman poets and even a few Roman novelists, we probably know something about individual Roman painters too—though I don't. The work that has survived, and it's marvelous work, is all anonymous. We don't know who did the murals in Pompeii. What we do know is that those were the best paintings that were done between Lascaux and Giotto—and that's quite a span.

We don't know anything about the Egyptian painters. There was very considerable Egyptian painting, though held to a rigid formula that was not permitted to deviate for a staggering three thousand years.

Zinos-Amaro: Why don't we know the names of Egyptian painters? Were they considered artists in their society?

Silverberg: We just don't know them, nobody preserved them. What we know are the names of the Pharaohs and public officials. The painters were considered artisans, not artists. The lack of variation in Egyptian art from the fourth dynasty on to the Ptolemaic period probably indicates that they were told what to do, and if they attempted to deviate from that they would be driven from the temple.

Of course in a sense that was true in the Renaissance too. You painted within the narrative. You did not, as Max Ernst did, show the baby Jesus biting the breast of the Virgin. If you did, woe betide you!

Zinos-Amaro: I wanted to turn to the subject of classical music now. In the dust jackets of some of your early non-fiction works, like your biography of Socrates, it says that one of your hobbies was "collecting classical music records." You've written about striking up a friendship with Bob Lowndes by way of your shared love of classical music. When did your interest in music start, and did you study musical theory?

Silverberg: I don't think that collecting classical records is quite an accurate description of what I was doing, by the way. I do have a collection of classical records, but my goal was to hear the music, and the way you do that is to accumulate the objects on which that music is preserved.

I did study musical theory but it was a great disaster. When I was ten, at my parents' urgings I took up the study of the clarinet. I played the way any untalented ten-year-old would play. My instructor, who was a medical student who was picking up some cash on the side, also instructed me in musical theory. I learned a lot about dominant sevenths and all of that. None of it stuck. My sense of pitch is not trustworthy. I can tell that note from that other note, but I can't sing, for example. Dr. Mamloks' instruction and theory did not remain with me very long, nor did the playing of the clarinet. But listening to music as a consumer, the way I can go to a museum without being able to paint, was very important to me from the time I discovered there was such a thing as music.

I remember the biggest impact came when I was perhaps fifteen and I went to see *Fantasia*. I had been taken to see *Fantasia* when I was a little boy—it came out when I was four. But I went to see it again in my middle teens. And there was the Beethoven *Pastoral*, the *Le Sacre du printemps*, the *Toccata and Fugue in D Minor*, *Night on Bald Mountain*, all done with visual effects. I thought, "This is all wonderful stuff. I will go out immediately and get the LP records." LPs were just a couple of years old. And I did, and that began my collecting. I formed a collection of classical records, but the true collector, which

I never was, would go hunting down 78 RPMs and rare albums and things like that. I was interested in the music.

Zinos-Amaro: Your work is certainly peppered with references to classical music. Eli in *The Book of Skulls*, for example, mentions Berg, Schoenberg and Xenakis—I was nineteen when I read that. Webern, Penderecki and Stockhausen are also mentioned. You featured Pergolesi himself as a character in "Gianni." So your interest in classical music clearly manifests in your science fiction writing. But I don't see the same happening with painting, sculpture, film or other forms of art. Am I just missing the other references?

Silverberg: No, you're not missing them. But what my characters talk about relates to who they are. In *The Book of Skulls* they're college boys and they're more likely to talk about composers than the movie they just saw. It's a good thing, because those movies would mean nothing to today's readers, but some of them still know who Berg and Schoenberg were. My characters are not likely to describe a landscape as something out of Monet. I don't think that would be a useful narrative step.

Zinos-Amaro: But you design the characters. Why couldn't it potentially be a useful step?

Silverberg: Well, a lot of it is science fiction. *The Book of Skulls* is set in 1971-1972, but *The Face of the Waters* is set on Hydros, a planet far away, in the remote future. I'm not going to be talking about Turner and I'm not going to be talking about Wagner. I think you may have the wrong end of the stick when you talk about the effect of music on me. Where the music has fed into my work is not so much references to particular composers, which is a kind of stamp collecting—"oh yes, I know who Beethoven is"—but where the compositions themselves are playing in my head as I'm writing. I never play music when I write, or when I did. I sit in my office with my back to the garden.

But I can hear the music. Particularly in the climactic pages of a novel something is playing in my head. There's an essay I wrote called "The Sense of an Ending" that talks about that. I find it often very useful to refer to some specific passage to give me the tone, the pace. Karen was writing a novel twenty years ago and she was having trouble with the ending. I suggested a way for her to handle it that involved listening to a passage near the end of Benjamin Britten's *Peter Grimes*. I said, "Listen to what that man is saying to Peter Grimes. He's saying, 'Go out and drown yourself,'" which is what Peter Grimes does. "Listen to the way he's saying, 'Take the boat, Peter. Go offshore. *Sink* the boat.'" It's a kind of Sprechstimme, he's not really singing it. "Listen to that, it will give you the tone for the passage you have to write." This was a revelation to her.

Zinos-Amaro: I find this remarkable. You can just evoke the music mentally?

Silverberg: Well how else, Alvaro, telepathically? [laughs] I listen to the music, try to remember what it sounds like. I can summon it up, like Glendower from the vasty deep, and sometimes it comes. *The World Inside*, which I wrote forty-five years ago, so I can't be terribly specific, is an example of when this happened. One of the sections involves an actual musician, named Dillon Chrimes. The rhythm of the prose was generated by whatever music I summoned up when I was writing that.

When this happens, the music feeds the scene. As I enter a scene, suddenly I can hear Brünnhilde about to march into the flames on top of her horse. I can hear the rhythm, the beat, and I'm writing to that rhythm. I try to draw for my writing on everything that will provide another layer of texture.

Zinos-Amaro: You've attended a lot of classical concerts through the years. Are there any performances that stand out for you?

Silverberg: Yes, and I've been treated to a couple of them right here in San Francisco in latter days. Michael Tilson Thomas did a Mahler Second that left me slack-jawed and also an astounding *Le Sacre du printemps*. I can go back to my teens for other legendary performances, like Tchaikovsky's Fifth at the Brooklyn Academy of Music, circa 1952; Charles Munch was conducting, and though this happened sixty-three years ago, I even remember who I went with, so it certainly left an impression on me. Also a *Rosenkavalier* at the Met in 1957 or so that still destroys all subsequent *Rosenkavaliers* that I've seen. All wonderful experiences.

That's what a writer's material is made of, the things that the writer has done and seen and felt and which he's able to find at the moment he needs them.

Zinos-Amaro: Film is another art form I'd like to talk about. Going back through fifteen years of email exchanges with you, I found an email from October 2003 where you mentioned you skip most contemporary American movies, because they are extreme in that they are "either full of explosions and car chases" or "soppy sentimentality." At that time you wrote about watching mostly European movies from the 1925-45 period. What are some of your favorites, and why this period?

Silverberg: I would extend the period quite a bit. I would extend it to 1970 or so because if you cut it off at '45 you exclude Bergman, Fellini, and Kurosawa and that really does decapitate modern movies. Incidentally, I watched a movie from 1943 last night that I'd never heard of before, a French movie about a painter selling his soul to the devil, called *Carnival of Sinners*.

1925 roughly starts us with the great German movies, including Fritz Lang's *Die Nibelungen*, which is Wagner without the music. All of the German movies, the UFA productions, and the Russian ones—Eisenstein and Dovzhenko—begin in the mid-'20s. Silent movies have an entirely different texture from what followed.

We move forward to the Hollywood movies of the '30s—the Busby Berkeley movies, the *Thin Man* stuff—and find a certain period charm. These movies are from an era before I was born, and I was born quite a while ago. The portrayals of that world, its telephones, its cars, its furnishings, I find fascinating.

Zinos-Amaro: Charlie Chaplin?

Silverberg: Chaplin never spoke to me. Buster Keaton was the comedian I responded to. I don't much enjoy funny movies, but Keaton is something special. The Three Stooges, no; Buster Keaton, yes.

Then there's a great gap for me in American movies from roughly 1945 to 1970. I saw very few Hollywood movies; I didn't need to, there were more than I could see coming in from overseas. The only American movies of that period that I go back and see now, and there aren't many, are those that I saw in my childhood that I want to revisit. John Ford's *Stage Coach* and *My Darling Clementine*—a lot of Westerns, surprisingly. And *King Kong*. I don't know how many times I've seen *King Kong* but it always, always transfixes me. The first time I saw it I was ten years old and they played it in a double bill with *Son of Kong*, the mediocre sequel. I went to see a matinee of *King Kong*, sat through *Son of Kong*, and then sat through *King Kong* again, that very same day! You could do that then, because movies ran consecutively in the theater. I got home quite late and there was quite a discussion about the hour at which I returned.

Zinos-Amaro: You would go on such outings by yourself when you were ten?

Silverberg: By myself, or with some friends perhaps. The world was much safer then. We went everywhere by ourselves. My friend Saul Diskin and I would take long excursions throughout Brooklyn at the age of nine and nobody said anything about it. Wouldn't do that now. But by the time I reached college—now we're talking about the period from 1952 to 1956—we're beginning to get the influx of postwar European movies: Rossellini, Jean Renoir, various other Italian directors who are not remembered, the first Fellini movies, Luis Buñuel. There was such richness, and of course I lived in New York, not West Boondock, and so had everything available. New York at that time had a theater near Carnegie Hall, the Toho theater, that showed nothing but Japanese movies. There was another Toho in San Francisco that was still in its last gasp when I moved out here. So of course I saw all the Kurosawa movies and movies by lesser directors. The first Japanese movies that came, like *Gate of Hell* or *Ugetsu*, were not Kurosawa, they were made at other studios. Great visual treats. I still try to go the movies, and I see on average about one and a half movies per week. One at home usually, courtesy of Netflix, one in the theaters. But of course the supply is diminishing, because I prefer subtitled movies and that filters out a great deal of the audience.

Zinos-Amaro: You mentioned that American gap. Was that just because European and Japanese cinema captivated you more?

Silverberg: There wasn't much that was good. Remember, I was a college boy going to an Ivy League school and though I could respond to the mythic dimension of the Western, let's say, there was not much about the typical gangster movie that I wanted to see. There were *some* good ones in that period, like *Beat the Devil* or *The African Queen*.

Then later, in 1970 or thereabouts, there was a great renaissance in American filmmaking. We had *Midnight Cowboy*, *Easy Rider*, *The Graduate* and *Petulia* and scads of movies that were pitched rather differently from the movies of the '40s and '50s, which were aimed at twelve-year-olds.

Don't forget that movies, even for a fairly sophisticated New Yorker, provide a window on the world. It's a way of seeing that which you can't see, like the Eiffel tower—and during the War you couldn't go anywhere, and after the War I was busy with college for a while. A trip from New York to Philadelphia was a major outing for me, as I was saying last time. Starting in 1957, when I made my first European trip, I began to go everywhere, and let movies be my guide to some degree. I saw what Paris looked like in the movies and thought, "I'll go there," and found it looked even better.

Zinos-Amaro: You've just touched on one of the ways that cinema has served you, by allowing vicarious travel. What are other purposes or benefits you see in the film experience?

Silverberg: There is the narrative value. A movie like *The Seven Samurai* is a very exciting battle story involving some very interesting and distinctive characters—a great movie. A movie like *La Dolce Vita*—which I first saw in Rome, incidentally, without subtitles—portrays an alien society. I was a professional writer at the time of *La Dolce Vita* and could impose a narrative on the episodic scenes. When we reach the final scene, Marcello is on one side of a little coastal stream and there's a young girl on the other side and some kind of sea monster has washed up between them. He's trying to speak to her and she can't hear him. The girl is calling things to Marcello across the stream and he can't hear her. That failure of communication, which is the last thing you see, is that moment of perception that *I* found in the movie of Marcello, having traversed the Roman decadent society of 1959, finally face-to-face with the fact that he can't reach anybody, and nobody can reach him. Prior to that there's the character of the philosopher who kills himself, played by the French actor Alain Cuny, and the wonderful goofy moment of the Christ dangled from the helicopter in the opening. So everything is building to Marcello's isolation within this pleasure-loving but defeated society. I could find a story there, even episodic as it was.

Zinos-Amaro: There are movies where it's much harder to impose a narrative, like *Last Year at Marienbad*.

Silverberg: Well that's a special case, an extreme case which we might even say is a *reductio ad absurdum*. But yes, besides the narrative value there is the formal aspect: the editing, the lighting, and so on.

Zinos-Amaro: Is that something you pay attention to?

Silverberg: I do to the limit of a layman's understanding of how movies are made. The one craft I really understand is writing. I'm not a movie-maker, a composer or a painter, so I have to come to these things as an amateur. But I can perceive how the editing is done. I can look at what Kurosawa is doing and think, "What a marvelous camera angle that is," which in some ways knocks me out of the story, but I can't help that.

Zinos-Amaro: Do you experience the cathartic response we were talking about before?

Silverberg: Oh yes, if that movie gets me to that place, i.e. if it's a competent movie. I saw a movie recently called *Diplomacy*. It's a movie about Hitler's order to destroy Paris as the Germans retreated under the American invasion. There's a different version of it, called *Is Paris Burning?*, which I never saw. *Diplomacy*, an extremely elegantly made movie, is largely a dialog between the German general and the French official who is attempting to convince him to leave Paris alone. I knew Paris had not been destroyed by the Germans. I've been to Paris many times and it's there, looking just like itself. But the film, as conveyed through these two splendid actors and these beautifully drawn characters, had me in suspense. Will the German give the order, throw the switch and destroy Paris? And when it doesn't happen, and he is turned, he is finally convinced that this isn't how he wants to be remembered in history—the man who destroyed Paris at Hitler's orders—there was great cathartic release. And yet I knew all along how it had to come out. Well, that's good writing and directing.

Zinos-Amaro: One theory about how movies entrance us is the dream theory of film. You're in a dark environment, looking *into* a screen (which is different from looking *at* something), and you enter a dream-like state.

Silverberg: When I was a small boy I remember coming out of movies—I saw a lot of Westerns—and stepping out into the day-light (I only went to matinees) and having to adapt to the presence of Brooklyn around me. I was no longer in a concentration camp somewhere in Germany, or an island somewhere in the Pacific. It was a jolt, a difficult transition, and I noticed it very consciously when I was ten. "I'm still in the movie," I would think. Less so now. I'm pretty aware of the boundary between movie and reality. But it is a kind of dream-like state.

Zinos-Amaro: To follow the implication in reverse, do you ever have dreams that are film-like?

Silverberg: I have dreams that are fiction-like [laughs].

Zinos-Amaro: You mean you don't dream realities?

Silverberg: Of course they're realities—and sometimes saleable realities. I wrote a whole novel that was drawn from a series of dreams that I had during the two or three weeks that I was writing the book. I remember my dreams very well and many of them are extremely vivid and useful. I have dreamed whole sections of the book I'm writing. On more than one occasion I've dreamed an entire novel, the writing of it. I can remember starting on page one and during the course of that dream—which may have lasted two and a quarter seconds—pro-ducing the whole thing and thinking, "This is pretty good. I'll tran-scribe it as soon as I wake up." Of course I can't remember a word of it when I awaken.

Last night it was necessary for me to get to Trafalgar Square, not from California, but wherever I was in London, and there was some difficulty in making the journey. I drew up a very intricate route on the tube that involved going all around Robin Hood's barn and late in the dream I thought, "It's too complicated getting there by tube. I'll just walk there." I've done it many a time; it's about a fifteen-minute walk from Grosvenor Square, where my hotel is, to Trafalgar Square, where whatever important thing was going on. That would not have formed a very interesting part of a story but it was certainly very vivid while it was going on. I do sometimes when I'm in London plot out a tube route for myself, but it's not that hard.

Zinos-Amaro: Anything else you'd like to add about how film has affected your life?

Silverberg: There are eight books and stories of mine under film option now and it would change my life if one of them became a spectacular hit, but so far . . . It's now the all-time record. At the moment they are *The Book of Skulls*, *Dying Inside*—which I can't see as a movie, but that's not my problem—"How It Was When the Past Went Away," "Passengers," *Downward to the Earth*, *The World Inside*, "Needle in a Timestack" and *Hawksbill Station*. I usually have something or other under option, but never before eight at once.

Zinos-Amaro: I had heard that *The World Inside* might become a television series.

Silverberg: HBO was quite seriously interested in it for a while. They even had a producer. What killed that was *Game of Thrones*. They decided, "We have enough of that fantasy stuff now, we don't need another one."

Zinos-Amaro: We have been talking a lot of about narrative. In your autobiographical essay "The Making of a Science-Fiction Writer" you wrote the following: "The storytelling art evolved as a way of interpreting the world—as a way of creating order out of the chaos that the cruel or merely absentminded gods handed us long ago. To perform the task effectively, the writer must peer into the heart of the chaos; the writer must know something about the world." What do you mean by chaos in this context?

Silverberg: Have you ever been to Times Square in the middle of the afternoon, watching people go in all directions? Everybody in Times Square—or Trafalgar Square, or Piazza Venezia—is bound on some purpose of his own, unrelated to anybody else's, and to make sense of that frenetic activity requires imposing an organization. The world is a very busy, crowded place and we don't generally understand what's happening in it unless we make contact with what's going on about us. A story is an artificially imposed order in which the various characters are bound on purposes that we do perceive, eventually—we may not perceive them at the beginning. That's what I mean by order from chaos.

Zinos-Amaro: In a 1986 essay called "Becoming a Writer" you wrote that "The moment a writer strops growing, he starts to shrink." Can you say a little bit more about that?

Silverberg: I think you're handed most of your material in your first twenty or thirty years. New experiences happen all the time, not always pleasant ones, but the ones that shape you, the ones that define you, happen early. If you are a successful writer, and I was one, you tend to spend more of your time at home writing and less out in the world being buffeted by the chaos I spoke of moments ago. And so you're not gaining new material. I've had plenty of things happen to me in the second half of my life that didn't happen in the first: I had a fire turn me out of my house when I was thirty-three, I moved from one end of the country to another when I was thirty-five, I had a divorce when I was fifty-one. But I don't think these experiences are formative the way your first day at school is, or an early romance, or an early failed romance. They just add to the accumulation of stuff that has happened to you. They're not the deep part of the well that you draw on in creating a story and a character. And therefore your later work tends to be reprocessing of things you've done before.

Zinos-Amaro: How does the writer grow, then? Is it craft, technique?

Silverberg: Up to a point the craft and technique can expand your ability. I think I've forgotten a lot of tricks I used to use! But I've been around a long time. After a while the technique doesn't improve. What the writer needs is the reservoir of experience that he will manipulate using the craft at his command. Occasionally an older writer will surprise. Heinlein, when he wrote *The Moon Is a Harsh Mistress*, wrote it in a tone of voice that was nothing like anything he had ever used before, and that was quite surprising. He was fifty-six or so then. But very few writers write anything worthwhile in the later years.

There's nothing really wrong with going back to the same stuff if it's good stuff. The later Sherlock Holmes stories are just as good, I suspect, as the early ones. Simenon wrote seventy-five novels about Maigret and they're all fun to read. But you're not growing, you're not changing. And if you do change, you're going to get some ugly fan letters. *Lord Valentine's Castle*, coming after a four-and-a-half-year hiatus, was a consciously chosen departure from what I'd written before. When it was published I got a letter from a woman who said, "I read *Lord Valentine's Castle* and then I read *Dying Inside*. How dare you write a book like that? I was expecting more *Lord Valentine's Castle*, and instead I get this thing." I didn't answer her. She had read them in the wrong order, of course, but she was disturbed that I had changed path.

Zinos-Amaro: Is the writer's growth in the eyes of the reader?

Silverberg: Well sometimes the readers disappoint one. That can't be helped. I was reading in *The Wall Street Journal* today about the information that circulates in the world of the stock market, and they talk about how the brokers will estimate the earnings that a company is expected to have in the coming quarter or year. If the earnings miss the estimate the stock will go down. The writer said, rather cleverly, that it isn't the earnings that miss the estimate, but that the estimate misses the earnings. So sometimes the audience fails the writer. Nothing can be done about that.

Zinos-Amaro: [laughs] I think Oscar Wilde once remarked that one of his plays was a great success but the audience was a dismal failure. So are we saying it's simply not possible for the writer to grow past a certain age?

Silverberg: Most of them don't. Late Hemingway, late Faulkner, late Saul Bellow, we're talking about some of our greatest writers now. Shakespeare wrote the *The Tempest* when he was fifty-two or so and retired. Roth gave it up at eighty, but he might as well have done so ten years earlier without harming his reputation.

Zinos-Amaro: Late Henry James?

Silverberg: That's a special case. He entered into what I would call a kind of decadence, an over-elaboration of the technique.

Zinos-Amaro: Late Nabokov?

Silverberg: He was fifty-five when he wrote *Lolita*, fifty-seven when he wrote *Pnin*. This is not exactly deep in old age. And also his life was interrupted by his exile from Russia. *Ada or Ardor* I think is a great failure of a novel that he wrote when he was seventy. It's a science fiction novel in a way; it takes place in a parallel world. So you see, his best work was done before he was sixty.

Zinos-Amaro: One can at least produce good work for several decades.

Silverberg: I think most writers do their strongest work say between thirty-five and fifty. Certainly I did. Plenty of my work later than that needs no apology but after I wrote *Star of Gypsies*, when I was about sixty, I started to run out of steam. There was still *The Face of the Waters* to come, and other books. *The Alien Years* was about the last gasp. Though there's much that I like in *The Alien Years*—I took out the best parts and made them into short stories, and I'm very proud of them—it does not have, line by line, the intensity of what I was doing twenty years earlier.

So I stopped writing, aware that there is nothing further that I wanted to say in the world of science fiction. I'm out of touch with contemporary society—which is another good reason I don't think I should be writing any more. The science fiction writer, in building his extrapolations, has to have a starting point in the present. I don't have a cell phone. I'm not sure what Wi-Fi is. I can't do reasonable extrapolation from a world if I don't understand it. I'm not part of the world of today's readers—but I *was* part of their world. In fact, I helped to create their world. Somebody was once collecting epitaphs of living people and asked me to write an epitaph for myself. I said, "Because he wrote so much about the future, he was condemned to live in it."

Yes, I can use the Internet, I can use DVR, I have a bionic circulatory system, so a lot of benefits have to come from the twenty-first century, but I certainly don't feel at home here.

I've already lived considerably longer than Faulkner, Hemingway, James and Shakespeare—just to name a few of my colleagues!

Now, sometimes you don't recognize all this, and you go staggering on, writing one feeble book after another.

Zinos-Amaro: If the books keep getting published, do the readers recognize it?

Silverberg: It's hard to tell. I don't think late Heinlein is very impressive but yet they sold millions of copies. And sometime in that late run of novels he did *Friday*, which was a very vigorous book.

Zinos-Amaro: Late Clarke or Dick?

Silverberg: I was never much of an admirer of Clarke's work. Late Dick is a special case; it's esoteric mysticism. What he's writing in his late years is almost discontinuous from what he was writing before. And also it's not late Dick—he died at fifty-four.

Zinos-Amaro: Jack Williamson?

Silverberg: Another exception that proves the rule. My God, the guy won the Hugo and the Nebula when he was ninety-one! Nobody else has done that. Nobody else, I think, ever will.

What I began to fear for myself, and it was probably an unrealistic fear, is that I'd publish a book and it would be so weak that it would retroactively invalidate all my other stuff. People would read it and say, "I can't believe he was *ever* any good." Well I didn't write that book. Also, and I don't mean this to sound defensive, I wrote enough. It isn't as though I had a sketchy career. I was not a shirker.

Zinos-Amaro: In your seven decades as a reader, who are some of the overlooked or obscure writers that stand out? I've heard you talk about Ward Just, for example.

Silverberg: I read a lot of Ward Just in the eighties and I think he's still published, but somehow I lost track of him, probably because he started doing the same book over and over. Ward Just provided insight into the world of Washington political society of interest to me, that I see only from a great distance. Louis Begley is another one. Begley is a curious case because he's Jewish, but he offers a look at the world of WASP privilege, the New York high WASP lawyer world, which he found his entree into. I find that world of some interest. I'm hardly part of it myself, but because writers live outside the class system, generally, I've been able to move in parallel circles. Though I'm an alien in them, I'm accepted. But these writers, Just and Begley, are quite visible.

Anthony Trollope is hardly an obscure writer, but nobody much reads him any more, except I do. What Trollope gave me was a portrait of the Victorian world I find fascinating. And elegant plot construction. The huge Trollope novels always reach a proper resolution, and I admire that in a writer. He doesn't drop a stitch.

I've written about *Hadrian the Seventh* by Frederick Rolfe. Now there was a really neglected writer, a paranoid writer. Crazy man, great writer. Luckily for him, posthumously his one great book was rediscovered. I've read a lot of his other works and they weren't as good.

I've also enjoyed the works of W. M. Spackman and Ivy Compton-Burnett, but I don't know how neglected these are. I begin to think that anybody who is not writing for the Oprah Winfrey book club is a neglected writer or an unknown writer now.

Zinos-Amaro: I know you waited a long time to read *War and Peace*. I believe you read it in 2002 for the first time. Why the wait, and are there other classics of that magnitude lying in store for you?

Silverberg: *War and Peace* had a talismanic value for me. Somebody would always ask me, "Have you read such and such?" Tolkien, for example. And I would say, "Well you know, I haven't even read *War and Peace* yet, and that's the greatest novel there is." That was my defense against not having read *Stranger in a Strange Land* or *Lord of the Rings*. And then I thought, "That works very well. It's very convincing. But on the other hand, here I am getting older and older, and I've never read *War and Peace*!" So I thought, "Read *War and Peace*." And I did. And behold, it is the greatest novel ever written, or at least the greatest novel I've ever read.

I don't think there's much else now that I haven't read of that sort.

I've read the Brontës, for example. I've been through Dickens several times. I've pushed my way through Proust twice, two different translations. I'm glad to have read it, but I can't say that I was eager to pull the next volume down from the shelf. I like to reread classics. I was looking at Thomas Mann's *Buddenbrooks* just the other day, thinking, "I should make one more tour through *Buddenbrooks*," which I had read in college and then subsequently. One late book by Mann that I found very pleasing, by the way, was *Confessions of Felix Krull*. He wrote the first ten or fifteen thousand words in his twenties and late in life picked up right where he stopped, continued and finished it! *Doctor Faustus* is also late Mann, and a great novel. I'd like to read Gibbon once more. But Gibbon is very large and I don't have much time. I'd like to read *Don Quixote* once more. I read Rabelais earlier this year for the third time. It was wonderful, and that's my farewell to Rabelais. At eighty you know you don't have thirty or forty years of reading time ahead; you have to judge your consumption. I've never read Thackeray. And so I think when I've finished what I'm reading now I'll pull down *Vanity Fair* and give it a try.

Zinos-Amaro: That's an interesting phrase, "my farewell." You're aware of saying goodbye to certain writers these days?

Silverberg: My whole life is a series of farewells now.

Zinos-Amaro: And you're conscious of this during each experience.

Silverberg: Yes. I know I'll never have time to read Rabelais again. I probably will never have time to go to Berlin again. I've been there three times, and that's probably enough. I'm fairly healthy, reasonably vigorous for an old man, but I don't have infinite time. I'm conscious frequently that this is probably the last time I'll have this particular experience. Now, I'm not going to think that about Paris, because I'll keep struggling to go back to Paris as long as I can. But Washington,

D.C.? No. Probably not Chicago. I'd like to see *Seven Samurai* once more, but not twice more. It's inherent in the process of getting to the end of your life that you're saying goodbye to things all the time. If I were Jack Williamson, I'd still have eighteen years left.

Zinos-Amaro: I know you enjoy reading biographies, especially of artists of one type or another. What are some of the best biographies you've read?

Silverberg: I do gobble them up. There's a two-volume biography of Nabokov by Brian Boyd that I think is splendid. Another one is a biography of Sinclair Lewis by Mark Shorer. Curiously enough, Sinclair Lewis is not a writer that I read, but the biography brought him to life. I particularly like the biographies that have a tragic arc: the writer achieves great popularity and financial success, and then somehow fizzles it all away and ends in a daze of alcoholism or poverty. That's the Sinclair Lewis story. I've never ready any Dreiser, but his career is of interest to me: the coming out of nowhere, the success, the decline. W. A. Swanberg's biography of Dreiser captures this.

I've read about Faulkner's life. And Fitzgerald. I keep reading Fitzgerald biographies over and over. I'm very fond of his work, his elegant prose. A couple of splendid novels: *Gatsby* and *Tender is the Night*. But he didn't last very long.

I've read a number of books about Dickens, who is particularly interesting to me because he became his own publisher. He bought back the rights to his books, and he was a terrific businessman. Worked himself to death, died at fifty-eight. He didn't have to worry about late-life decline; he didn't get there. Trollope wrote an ill-advised autobiography. He told exactly how he wrote his books. He'd start at five in the morning and write two hundred and fifty words an hour, or whatever it was, and then he'd pack up and go to his job at the post office, where he was a very important executive. This was like the Wizard of Oz taking the curtain off.

I'm reading now, not for the first time, the memoirs of Albert

Speer, Hitler's architect. Not a biography, it's an autobiography, but a wonderful portrayal of the court of Hitler, the monsters that surrounded him. Speer was not particularly a Nazi, just happened to be caught up in it all for the glory of the architecture, and there he is among Goering and Goebbels and Himmler and a lot of very much larger-than-life dragons.

I see a new biography of Bellow starting up, many volumes apparently.

I'm eager to read the forthcoming Philip Roth biography. He had a very turbulent life but he's finishing well. He's rich, famous, old, seems happy.

Zinos-Amaro: Has he avoided that retroactive damage you were talking about before?

Silverberg: He wrote weak novels toward the end but I think people will forgive him.

There was an Updike biography that I read last year by Begley's son, Adam Begley. Fine, but just not quite good enough, biography, because the second wife suppressed a lot of material that could have been used.

Zinos-Amaro: There was a big new biography of Joyce a few years ago by Gordon Bowker.

Silverberg: I've read Richard Ellman's book on Joyce. I had the first edition of it, which he later expanded. Some of this is intimidating. I read a lot, but there's a lot to read.

Zinos-Amaro: What about the lives of composers or other artists?

Silverberg: I'm hampered with composers to some degree by my lack of technical musical knowledge. I cannot follow the structural complexities of modulating from one key to another, for example. I have an approximate idea of what's meant but I don't hear it. Beethoven, of course, interests me greatly. Complicated, tormented man. I like the novelistic aspects of biographies.

Zinos-Amaro: So perhaps Bach is not your favorite biographical subject!

Silverberg: I've never read a biography of Bach. Great, great artist, sat there year after year pumping out masterpieces. Twenty kids, two hundred and seventeen cantatas—not a very tragic arc.

I read Leon Edel's five-volume biography of Henry James. James did not have a very dramatic life, but he was an interesting man, a brilliant man. He traveled a lot, he moved in interesting circles overseas, he wrote several great novels: *The Wings of the Dove* and *The Portrait of a Lady*, which I think is his greatest work. (And a couple of novels I couldn't manage to read—but I'll forgive him those, because maybe it's my fault that *The Ambassadors* feels so ornate). James did not have great commercial success. He was a writer's writer and lived comfortably but his books did not sell very well, unlike those of the various bestselling writers of that period who are totally forgotten. He wanted to be a playwright, and wrote a play, *Guy Domville*, that apparently was so preposterous that it was booed off the stage on opening night; it was quite traumatic for him.

I have a very tempting biography of Mahler and I do want to get to that.

Zinos-Amaro: We've talked about writers and a little about recognition. I wanted to walk through the list of Nobel Prize winners with you and get your brief thoughts on some of them, starting from the present and working back.

Silverberg: Okay.

Zinos-Amaro: Alice Munro.

Silverberg: I've read many of her short stories and think she's a very good writer. I'm not eager to enter the world of shabby lower middle-class Canadian life she portrays, but she writes brilliantly.

Zinos-Amaro: Mo Yan.

Silverberg: Never had heard of him before.

Zinos-Amaro: Tomas Tranströmer.

Silverberg: A Swedish poet. I don't keep up with contemporary poetry.

Zinos-Amaro: Mario Vargas Llosa.

Silverberg: Yes, I've read several of his novels. Not my favorite Latin American works. I prefer Garcia Marquez's.

Zinos-Amaro: Samuel Beckett.

Silverberg: I'm less fond of Beckett than I once was. I saw the original American production of *Waiting for Godot*, with Bert Lahr and E. G. Marshall. I thought, "Whatever this is about, it's fascinating." *Endgame* too. *Krapp's Last Tape*. A fine playwright. But his prose doesn't sing to me. I couldn't get much beyond the first novel in his trilogy, *Molloy*. Of course in his plays he's in collaboration with his actors.

Zinos-Amaro: Hermann Hesse.

Silverberg: I read *The Glass Bead Game*—it had some other title when I read it. A kind of fantasy novel. He, for me, is a one-book writer. I never went on to *Steppenwolf*, which everyone was reading at the time. *Siddhartha* was for the kids of the '60s; college reading, like Tolkien.

Zinos-Amaro: Heinrich Böll.

Silverberg: I've read his short stories, but not his novels. Capable writer. I tend to like German fiction. Günter Grass, for example. I enjoyed *The Tin Drum* and *The Flounder*, two great panoramic novels. I like the novel to show me the world. Somebody talking about Mahler symphonies said a symphony is a world. Well, not if it's a Haydn symphony.

Zinos-Amaro: Golding and Eliot I know you like.

Silverberg: Yes.

Zinos-Amaro: André Gide.

Silverberg: Clever writer. I've read his journals. Very fine observer of the mid-century scene. *Lafcadio's Adventures* is a sly novel about a man who pushes somebody off a train just for the fun of it.

Zinos-Amaro: Juan Ramón Jiménez.

Silverberg: No. I did read Cela fifty years ago, but don't remember it well.

Zinos-Amaro: Isaac Bashevis Singer.

Silverberg: Oh, he's a very inspiring writer because the world that he writes about could be from another planet—the world of the shtetl. I was reading a book of Singer's no more than five years ago, a collection of short stories, and as I was reading it, I thought, "Gee, writing short stories is a really good thing to do. I should do another one." I don't get that feeling too often. I took a few aspirins and it went away. But Singer did inspire that in me. Such a splendid storyteller and he's so insinuating. When he tells you about his characters, you cannot but listen.

Zinos-Amaro: Nadine Gordimer. Quite prolific in both fiction and non-fiction.

Silverberg: I've only read her short stories. She's appeared frequently in *The New Yorker*. Very capable writer. She manages to show the complexities of white life and black life in South Africa.

Zinos-Amaro: Naguib Mahfouz.

Silverberg: Never read a word of him.

Zinos-Amaro: Elias Canetti.

Silverberg: *Auto-da-Fé* I've read. It's about a crusty old Sinologist living in Vienna or Berlin, living in a vast library of books on China, which his housekeeper eventually sets fire to. Interesting novel, but the burning of books gives me the quease. Canetti, I'm told, was an important literary figure. He wrote many other books, but I haven't read them.

Zinos-Amaro: What about Patrick White?

Silverberg: I read *Voss*. His writing style is determinedly clumsy. I don't believe he's writing clumsily because he can't help it; I think he *wants* to. *Voss* is about an obsessive German who marches across the middle of Australia in the early nineteenth century, patterned on a historical figure, and meets an unhappy ending. Very strong novel, but, gee, I don't want to read any more of his books. Here's a case where every sentence set my teeth on edge, but the story itself is quite powerful.

Zinos-Amaro: Boris Pasternak.

Silverberg: I read *Doctor Zhivago* recently, the original Max Hayward and Manya Harari translation. There has been a later translation by Richard Pevear and his wife Larissa Volokhonsky, who are retranslating all of the classic Russian novels. I compared the reviews of the two translations, and what I found was that the Hayward translation was considered to be inaccurate but faithful to the atmosphere, while the newer translation is literal but dull. A review of the Hayward translation pointed out that there are certain things about Russian word order that are not common to English word order. Russians often have a Teutonic system of putting the verb miles away from the subject and Hayward didn't follow that, which made it much more readable, but it didn't sound like the original. Pevear and Volokhonsky have followed that, which creates a very clumsy structure. I also hunted up the review by Nabokov, who had contempt for the entire book. But I didn't. I thought it was very exciting.

Zinos-Amaro: To make a small digression into science fiction: I recently read Joanna Russ' short novel *We Who Are About To*, and it's certainly vigorous prose, much in the modernist tradition.

Silverberg: I thought her novel *And Chaos Died* was brilliant and said so in a blurb for an early edition. I liked her short stories, too, and published one or two in the anthology series I edited, *New Dimensions*. We were very good friends in my New York days. Later I had less contact with her. Last time I saw her we had a friendly hug.

Zinos-Amaro: Coming back to our Nobel list: Churchill.

Silverberg: Splendid writer. Wonderful vigorous prose style. I've read his four-volume *A History of the English-Speaking Peoples*; a pretty fast-moving four volumes, and of course it's familiar territory also.

I've read a lot of Churchill but the one I'll probably never read, which I meant to long ago, was his five-volume history of World War I, *The World Crisis*. I have read his six-volume *The Second World War* on World War II, but World War I is a very difficult war to understand— I think they didn't understand it while it was going on. But it's too late in my life now for six-volume projects.

Zinos-Amaro: Eugene O'Neill.

Silverberg: Yes. I'm a great admirer of his more tormented plays. *Long Day's Journey into Night* I think was posthumously produced, and I saw it in a splendid production with Jason Robards, Jr. and Fredric March. And the other great one, *The Iceman Cometh*. Very intense experiences, these plays, even to read, but I think far more so to see.

Zinos-Amaro: Luigi Pirandello.

Silverberg: He used to be a big favorite of mine in my college days because of his Phildickian attitude toward reality. I put it that way because of our context; in fact Phil Dick was a Pirandellian writer. I'm not sure if anyone produces Pirandello any more. *Six Characters in Search of An Author*, well, the title itself tells you that he's playing with reality. And one called *Henry IV*—really *Enrico IV*—about a man who has the delusion that he is Henry IV of France and manages to carry it off very successfully. I haven't read Pirandello maybe since the '50s. It certainly caught my attention then.

Zinos-Amaro: I discovered his work through science fiction; the *Twilight Zone* episode "Five Characters in Search of an Exit."

Silverberg: Pirandello was still an active part of our culture in the early *Twilight Zone* days. Somebody like Rod Serling would have known about him. But these days nobody talks about Pirandello's work.

Zinos-Amaro: Given your interest in Norse literature, what about Sigrid Undset?

Silverberg: *Kristin Lavransdatter*, right? She was widely read before my time. I haven't read her work. My interest in Norse literature is largely mythical, ends somewhere in the thirteenth century. Though I shouldn't really say that, because we have Ibsen and Strindberg and I've certainly read plenty of them.

Zinos-Amaro: We haven't talked about Shaw.

Silverberg: Irresistible. I've read all of Shaw, and one or two biographies of him. But it's the plays that interest me. There was a lovely Penguin set that was issued in the '40s with about twenty of his plays, and I got that when I was in college. I still have it on the shelf—dark purple books. Every now and then I pull a Shaw down. In contrast to what I said about O'Neill, Shaw, I think, is better read than seen. Not that it's unpleasant to watch one of his plays, but the texts of his plays, with their introductions at great length, and their stage directions, are extremely entertaining, and that stuff doesn't get produced onstage. There's a science fiction play called *Back to Methuselah*, which takes place in a world in which people are born at age eighteen from eggs and live to be three hundred years old. It's not one of his great plays but it's a charming science fictional *jeu d'esprit*. The great play, I think, is *Man and Superman*, which is too long to produce. There's an interpolated section—"Don Juan in Hell"—that was taken out and produced as a separate play. But the others, like *Heartbreak House* and *Candida* and *Pygmalion* and ten more, are endlessly entertaining.

Zinos-Amaro: Kipling?

Silverberg: I still read him. I read *Kim* somewhere in the last twenty years, and I read his short stories all the time. I even did an imitation Kipling story as one of my last short stories, "Smithers and the Ghosts of the Thar," for *Ghosts by Gaslight*, edited by Jack Dann and Nick Gevers. I soaked up the Indian background from several of his stories for that.

But really, as we can see, the list of Nobel winners is notorious for its exclusions. The non-winners are often more interesting and include many of the greatest writers of the twentieth century. Borges, Tolstoy, Joyce, Lawrence, Graham Greene, Conrad, Proust, Virginia Woolf, Philip Roth.

Zinos-Amaro: You'd place D. H. Lawrence in that list of all-time greats? He seems to be falling somewhat in disfavor these days with the academy.

Silverberg: I'd certainly put him up there with someone like Henrik Pontoppidan! Lawrence is a very complicated writer, and a heavy-handed writer. But not a trivial writer at all. I think *Women in Love* may be his best novel. Of course I read *Lady Chatterly's Lover* because it was banned but that one just seems silly to me. I've read his travel books too—*Sea and Sardinia*, *Sketches of Etruscan Places*—but his novels are what we talk about when we talk about Lawrence. *Sons and Lovers*. There is a novella by Lawrence called "The Man Who Died," also published under the title of "The Escaped Cock," which is quite a blasphemous book. Jesus survives the crucifixion, goes off to Egypt, and has a romance with a priestess of Isis. Very Lawrencian story indeed; strongly erotic, strongly Mediterranean, the sun throbs throughout that book. It's only eighty or ninety pages. I don't know if it's widely known but it's been published in various editions under various titles.

Zinos-Amaro: Lawrence was friends with Aldous Huxley, whom we haven't discussed.

Silverberg: I didn't know that. *Brave New World* is one of the great science fiction novels. I read in my teens and twenties a lot of

Huxley that I probably didn't understand much of: *Antic Hay*; another science fiction novel, about immortality, called *After Many a Summer*; *Point Counter Point*. I thought he was a wonderful novelist, but I wonder now whether I still would.

Zinos-Amaro: Two writers whose works you keep coming to, also not Nobel winners, are Zola and Balzac. Balzac died before the Nobel for Literature started in 1901, so he wasn't eligible for the prize. Zola was nominated in both 1901 and 1902 but didn't win, so he legitimately belongs on your loser's list.

Silverberg: Neither of these writers was a great stylist. What I admired about both of them was their prolificity. I always am drawn to the very prolific writers, and that's not hard to understand to anyone who has looked at my bibliography.

Balzac, who preceded Zola by a generation, was determined to set down in his novels a portrait of French life in the first half of the nineteenth century. He lived only in the first half of the nineteenth century—1799 to 1850. And he left us close to a hundred books—he wrote at a staggering rate, which is why he's not much of a stylist—that provide a wonderful panorama of every aspect of French life from the working class to the aristocracy. Only about half of them have ever been translated into English, and a lot of the translations are nineteenth century translations that are suspect for one ground or another. Penguin has done at least a dozen of them, which I've read, and several of them are among the novels for which I have the highest regard. *Lost Illusions*, which I think is his greatest novel, is about a young writer who comes to Paris and has a career. Its sequel has been translated as *The Harlot High and Low*—though I think the more accurate translation of the original would be something like *The Splendor and Misery of Cortesans*. These are long novels, very rich. They've had no impact on my career at all but are books I've enjoyed reading and hope to read again someday. What interests me about Balzac is his insight into human greed, questions of inheritance, investments.

Very shrewd insight into all that nasty stuff that the French are so good at!

Zola, I think, may be half an order of magnitude down as an artist, but had the same goal of, through a long series of novels, depicting France in the *second* half of the nineteenth century. He built his entire series of twenty or so books, of which I've read about a half, around two families stemming from the same ancestors. One family became depraved and corrupt, while the other went in the other direction; you have the Rougons and the Macquart.

Zinos-Amaro: I've read only a few novels by each of these writers, but it seems to be that Zola is somehow darker. Is that because Zola's time was intrinsically darker than Balzac's, and he's just reflecting that, or is it his psychological constitution?

Silverberg: I think Zola *was* a darker writer. But the most recent Balzac I've read, not for the first time, is *Le Père Goriot*, a terribly sad novel about Father Goriot and his two wayward daughters and the trouble those girls bring upon him. As for Zola, the famous novel is *Nana*, filmed a number of times, about the high-bracket courtesan who is actually the daughter of the drunkard of an earlier novel. You see the genetic evolution from novel to novel. What's most fascinating to me about both of these writers is the continuity in the series, explicitly in Zola because he's writing about two families that are interwoven. In Balzac the same characters keep popping up in novel after novel. You see them from different perspectives. And though I say these writers didn't have any impact on my career, *had* I continued writing about Majipoor, I might have attempted a Balzacian interweaving of characters. Certainly I was tempted. But I've now stopped writing about Majipoor.

Zinos-Amaro: Majipoor has many influences, including classics like *The Odyssey*. You've written about Greek and Roman works in your essays. I wanted to ask you about some specific ancient classics and their literary progeny—I've made a short eclectic list. For example, Menander's comedies.

Silverberg: I read both Menander and the Roman playwright Plautus in college, now a long time ago. One of them—I think it's Plautus—wrote the play from which *The Comedy of Errors* was adapted by Billy Shakespeare. When I talk about the Greek playwrights I generally talk about the serious ones, not the comedians. Aristophanes, whom I do talk about, was a comic writer, but he was a very serious kind of writer.

Zinos-Amaro: Lucretius' *On the Nature of Things.*

Silverberg: Yes, I read that a couple of years ago, and I believe I wrote a column about it. Very interesting, very difficult book. Very profound and atheistic book.

Zinos-Amaro: Virgil's *Eclogues.*

Silverberg: I've read the *Eclogues.* The *Eclogues* are pastoral poems, in one of which Virgil allegedly foretells the coming of Jesus. The other Virgil I've read, of course, and I've read it a number of times, is *The Aeneid.* I've quoted from it in my work.

Zinos-Amaro: Juvenal's *Satires.*

Silverberg: Yeah I've read those. Nasty, dark, corrosive poems about Rome in its nasty, corrosive days.

Zinos-Amaro: You've talked about travel and history books like Herotodus. What about Pausanias's *Description of Greece?*

Silverberg: Funny, I looked that up online not long ago. He provides a tour of the entire classical world. Somehow it came to my attention and I looked at the edition available on the Internet. I thought, "I will never read this." I have to plot plausible lifespan against available books, and fascinating though it is, I'll never read it. If I were still writing non-fiction books about the ancient world I probably would have reached for Pausanias.

You really should read Herodotus. Great fun.

Zinos-Amaro: I have the landmark edition, thanks to you. Did you ever check out Thomas de Quincey's essay "Modern Greece"?

Silverberg: The only de Quincey I've read is *Confessions of an English Opium-Eater*, which wasn't as trippy as I wanted it to be.

Zinos-Amaro: Frazer's *Golden Bough.*

Silverberg: You don't read that, you just sort of explore it. I have the abridged one-volume edition which I've dipped into now and again.

Zinos-Amaro: You've written at length about the influence of H. D. F. Kitto's *Greek Tragedy* on you during your formative years. What about Kitto's *In the Mountains of Greece*?

Silverberg: *Greek Tragedy* was indeed life-changing for me, and I'm also aware of Kitto's general history, *The Greeks*. Have not heard of this one, which sounds like a travel book. For a literary account of travel in Greece, I recommend Patrick Leigh Fermor. When he was 19 he *walked* from Holland to Turkey, getting to see the last gasp of old Europe before Hitler ruined it, and decades later he transformed his journals into two brilliant books, both in print. Unfortunately he didn't write the third volume, Romania to Turkey. A marvelous writer, wonderfully resonant prose, and his adventures will, I think, fascinate you.

Zinos-Amaro: I'll make sure to check him out; thank you. To come to a more recent work, Herman Broch's *The Death of Virgil.*

Silverberg: I found it very hard going. Said to be one of the great twentieth-century novels. Somewhere in the last fifteen years I read it, but I was forcing myself all the way and I don't recall why.

Zinos-Amaro: Have you seen Claudette Colbert's *Cleopatra*?

Silverberg: We saw it recently; may have it on DVD. It's a Cecil B. DeMille movie and it's a lot of fun—far more entertaining than the Elizabeth Taylor *Cleopatra* of twenty years later.

Zinos-Amaro: Lastly, how about works by Mary Renault?

Silverberg: *The Bull from the Sea* and *The King Must Die* are about Theseus. I did read them a number of times and she had some influence on my Gilgamesh book. She wrote several books about Alexander, which I haven't read.

Zinos-Amaro: We've talked at length about literature and I'd like to shift to early science fiction for a moment. I know that during the last few years you've been avidly reading Jules Verne and collecting various editions of his works. What prompted this?

Silverberg: I thought I would read *20,000 Leagues Under the Sea* again, after all these years. Somehow I heard that the translation was untrustworthy.

Zinos-Amaro: As it happens I recently discovered that my edition of Verne's *20,000 Leagues Under the Sea* is abridged; very frustrating.

Silverberg: Mercier Lewis, the original translator of early editions, left out about twenty-five percent of the content. He compressed a lot of the scientific cataloging stuff. Dr. Aronnax would list all of the fish they saw and the translator would shorten it. But also where he didn't understand he'd make up his own translation. For example, there's a reference to "the Badlands of Nebraska," when Nebraska was not widely known in 1873. I think this was translated as "the disagreeable territory of Nebraska."

Incidentally, I once translated the Latin portions of Krafft-Ebing's *Psychopathia Sexualis* in the time when it became legal to publish it, and a lot of the technical terms that he put into Latin I didn't learn when I was studying Latin, so I made up my own translations. Very tempting.

Zinos-Amaro: How did you come to translate that?

Silverberg: A paperback publisher wanted to rush into print an edition of Krafft-Ebing that had the Latin translated, and he approached me. "I know some Latin," I said, and I did, but I didn't translate it very accurately.

Zinos-Amaro: Are you credited as a translator?

Silverberg: Oh, no. And it's a good thing, too, because eventually a legitimate translation came out from G. P Putnam, and the translator was my high school Latin teacher!

Anyway, to come back to the Verne, there are other translation errors. For example, "making a detour"—"faire un crochet"—was literalized as "making a curve." "The Captain pressing an electric bell" becomes the "The Captain pressing an electric clock." "A quiet study" becomes "a quiet repository of labor."

Zinos-Amaro: These errors remind me of the essay you wrote on the Babel translator, "The Quality of Pity is Not Folded."

Silverberg: Yes, but this is not a machine doing it!

When I first heard that the translation of *20,000 Leagues* was untrustworthy I was in France and I saw some fine French first editions.

I thought, "How beautiful they are. Why don't I buy some of these?", not understanding quite how expensive they were. But after a while it didn't matter. Simultaneously I began accumulating translations and buying the French editions. After all, I need *some* new obsession to keep me distracted. I can't get any more plants; the garden is full.

Zinos-Amaro: Do you compare the texts of different editions?

Silverberg: Oh yes. When I began collecting all the Verne books I came in contact with an academic named Arthur Evans, who has done some science fiction anthologies and who is the big American expert on this stuff, and he sent me some helpful material. There's an essay in an issue of *Science Fiction Studies* devoted to Verne that does some comparing and lists the recommended modern translations. I have collected most of the nineteenth-century translations, whatever their deficiencies are, because I like the binding. But where there is a modern translation I get that and that's the one I read.

Zinos-Amaro: Any lesser-known titles you might recommend to science fiction readers?

Silverberg: In fact very little Verne is science fiction. Only six or seven of his dozens of novels could really be labeled science fiction. But there's a wild one called *Hector Servadac*, which Gernsback published in early *Amazing Stories* as *Off on a Comet*. A comet strikes the Mediterranean and essentially scrapes all of North Africa away from the Earth, attaches it to itself and goes out on an orbit of its own that takes it beyond the orbit of Jupiter. On the way back it passes the Earth again, hits the Earth again, and drops it off! It's a bizarrely improbable story, but he does it with a straight face with a cast of French characters and English characters, Englishmen stationed at Malta and Frenchmen stationed at Tunisia or Algeria. They meet up there and it gets colder and colder as they get farther out. Is there a trustworthy translation of that? Apparently not. Edward Roth's translation from 1877, now back in print from Dover, gets a black dot in this rating scheme, which means "No." The Ace edition from 1957 was abridged. The version I read, the British translation, receives no symbol, meaning, "it's okay."

Zinos-Amaro: And Verne's non-sf? You've mentioned *Captain Hatteras* to me in conversation.

Silverberg: Yes, *Captain Hatteras* is one of his best books. Last year I read a collection of Verne's little-known short stories, *Dr. Ox*. They are early work and not very good, but one of them, "A Winter Amidst the Ice," is fascinating because he reworked its themes into *Captain Hatteras* fifteen years later.

Verne is a great storyteller. I've read now eight or nine of his novels, including one very recently called *An Antarctic Mystery*, which in French was *The Sphinx of the Antarctic*, a more accurate title. It's a sequel to Poe's *The Narrative of Arthur Gordon Pym*. Verne removes everything from *Arthur Gordon Pym* that is fantastic or unscientific and explains it all. It's a good story. Verne has never ever failed to hold my attention.

Zinos-Amaro: Speaking of editions, I saw that the Bison Frontiers of Imagination series from the University of Nebraska Press has put out some interesting Verne titles. *Magellania*, for example.

Silverberg: I did some introductions for some other books of theirs, including a French end-of-the-world novel I found very exciting, Camille Flammarion's *Omega*. That's a good series. I don't actually have *Magellania* yet. *Magellania* is an unpublished Verne manuscript, posthumously edited by his son, who was also a writer. This is Verne's original version, and one of these days I'll pick it up.

Most of the modern Verne translations were done by Wesleyan University Press, under the auspices of Arthur Evans. Those are the ones I read, because I know he's a reliable scholar. He wrote an article trashing the nineteenth-century translations. *Mysterious Island*, which is not really science fiction but has Captain Nemo in it, I thought was an extremely compelling novel.

Zinos-Amaro: Have you seen the Bison book *The Man with the Strange Head and Other Early Science Fiction Stories* by Miles J. Breuer?

Silverberg: Breuer was quite a good writer, capable for his time. His most famous piece is "The Gostak and the Doshes," a short story from *Amazing*, 1930, about semantics, explaining how the gostak distims the doshes, but the doshes don't distim the gostak. A very funny story. I was briefly involved in Breuer's post-life career. One of my anthologies includes "The Gostak and the Doshes," for which Forry Ackerman gave me permission, claiming to be the agent for the estate. A few years later I got a letter from either Breuer's daughter or grand-daughter, saying, "It seems you have published my ancestor's story in your anthology. Who is this Forrest J. Ackerman?" Apparently he had no right to grant me the permission. What he would normally do with Gernsback material was to grant permission to any anthologist who asked, and should there be a complaint, he would patch it up with the actual owner of the rights. He claimed to represent a lot of people—Hubbard, for example, Lovecraft, even Heinlein. In the two-volume Heinlein biography Heinlein talks about how he attempted repeatedly to shake off Ackerman, who in the '50s would offer his stories to Hollywood producers. This is quite destructive, because when a non-legitimate agent starts offering the stories, the studio begins to wonder, "Is the title clear? Who has the right to represent it?" It's not so easy to prove it sometimes.

Over the years, many of my books have been optioned for movie productions, though we don't see many productions. Big studios require very elaborate evidence that the title is clear, that you haven't granted the dramatic rights to three different studios, or that you haven't handed them away as collateral for a loan. One time I received a list of requests that I was to fulfill, one of which said, "We need a letter from Helen Silverberg demonstrating that she owns no rights in this book." I sent them back a letter saying, "You want a letter from my *mother* saying you can make this movie?" They had mistaken my mother's name for my ex-wife's name. Indeed it was reasonable to wonder whether if in some divorce settlement I had handed away a share in the dramatic rights to this book. Of course my mother was dead at the time. They did see the absurdity of it once I explained who Helen Silverberg was.

Zinos-Amaro: "Trust me, my mom says it's okay, you can move forward with production."

Silverberg: "And I'm not playing hooky."

CHAPTER 3
In the Continuum

Alvaro Zinos-Amaro. I'd like to begin today's conversation by discussing some of your habits. What are some of the more deeply ingrained aspects of your daily existence?

Robert Silverberg. I awaken early in the morning. I eat regular meals. When at home, I have the same breakfast every day. I have the same sandwich for lunch every day. When I'm traveling, of course, anything goes.

Zinos-Amaro: Every day means Monday through Sunday?

Silverberg: Yes. In the evening we rarely eat home during the week, so we run the range of Bay area ethnic restaurants. It could be Thai one night, Indonesian the next, and so on right through—we try not to repeat. Saturday night we usually stay home because I'm not fond of crowds and chaos and since most people are out Saturday night, I do the reverse. Though once upon a time I cooked, I gave it up about twenty-five years ago. Karen is the chef now, and she whips up something for Saturday night dinner, and sometimes Friday night. As the Bay area population has increased in recent years, particularly Oakland has had an increase in non-housebroken diners, and we end to shy away from local restaurants on Friday nights because they're crowded and loud.

Zinos-Amaro: As part of this pattern, when do you do your reading? After lunch? In the morning?

Silverberg: It varies now, because the work schedule has been subtracted from the daily routine. In the days when I was writing, I would finish breakfast at 7:45 am, and at 8:00 I'd make a quick trip to the post office, which in those days delivered the postal box mail early. I'd pick up the morning mail and look through it very quickly. By 8:30 I was at my desk. Nothing could interfere with that. I never had an Internet connection in the office, and I never answered the phone. What I did was sit down at my desk with my back to the scenery and work from 8:30 to noon with as few interruptions as I could manage. Sometimes I'd get up and pace around the floor. But that was about it. So that occupied morning. Then I'd come back tired. I knew when it was time to stop because I couldn't go on. I was working very intensely. In that 8:30-to-12 span I'd try to do six or seven double-spaced pages of first draft material, as my daily output.

Zinos-Amaro: Roughly fifteen hundred to two thousand words?

Silverberg: Yeah. It was about two hundred and sixty words to a page. Of course, in earlier times I would write in the afternoon too, and I would get five thousand words done. That's when I was really prolific. But as I got older, I asked less of myself.

So I'd come over from the office at noon, make lunch, rest, and in the afternoon do some gardening, do some swimming, do some reading. Nowadays I do go to the office every day. The mail comes later so I go to the office about 7:30 am. I put in an hour of bookkeeping and filing. Still a lot of professional stuff to do. In fact, sometimes too much. The columns I write are seven manuscript pages. In olden times that would be a morning's work. Now I spread them out over three days. I don't want to make demands on myself that I don't need to make. I'll do a couple of pages, the next day the middle three, and then the next day wrap it up. I used to proofread it, but now I outsource that.

Zinos-Amaro: I'm somewhat familiar with that outsourcing part . . .

Silverberg: When it's done I email it to *Asimov's*. The whole business of putting manuscripts into manila envelopes and taking them to the post office has vanished from my life, but it was very important once upon a time. In fact, I remember when I was trying to sell a story, before my career began. I sent it to Sam Moskowitz, the editor of *Science-Fiction Plus*, a Gernsback magazine of 1953. He was very sympathetic to my aspirations, and I thought, "Someday he'll buy a story of mine." Probably if the magazine had lasted he would have. I remember holding that manila envelope in my hand and putting it in the slot of the street mailbox, thinking, "Please, Sam, buy this story." But he didn't. The manila envelopes are no more, and I don't utter any prayers as I shoot the email to New York.

The rest of the daily routine: the afternoon I usually spend reading on the couch. There's the reading heap.

Zinos-Amaro: Is there a drink with that?

Silverberg: There *is* customarily a drink, yes. In fact this is a custom that goes back to the beginning of my career, when I would work until three in the afternoon, and I would mix myself a drink sometimes, or just pour it. I still have the drink somewhere between three and four-thirty. Then it's dinner time, and comes the great family debate, "Where are we going to eat tonight?"

It's a hard life, full of stress and decision-making.

Zinos-Amaro: I see that! I'm assuming you keep track of where you've eaten?

Silverberg: Yes, I have a restaurant diary.

Zinos-Amaro: How far back does it go?

Silverberg: I started keeping it in the seventies.

Zinos-Amaro: So we could look up any date and find out where you ate (if you weren't traveling).

Silverberg: That's right.

Zinos-Amaro: Do you make some notes regarding the experience?

Silverberg: No. Unless it's an unfamiliar restaurant where we've been for the first time, and I'm not likely to recognize the name if I look through it, and I didn't like it. Then I might put down, "Don't go back."

Zinos-Amaro: Do you use an actual diary, or if not, what do you use for this restaurant log?

Silverberg: For this I'm indebted to DAW Books, for whom I've never written. Karen wrote some books for DAW, but I never did. Betsy Wollheim of DAW Books sends me the DAW promotional calendar every year.

Zinos-Amaro: So even here there's a science fiction angle.

Silverberg: Sometimes the calendar is a little late coming. She usually sends it at Christmas time. But sometimes I don't get it until January 2nd or 3rd. I've let Betsy know that the calendar is very important to me and I don't want to be dropped from the mailing list! Of course, I'm a friend of the family. Knew Betsy when she was a little girl, when her father was publishing me fifty years ago. Betsy's mother Elsie was a dear friend of mine.

Here in my dotage I forget things. Sometimes I forget where we ate last night, and in the morning when I'm entering last night's restaurant diary entry, I'll call to Karen, who's usually within reach, and say, "Where did we eat last night??" She usually remembers. And if not, I keep the credit card slips on my dresser. You noticed last night that when we had dinner I wasn't given the duplicate credit card slip, and I took their accounting slip instead, because I wanted *some* memorandum of where we'd eaten.

Zinos-Amaro: How long do those get stored?

Silverberg: I put them on the dresser and sometimes they accumulate there for a week or two. Then I gather them up, I make sure I've entered every one of them in the bedroom, and then I throw them away. The restaurant last night was called Ghazal. I remembered later in the evening that "ghazal" is a Persian verse form. India is not very far from Persia, and I suppose they have ghazals too. Of course it may mean something else entirely. It might mean "sacred cow with purple spots." But I wonder if it *is* named for the poetry. American poets were writing in ghazals for a while. It was a fad in the '70s, the way sestinas suddenly became popular. I've never written any poetry, but I would imagine writing a sestina would be a terrific headache.

Zinos-Amaro: When did your affinity for sophisticated culinary experiences begin?

Silverberg: I went to college at Columbia, which is not only in Manhattan but is in a fairly sophisticated corner of Manhattan, on the Upper West Side, where there were restaurants of all varieties around. I had to have dinner every night when I was in college, so I began eating at the local Chinese, Japanese, even Vietnamese restaurants at that early date, and I've simply continued. Last night we had an Indian dinner. I remember the first Indian dinner, which was shortly after my graduation from college. There were six of us: my previous wife's two college roommates, their husbands, and the two of us. We went to an Indian restaurant in the Times Square area and were *astounded* by how hot the food was. People were falling to the floor. I've never been able to duplicate a meal that hot, because I was caught by surprise and I've adapted to the heat of Indian food. Last night I ordered extra hot and of course it wasn't to me extra hot.

Zinos-Amaro: How about your penchant for tailored clothes, did that start around the same time?

Silverberg: I've gone through phases. In my twenties, living in Manhattan, not eating only at small ethnic restaurants, but at the high-level French restaurants sprinkled all through Manhattan then, I dressed accordingly. That meant a suit and tie. A suit and tie in the '50s was not an unusual costume. Now people will point at you on the streets.

Then, as the world got weirder in the late '60s, I was visiting Los Angeles in 1969 and spending the day with Harlan Ellison, who was dressed in the regalia of the era, a body-shirt of many colors, striped pants and whatnot. He said, "You know, this is the first time since the Middle Ages that men have been allowed to dress flamboyantly, why don't you take advantage of that?" He took me to one of his favorite clothing stores and I bought some very flamboyant clothes. I still have some it in what Karen calls "the Clothing Museum." I'm much bulkier now than I was then, when I was built about the way you are, very slender. So of course I can't fit those shirts any more. The waistline has expanded from hardly anything at all to the thirty-four that it is now, so I can't wear those clothes. It would certainly be bizarre if I tried at my age!

Through the seventies, in my new California incarnation, the formality of New York restaurants was no longer required, and I wore the weird clothes of the era. I gave up wearing shoes and wore sandals—until 1979. The WorldCon was in London and I thought, "They're not going to put up with any of this here." So I bought shoes and conventional grown-up clothing. At the WorldCon, as I unveiled my shoes, some people who hadn't been to many of the earlier cons had never *seen* me wearing shoes. Andy Porter, who had, was so astounded I had reverted to shoe-wearing that he took a picture of my feet and ran the picture on the front page of *Science Fiction Chronicle*, which was his competitor to *Locus*.

In 1975, I was invited to an academic conference in Denver in April. The same conference, by the way, where I was told that "Born With the Dead" had won the Nebula. I flew from here to Denver. April here is, of course, extremely pleasant. I got off the plane in Denver wearing a little jeans jacket and my sandals and found myself in the middle of a snowstorm. Because of the oddities of Denver weather, the next day it was seventy-five degrees there and the snow was gone. Getting off the plane was unpleasant. I decided not to go back during snow season and have avoided it ever since.

As far as how I dress now: I'm still in California, and most people dress like street people here. But at the appropriate restaurant, almost as an act of rebellion, I will wear a suit and a tie. Or when we go the opera.

One thing I do resent, though. When I was twenty-six, and eating at the best restaurants in New York, everybody else there was considerably older and behaved like an adult. When one went into the Richelieu or Pavillon or any of the other great French restaurants of the 1950s and '60s, everybody was speaking quietly and behaving as one does in a real restaurant. Of course, I didn't want to be offensive—not that I have ever been one for shouting in restaurants—but I behaved in the way the older people around me did. Now I'm the older person. In fact, I'm usually the *oldest* person in the restaurant by ten or fifteen years, and all around me are people in their thirties and forties who are behaving like barbarians, shouting, telling loud foolish jokes and laughing uproariously at them as though they were really funny, dressed in jeans, sweatshirts, sneakers . . . I feel that it's unfair that when I was young I willingly conformed to the ethnology of the serious restaurant but now that I'm not only older, but old, nobody around me is behaving anything but like high-school boys and girls! It's completely unbalanced. We'll choose our restaurant sometimes to avoid the youth culture. The youth culture seems to be everybody up to about forty.

Zinos-Amaro: When throughout these various phases did you decide your clothes would be tailored, rather than bought off the rack?

Silverberg: Right at the beginning. Remember that I started my career, while at an Ivy League college, with enormous commercial success. And I lived in Manhattan, in what we now call the "Mad Men" era, when people behaved in a rather different style from California, 2015. Since I had the money and I saw no point in dressing down, I went to Brooks Brothers, let's say, and bought my suits there. In college, by the way, I wore white bucks and chinos, but stopped that on graduation day. Right now I'm wearing khaki-colored jeans, which I wear a great deal, but we didn't have those then. There were just blue jeans, or dungarees as we called them, and that was working-class stuff.

Most of what I buy, I buy overseas. If I'm in London, which has some of the world's best tailors, I'll buy it there, or in Italy. We were walking through the airport in Rome on our way to get a flight to Sardinia and there was a very handsome jacket in the window, and Karen said, "Bob, you need that." I wear it quite a lot, though it happens to be at the cleaner right now. Fortunately for me, my size has not changed conspicuously as I've aged. I've put on weight, of course, but I can still wear clothing twenty years old, if it's in good repair.

Zinos-Amaro: We've been talking about your daily habits. I'm curious if the heart attack you had a few years ago has changed your daily routine in any way.

Silverberg: Not really. "Heart attack," by the way, sounds to me terribly serious, the way "eighty years old" sounds terribly serious. Karen will say it *was* terribly serious. These things have undertones that are very serious. The heart attack was in fact dealt with within an hour or two. The appropriate repairs were made, the circulation was restored, and I was saved. Sometimes a heart attack, I understand, involves excruciating pain in the chest and serious damage to the heart muscle. Neither of these things happened. What I felt was discomfort. Enough discomfort to say, "Karen, I don't feel well." I couldn't walk. Something bad was happening. But I was not aware that a heart attack was happening, because it didn't correspond to my notion of what that would be. But others were, and I was taken away to the hospital and a stent was inserted. There have been no permanent consequences. I function normally, I climb stairs, I do all those things. I do take a statin now. At first I couldn't find one that didn't have terrible side effects. When my doctor said, "You should really be reducing your cholesterol," I tried various statins, and they all were brutal. The cardiologist here discovered one that didn't have the side effects, so I take it, and my cholesterol is down.

A year and half later, I'm still here. What *has* changed is the fact that I'm a year and a half older. I'm getting up into a "serious" age where you just don't have much stamina. There's no pill that will fix that. I've cut back on the time I spend in the garden. I swim every day but I don't swim fifty laps. I don't, like some lunatics, go out and run miles and miles. I'm reasonably energetic for a man my age, but I can *feel* the difference.

I'm very rigorous in my routines, and my habits are essentially unchanged. You don't produce the number of books and stories that I did without regularity and routine. You don't wait for inspiration and bat out something every now and then and run up a bibliography that's the size of the telephone book. All of my life was built around the writing routine. And though that's been subtracted now, the regularity is irreversible.

Zinos-Amaro: In an essay you published in 1974, you talked about the various crises in your life: "Worst of all, the strain of these perplexities was affecting my health: a whole assortment of psychosomatic troubles began plaguing me." What were some of these psychosomatic ailments?

Silverberg: A plugged artery that cuts off circulation to your heart is not psychosomatic. That's a mechanical failure. But when the endocrine system begins changing its function, that can be governed by the brain, and the intensity of the hormonal secretions can change. I do think it's the result of psychological pressure. In 1966 I wrote a book, now completely forgotten, about the Great Wall of China. A not very satisfactory scholarly work, but it did cover an enormous amount of material.

Zinos-Amaro: Weren't there two editions of that book?

Silverberg: Yes. I cut it down for younger readers. I worked with terrible intensity on that book, and around the time I finished it my thyroid gland began to malfunction. I lost weight and felt the hyper-thyroid symptoms, which are quite exhausting. That was, I believe, the result of overwork, and it was cured by medication. Several times in the intervening few years, one stress or another—my first marriage was coming apart—my body would react with something unpleasant. I had a fire in 1968, a move to California a few years later, I had career problems, and so on. My body would react badly to this. I won't go into terrific anatomical detail, but for example I had back trouble in the early seventies, which I don't now. The back would get stiff, and if I bent over I'd have a great deal of trouble unbending. I'm quite a skeptic about most medical treatments, but since nothing else worked I went to a chiropractor that had been recommended to me by a Bay area person, and what he did was essentially pass his hands through the air over me—I was hoping for some kind of intensive massage that would put everything back where it belonged. So the chiropractor did not succeed in fixing my aching back, but my divorce did.

Zinos-Amaro: You mentioned career troubles. In a piece gathered in *Other Spaces, Other Times*, you write that "most publishing deals, [...] begin with high hopes, warm feelings, and glowing promises, and generally end with catastrophic bungling on the publisher's part and disappointment for the writer." That seems perhaps a harsh view. Is that really true of most publishing deals?

Silverberg: True of mine. I've had some lovely publishing relationships. Lou Aronica of Bantam, Don Fine of Arbor House and then Donald I. Fine Co., Malcolm Edwards of several British publishing companies. Though there was some conflict eventually with the very abrasive Don Fine, I'm still on very good terms with Lou Aronica and Malcolm Edwards. But the publishing history of those books shows that the high hopes engendered by the large advances were not sustained by the promotion, the packaging, all the rest. Generally I would find as the relationship went along that they're not printing many copies, not advertising anything, putting the wrong cover on the book. In the case of one of my Bantam books I was given a cover painting by one of the most famous artists of the era, a man who won a Hugo every year as best artist and who *was* a splendid artist. But the illustration was completely inappropriate for the book. It was a kind of sexy high-priestess-of-the-fantasy-cult thing for a book about the greenhouse effect.

Zinos-Amaro: *Hot Sky at Midnight.*

Silverberg: Yeah. I asked to have the cover replaced, but it couldn't be done, because they'd spent a lot of money on the commission.

In general I've found that though the person with whom I conducted the publishing relationship was always extremely amiable and eager to work with me, and understood what I was doing, the rest of the people in the publishing process didn't do very well for me. There were about twenty reasons that I stopped writing, and that was one of them. The constant disappointment. Yes, I got big advances, but I didn't get corresponding big sales. In the case of *Lord Valentine's Castle*, which brought in the biggest advance I'd ever had, there was a stipulated advertising budget for the book in the contract. And then there were no ads. I waited for the ads and got in touch with my editor at Harper and said, "You were supposed to spend thirty-seven thousand dollars on ads. I don't see them." And he said, "We didn't do it? I'll have to look into that." They had never bought the ads. So then, after the book had been published, they put a small ad in the *Sunday Times Book Review*. This experience, replicated over a number of years, led to the sour remark you quoted.

Zinos-Amaro: In terms of your daily routine, we've corresponded about your inability to have an assistant around. You tried with Carter Scholz thirty years ago. What's the difficulty?

Silverberg: For one thing, when I was working, I couldn't have someone else in the office. But I'm not working. The filing is a severe issue. I was an enormously prolific writer. New editions come in, new contracts come in, queries, all sorts of things. All of this has to be dealt with, then filed in a proper place. If an assistant is doing the filing, I won't know *where* things are being filed. And I couldn't figure that out at all. Carter helped me organize the magazines that were all over the office. You see how chaos develops very quickly. Every day there's cartons of mail and I'm not always able to deal with it. But Carter got things organized. Shay Barsabe, who was Carol Roberts when I met her but changed her name along the way for reasons that I've never fully understood, was also invaluable in organizing things. She came in in the afternoon, when I was no longer working, and she helped me in the garden. Things here in California grow twenty-eight hours a day, and it's a big garden. Now I have a new garden assistant who's helping me once a week. It becomes essential now, because I no longer have the stamina to care for the garden. But I am, if not reclusive, at least somewhat insular. I like to be alone a lot. George R. R. Martin has three full-time assistants. It's a different temperament. George has very fine "minions," he calls them. Karen is very helpful and of course lives here full-time. [laughs]

But unfortunately I need to do it all myself, or I'll lose track of it. And I can't do it all myself. This paradox I'm stuck with.

Zinos-Amaro: In your column "Ancestral Voices," you wrote that, "We ought not to despise our literary ancestors, nor even to mock them, for they not only showed us the way but had real virtues of their own." Is this a problem today?

Silverberg: Last week there was a piece in *The Wall Street Journal* about Tom Stoppard. Stoppard said he is disgusted with the stupidity of the contemporary theater audience. They don't understand anything he's saying. Of course Stoppard is a very bright man who wrote plays that call for a certain amount of intelligence. He gave the example of a play he wrote called *Rosencrantz and Guildenstern Are Dead.* Well if you've never heard of a play called *Hamlet,* you don't know the reference to Rosencrantz and Guildenstern. What he said is that he's writing now for an audience that has no references to the past. And though—he's my age—he's continuing to write, I suppose, because he can't stop, he understands that he's not being met with comprehension by the younger audience. And sooner or later that's all there will be, the younger audience.

I've had the same experience in science fiction. There are, of course, extremely intelligent people reading science fiction. I know a few of them. But what I see being acclaimed in modern science fiction, such that I look at, doesn't impress me with its breadth of historical reference. If you don't understand the past it's very hard to extrapolate the future. There is now, aside from the general ignorance which pervades our culture, a political condemnation of the past. The attitudes of the past are considered obsolete and pernicious. A lot of fiction is criticized because the roles of the characters do not inspire the kind of self-esteem that is required of us today. Why this has not caused Shakespeare to be banned, I don't know. Here's *Othello,* in which the protagonist smothers his wife in a fit of jealousy: that's a terribly cruel, insensitive thing to do. The play should be banned because it offers a poor role model. King Lear is a silly old man and he does something very silly. He's really bad to the one daughter who is on his side, pays the price.

Zinos-Amaro: We shouldn't discuss *Macbeth* then.

Silverberg: Mrs. Macbeth *is* the model of a strong woman.

Zinos-Amaro: [laughs]

Silverberg: You see what I mean. When you start interpreting the work of the past in the political sensitivity of the present you mutilate our culture. It's very difficult for writers who are not deeply connected with the contemporary culture. I've given up. I do try to protect my own work against retroactive criticism of what was a legitimate depiction of human beings in a different era.

Zinos-Amaro: In another column, "When There Was No Internet," you said, "I believe it's important to maintain an awareness of the power and wondrousness of change, for those who fail to understand the meaning of change will be devoured by it." Have we been devoured by change?

Silverberg: *You* haven't! You're sitting there with your Mac-Book Air and your smartphone. I haven't exactly been devoured by change—I've been swept aside by it.

Zinos-Amaro: But you have an iMac. Let's not split hairs.

Silverberg: I have an iMac, yes. I also have an automobile and know how to drive it, and my father couldn't. When I fly to Europe, I do it aboard the latest Boeing model. I'm not deliberately living in the past. But most of it I'm not a part of any more. I haven't made the effort. I don't have a Facebook page. People write to me and want me to friend them and I can't do it. In fact, I don't even know how to notify them and say, "I'm sorry, I can't friend you!"

The language is changing around me. If I were writing now I'd have difficulty writing in twenty-first-century English. I don't like the use of "friend" as a verb. I would have to speak the way people speak if I wrote to them. So yes, I think that if you don't stay cool, you'll be swept aside. The world has changed out of all recognition around me, and so long as I know how to use the Internet and drive my car, the rest I don't need. But if I were fifty instead of eighty, I'd be scrambling to *connect*. In fact, when I was fifty, I *was* with it. I had a computer—with a ten-megabyte hard disk—before the current Hugo nominees were teething. I chuckle about that sometimes. The computers of the day had tape drives as their memories, and some of them had floppy disks. The computer salesman said, "You know, you really ought to get a hard disk." They were called Winchesters at that time—another obsolete term. I asked him what the value of the hard disk was. He said, "You can get a whole novel onto one." I had my choice between five megabytes and ten. It was staggeringly expensive. You could buy a car for the cost of that ten-megabyte hard disk. And yes, it did make all the difference. Instead of waiting for the tape drive to load, I had my novel right there. Now I laugh. I get emails that are nine megabytes large, and that's just a picture of something!

Zinos-Amaro: *I've* sent you ten-megabyte attachments: story scans, etc.

Silverberg: The iMac, with its zillion-gigabyte capacity, doesn't have a problem with them. But my 1982 hard disk wouldn't have known what to do with them.

Zinos-Amaro: We're speaking of changes in culture and technology. What about science, do you keep up with it?

Silverberg: I get the *New York Times* and the *Wall Street Journal*. If we're going to land a satellite on a comet, I'm going to follow that event.

Zinos-Amaro: Does something like that tickle you?

Silverberg: Oh yes. When the Hubble Space Telescope produced those spectacular color photos of galaxies it gave me the same shiver I got reading science fiction concepts when I was twelve years old. But I don't have a deep scientific background. I don't have a mathematical background. I know a little about biology and chemistry, and archaeology, if you call that a science, which I do. So it's difficult for me to understand the advances in atomic theory, for example, and some of it—string theory, for example, what little I know of it—strikes me as theology rather than science.

Zinos-Amaro: "Not even wrong," right?

Silverberg: [chuckles] Not even wrong. I no longer try to keep up with any advanced science. I just have a layman's knowledge of what's going on. I don't need more than that because I don't have a professional need for it.

Getting yourself to old age involves excusing yourself from a lot of things you once did. Saying, "I don't need to do this," or "I can't do this, so don't fool yourself into trying." One by one, you let go of a lot of things that you formerly did. Or if you're wise you do, instead of frantically running after them.

Zinos-Amaro: Is there anything you held onto too long, that you thought you could do but couldn't?

Silverberg: I hope not. I haven't tried to write any novels in close to ten years now.

Zinos-Amaro: Maybe you let that one go too early. You could still have the ability.

Silverberg: I might have the ability, but I don't have the will. I could push myself through and write a novel right now. But why? Imagine what my office would look like if I went in there for three hours a day and wrote fiction instead of tidying up mail! Imagine how much email would accumulate!

Zinos-Amaro: [laughs] We'll take care of the email and filing for you, Bob.

Silverberg: When I said a few minutes ago that I'm not on Facebook, I'm really not part of it—any of it. I live on as an observer, a stranger in a strange land. I've just come down from Mars. "Oh, look what they're doing now." I *can't* be part of it. I'm not out there in the social world. You see that stack of newspapers over there? I read them each day because otherwise I would have *no* idea what the world around me is like and I need to have some connection with it. I don't like a lot of what I see in the United States.

Zinos-Amaro: Have you ever considered living elsewhere?

Silverberg: I have on several occasions, but not seriously. We had a terrible freeze here in 1989 or 1990. Killed a great deal of the garden. I thought, "Why don't I just move to Australia? They don't have freezes in Sydney, and I've been there a number of times and it's a beautiful city. I can sell this house and get a really pretty place in Sydney." Then I realized Sydney is fourteen hours from anywhere, except Melbourne. That was the end of the Australian fantasy.

Zinos-Amaro: I was thinking more of Italy or France.

Silverberg: That periodically comes up. Along the Mediterranean coast, Italy or France, I could have essentially California climate, and I could eat very well there. Of course, moving this whole establishment, with the millions of books and artifacts, is unthinkable. But sometimes I'm tempted. I can at least make myself understood in Italian. And if I lived there I would become fluent. But Italy is a chaotic country and has big problems that I don't want to buy into at my age. Though I can read French in a halting way, I can't speak it, and I don't want to be inarticulate in the country where I live. Certainly there are areas like Antibes or Nice where I could live very happily and comfortably, but for the linguistic problem. I don't know what the tax situation is in those countries. I understand how to operate within the American tax system. So yes, I'd like to leave on occasion. There's lots of things I don't like about the United States. But this is where I live, and I'm not going to leave.

Zinos-Amaro: What's your engagement with world events? Do you follow specific news items assiduously?

Silverberg: I follow certain world events. I think there's a real threat in the radical Muslim world. It's one that's far more difficult to contain than either Nazism of Communism. We were able to destroy Hitler, wiped him out. We outlasted the Soviet Union and managed to push it until it fell apart of its own contradictions. Marx used to talk about the contradictions of capitalism, but it was the contradictions of Communism that did them in. The jihadists don't have a single nerve center that can be struck. We killed bin Laden, but it didn't matter, except to bin Laden. I fear the many-headedness of radical Islam and its irrational nature. Communism pretended to be an economic system. It didn't work and when its failure was apparent it fell apart. Ultimately the same thing will happen to radical Islam, but it may be hundreds of years. I hope we will corrupt them with our iPhones and our Facebook! But it's a slow process, and since we have atomic energy loose among us, it's possible they may do a lot of damage, and this troubles me. That's a story that I follow at a distance. I think we've made a terrible mess of coping with it. My hope is that we survive the present political administration and get on to a government that understands the nature of the menace.

I've been following the Greek economic crisis very closely. I have strong feelings about economic mismanagement. I've seen a lot of it in the United States. Although we are strong enough to survive it,

Greece is a pokey little country that does not have our resilience. I watch the personalities. The Greek Minister of Finance, whose name I can't pronounce, is a fascinating character. A man with an extraordinary face and an extraordinary mind. Very complicated and interesting to watch. I wish he were not doing what he's doing, but I do watch those stories. I do like to know a little of what's going on around me. I have some emotional involvement in this. I think, "The Greeks have done everything wrong. Let them be a lesson to us." We have the capacity to make the Greek error. Fortunately we have pulled back from the brink. We were headed there, I believe, six years ago.

Zinos-Amaro: This is taking us down the path of your political leanings. How would you describe your mix of social libertarianism and fiscal conservatism?

Silverberg: I'm a conservative in the old-fashioned way. I don't think there's anything conservative about trying to regulate people's lives and tell them how they may behave, so that aspect of modern conservatism is not for me. I'm fiscally conservative in that I believe that if you spend more than you take in you go broke. We see it happening before our eyes in Greece, and we nearly saw it happen in California. We've been rescued here, at least for the time being, by the glorious technology boom that is so profoundly hated by many of our left-wingers, but it's paying for us. And by the oddity of having brought Governor Brown back, in his old age, to rein in his own party!

The rest of my politics are libertarian in the sense that I believe people should be allowed to do whatever they want, however stupid it is, so long as it doesn't interfere with anyone else. I was frightened by the "occupy" movement because it seemed to me to have the seeds of the French or Russian revolutions: class warfare. Unfortunately I've had a successful business life, so I find myself the enemy. I don't like that. I'm not the enemy. I don't go out and oppress the masses, and I don't want the masses coming here and oppressing me. But the occupy movement was feckless and went nowhere.

Because I like the weather here so much, I have inserted myself into an area where I'm politically alienated. My friend Saul was quite far to the left—went down to Nicaragua to help the Sandinistas, that sort of person—and for his sins found himself living in Arizona, among the Goldwater people. And here I am in the Bay area, where I can walk for miles and not find anyone who's ever voted for a Republican.

We had dinner one night with friends, one of whom is fairly conservative himself, and he had two guests who have the usual Bay area political orientation. This was during the second Bush administration. His wife began talking in condemnation of everything the Bush people were doing, in the assumption that everybody agreed. You'd talk about it the way you'd say, "Isn't the drought a terrible thing?" No one's going to say, "We don't need rain ever." After she'd gone on for a while like this, I said, "I think you should know that not everybody at the table feels this way about the present administration. In fact, some of us voted for him." Astonishment! Flabbergastness! She looked at her husband and said, "I don't think I've ever had dinner with a Republican before." He very good-humoredly said, "Think of it as anthropology." I find it necessary now and then to shut a discussion down, when I find somebody is assuming that I'm on their side and I'm not. So I will have to say, "I'm just not one of you."

Zinos-Amaro: You prefer to shut the discussion down, instead of maybe explaining your position?

Silverberg: I'd rather not get into it at all. It's like the Jew standing among the Muslims saying, "I want to tell you why you've got the wrong ideas." I have one friend who shares my beliefs. He's a little bit harder right than I am on military matters, but otherwise we agree on most things. We were at a party out in his suburb with one of these people who feels freedom to condemn the opposite political view without understanding that there are actually some people who believe in it. She went on for a while, and then my friend said, "I think

you should know, Judith, that you're not among allies in this group."
The group being three people.

[Miranda, Bob and Karen's cat, jumps on the laptop and walks over the keyboard.]

Zinos-Amaro: Your cat just typed out the word "sw8ed."

Silverberg: It's the beginning of her memoirs. I was saying I don't generally solicit political discussions. One person with whom I do have interesting discussions, who's on the other side, is Terry Bisson. Terry is so far to the left that it wouldn't surprise me if he had some communism in his background. But he is an intelligent, articulate man, who'll say, "*Why* do you hold this position?" And I'll explain why I hold it.

Zinos-Amaro: Have those dialogues ever led either of you to reconsider your positions?

Silverberg: Not in the slightest. But at least I can say to him, "I feel that the positions that you advocate will not lead to the world that you want. Therefore, I believe that those are mistaken positions." I also discuss politics with Stan Robinson, who's very articulate. When politics is an intellectual matter, rather than an emotional one, I can have the conversations.

I want everyone to be prosperous. I believe that my ideas about the function of government and economics would lead to general prosperity, as in fact we saw during the time of the Clinton administration, where *despite* his core beliefs things got to be pretty good.

I don't see myself as a Republican, but I vote that way because I have no alternative. I vote for the candidate more likely to bring about my positions. Technically, I'm a registered Democrat! I want to have a voice in the government around me, and in the primary system there's no point in being a registered Republican here. That's like being invisible.

Zinos-Amaro: So what are some of your core ideas about the function of government? Can you summarize some of your main political positions?

Silverberg: The libertarian aspect of my beliefs involves the government interfering as little as possible in the free workings of the marketplace. When I say "as little as possible" this takes into account the fact that sometimes there are pathologies in the marketplace, as we saw in 2008, when we had the uncontrolled lending of money by the banks to people who couldn't possibly pay it back. It nearly brought the whole system down as a result.

Zinos-Amaro: Extreme deregulation.

Silverberg: Right. The government needed to step in and do something. And it did. My friends on the left were opposed to the intervention. "We're helping those evil banks." They would have discovered, as the Greeks are about to discover, that without a banking system you don't have a functioning society.

I oppose excessive government regulation, intrusive government regulation. You get some from the right also, though it has to do with things like abortion rather than the banking system. I favor reduction in taxes from where it was in ancient times. We once had a 91% tax bracket at the top. Nobody made enough money to be in that. But there was a point pre-Reagan where I was paying more than half my income in taxes. I thought, "This is wrong. I should be at least an equal partner in my own work!" I coped with that by stopping working. For five years during the Carter years I didn't work. It reduced my income, but also reduced the part of it that they were taking. I don't think we need to cut taxes below where they are now. It's a reasonable level. Having reached this level we have left people like me with enough money to spend to distribute it through the economy. I do believe in the trickle-down concept, and I let quite a lot of it trickle down.

Zinos-Amaro: What about taxes on corporations that keep a lot of their money overseas?

Silverberg: We have a trillion dollars or so parked overseas because we have the highest corporate tax rate in the world and the corporations just don't bring their money home. It's doing nobody any good, because they'll invest the money in new factories in foreign countries. I think if they were allowed to bring the money home they would expand production facilities here, to the benefit of the working class. They would probably increase the dividends they pay people like me, and I would spend the money.

Zinos-Amaro: When you say, "allowed to bring the money home," are you talking about a reduction in the corporate tax rates?

Silverberg: At the moment if they repatriate the income stored overseas, they're going to pay 35% of it in taxes. They won't do that. If they were given a tax amnesty, or a 5% rate, they would bring billions of dollars home. Instead they say, "We'll wait it out. We don't mind building our factory in France. It doesn't do anybody here any good, but so what? It's what the government is forcing us to do." This is what I mean by government counter-productiveness.

As for the corporate tax that they pay here, hardly any corporations do. The tax code is so stupidly written that they get away with it. They can write off a lot. That part of the corporate tax is really a myth. Where the tax code functions, it confiscates money from the productive and wastes it. If Hillary Clinton becomes elected, she won't have a Democratic congress, so it will be very hard for her to put anything through and increase the waste. In the first two years of the Obama administration, he *did* have a Democratic congress, but because of his own administrative incompetence he failed to put through the tax increase that he really wanted to put through. And then it was too late. They used up their two years punishing the banks for the crash, which simply removed lending power from the economy, and building the health care plan. I don't think Hillary will win, but if she does, I think she'll come in with a Republican congress and be completely helpless.

I do think there's a certain segment of the population that should be helped by the government. I don't think anyone should be left to starve in the streets. It's important to make that statement.

Zinos-Amaro: I can imagine some Republicans would disagree.

Silverberg: I don't know; I'm not an orthodox Republican in any way. My entire economic philosophy has to do with the greater good for the greatest number. And I don't think what's happened under Obama has been in that direction. There are a lot of people out there who are in much worse shape now than before he came in. That's because the economy is very wobbly. I don't think they understand what they're doing, and I don't think the Greeks understand it either. Theirs is a model for the extreme case of a polity that runs on high pension plans, high regulation and bad administration.

Zinos-Amaro: Did you follow the Spanish recession at all? The burst real estate bubble? The corruption?

Silverberg: I saw what the unemployment figures were in Spain. And driving along the Costa Brava, I could see the speculative buildings. I thought, "These people have done it very badly." But they're entitled to a certain amount of folly, I suppose, because they're still recovering from Franco. And so they all went amok once the boot was lifted from their necks. Greece too. They had the Colonels for a long time. But Spain will recover because Spain is a major country. Greece is a boondock. Ten million people. They produce olive oil and tourism.

The E. U. is certainly an interesting experiment. Convenient if you don't like getting visas all the time. And though the conservative of a different kind in me is saddened to see the mark and the franc and the peseta disappear, the euro is very handy.

Zinos-Amaro: You were talking before about government inter-ference. Should people be free to do essentially whatever they want as long as they're not hurting others?

Silverberg: I think they should be more sensible than most peo-ple are. I don't like the indiscriminate drug use that has such severe consequences for so many people. But I think it should all be legal.

Zinos-Amaro: So you'd support the legalization of heroin, for example?

Silverberg: Yes. All drugs. I don't think the criminalization of drugs has led to anything useful. It's just led to more criminals.

Zinos-Amaro: Tobacco consumption, domestically, has de-creased significantly over the years. After it was legalized, of course.

Silverberg: Tobacco has gone away largely on its own, yes. Of course, tobacco has been taxed into oblivion, to a large degree. I think anyone who smokes is stupid, but I wouldn't make it *illegal* for them to smoke; I just want it to be illegal for them to smoke near me, which has happened.

As for the rest of human behavior, I don't admire the breakdown of marriage as a custom among people who intend to have children. I believe that the old-fashioned legalities of marriage are useful for protecting the children against the chaos that is now engulfing them. But I'm very remote from that world.

Zinos-Amaro: Are you satisfied with what you perceive as the current separation of church and state?

Silverberg: Yeah. There are a lot of people—and unfortunately, many of them are Republicans—who would rather have a theocracy here. But we protect ourselves against that, and it shows no signs of happening. We have a lot of believers, and I'm not one of them. As somebody who regards the believers as deluded, I don't want them dictating how things should go.

Zinos-Amaro: What do you think our level of knowledge should be about a political candidate's religious beliefs? The question came up repeatedly in the last election.

Silverberg: Romney was badly maligned in that election because of his wealth. It was Newt Gingrich who did the job on him and said that he was a heartless exploiter of people, someone who will suck the life out of you, and the Democrats then campaigned against him on that basis. Romney made a lot of money through his own cleverness and he might, as President, have brought us back to a little more vigorous economic status. But that didn't happen.

The first time that religion mattered in an election involved Catholicism. There was a nineteenth-century candidate, James G. Blaine, who was accused of being the candidate of "Rum, Romanism, and Rebellion." They feared that he would be subservient to the Pope. He didn't get elected. Al Smith was the first serious Roman Catholic candidate, in 1928, and there was serious fear that as a Catholic he would take orders from the Vatican. Not true. Smith was an old-fashioned, somewhat corrupt politician, but I think he would take orders domestically. It came up again with Kennedy, who was officially a Catholic, but as we know from his private life, he didn't take orders from anybody. Kennedy broke the Catholic jinx.

I would not like to see a really dedicated believer as President. Santorum, for example. It won't happen.

Zinos-Amaro: Where do you think the second Bush was on that scale? Some of his statements were quite fervent.

Silverberg: Harmless. Here was a man who'd had a wild youth, alcoholism, a lot of partying; theoretically born again. I think he simply said, "Now I'm religious." Whether he even went to Church, I don't know. But his family are old-line Protestant aristocrats. They can keep religion in its compartment. The working-class people, like Santorum—for them it's an emotional matter, and they would try to get it on other people.

Zinos-Amaro: I think in some cases it might distort their opinion on particular issues, like climate change.

Silverberg: Yes. Santorum is at least a Catholic, which is regarded as a rational religion by millions of people. Somebody who belonged to a wackier cult I'd be very uneasy about. A Scientologist President, for example. But again, it won't happen.

Zinos-Amaro: You think we'll ever have an atheist President?

Silverberg: I think we've had a number of them. They just don't talk about it! Do you think Reagan got down on his knees each morning and prayed for guidance? I imagine a lot of them have lip-service beliefs. It's hard to believe that Bill Clinton would be genuinely religious.

Zinos-Amaro: That would depend on what the definition of "religious" is. Just kidding. Maybe if Big Macs were a religion, he'd be devout.

Silverberg: [laughs]

Zinos-Amaro: Getting back to the idea of an atheist President. I think the question behind my question is, will the United States in time become secular in the same way that some countries in Northern Europe are? Some of their economies appear quite robust.

Silverberg: I don't think we'll have an *openly* atheist President in the foreseeable future. In a country where when you take a poll and 70% believe in the existence of Satan, you're not going to get voters to support a candidate who can be attacked as godless.

Zinos-Amaro: What about a century from now?

Silverberg: I did say foreseeable future. Maybe in a thousand years it will all be irrelevant. After all, in the seventeenth century Europe was wracked by wars between Protestants and Catholics. They had a Thirty Years War. Those countries have a common currency today. In the Muslim world we have the Shias blowing up the Sunni's mosques and vice versa all the time. Some things change eventually. In Ireland it looked impossible that the Catholics and Protestants would ever talk to each other, and that seems to have calmed down. But in the United States the likelihood of an openly declared atheist even getting the nomination in the next hundred or two hundred years seems to me very small. This is lip service country. People pay lip service to religion if they're candidates, or corporate Presidents or whatever, and then there are the voters, for whom it's not lip service.

I don't see improvements in the education system, which would be needed. We have Creationism infiltrating the schools. In the right-left thing, the right is espousing irrationality. But the left has its own problems with diversity and cultural relativism. Instead of saying to the Creationists, "You are poisoning the minds of our children with nonsense," they're saying, "Well maybe you're entitled to believe what you believe." So we have both sides in the wrong direction. John Campbell used to talk about the opinion of the Universe. You can have *your* opinion, I can have *my* opinion, but it's the opinion of the Universe that matters. Moynihan said, "You are entitled to your own opinion, but you are not entitled to your own facts."

We had in the case of Rome a collection of gods that nobody believed in. There would be the appropriate sacrifices to Jupiter and then everybody would walk away and go about their Roman business. And then about 300 AD a cult came up from below and took control of the empire, because there was economic disturbance that the new cult promised to cope with. Christianity was a function of the lower classes rising up and the Emperor Constantine saying, "We have to co-opt this. I will become a Christian." And they stayed Christians thereafter, with the exception of Julian the Apostate, who said, "This is all nonsense. Let's bring back the old gods that nobody believes in." He had not a long reign. Since then we've had official Christianity, but in Europe nobody believes it any more. Maybe Pope Francis does, but the churches are empty. Here, though? Different story.

CHAPTER 4
Enwonderment

Alvaro Zinos-Amaro. "Enwonderment" is not a real word. You made it up in 1994. What were you attempting to convey with that word, and is it something you still think about today?

Robert Silverberg. There are words like "empowerment" that are bandied about very freely, especially here in California. Enlightenment is also frequently heard. As well as I can remember this, I thought I would create "enwonderment" as a kind of analogous noun that explains what science fiction is supposed to do.

Zinos-Amaro: I'd like to talk about how you've kept your own enwonderment alive during the last sixty years. I'm curious about your sense of community. For example, when you were writing in the popular archaeology field, did you feel a kinship with other popular archaeology authors?

Silverberg: Not at all. There were certain well-known popular archaeology writers, like C. W. Ceram or Leonard Cottrell, whose work I read, and I thought, "These people are doing very good work." But my connection was not to the community of popular archaeology or even to the community of archaeologists, but to the places themselves that I was writing about, and the spirit of recapturing the past, which for me is almost analogous to creating the future. Just looking in the other direction, to a remote and in fact inaccessible place.

Zinos-Amaro: Is the inaccessibility what gives it the sense of wonder? It can't be tainted by our contemporary existence; it's out of reach of everything going on right now.

Silverberg: Oh, definitely. I've talked about being a small boy and looking at the dinosaurs in the museum in New York and eventually, when I began to travel, going to the ancient places like Pompeii and Egypt. The future is, of course, totally inaccessible. It doesn't exist—yet. But the past, though it has existed and has left residues of itself, is in essence a construct. We reassemble the past out of the fragments and we tell a story to ourselves about what we think the past was like. But it's only a story. Some of it is more plausible than other parts. Some of it actually verges on the truth. Just as when we try to recreate what we were doing, let's say for me, in 1977—I was alive and quite grown-up—it would be in a way like creating 27,777. Some of it is just as imaginary at this point. I do my best to make it real, just as I would 27,777. But we are never able to do anything but an imaginative recreation of the past, or an imaginative creation of the future. And sometimes we don't even understand the present as we're living through it. In the very moment that we're doing things we don't know what we're doing. It is a source of wonder to me whenever I look at something distant, be it the past—the past for me is anything going back past Tuesday—and the future—which is say, next Monday—and trying to understand it.

Zinos-Amaro: In those moments are you suspending the intellectual knowledge that the past is just a story we're telling ourselves? Are you believing the story?

Silverberg: On one level I'm aware that it's just a story. Every work of history is selective. It's a selection of the available facts, arranged in a coherent pattern. I'm aware of that. But on the other hand

I've always tried to believe that when I think about the past I'm think-ing about someplace real. Someplace that actually existed, and that I have a valid understanding of it. Just as when I wrote about the future I tried to make it as plausible and consistent a future as was within my power. I think that's what divides the mediocre science fiction writer from the good one. The good one can make you believe that you're in the future, for the time being, because *he* does. And he knows he's not.

Zinos-Amaro: Has the science fiction world been your primary community?

Silverberg: The science fiction world has been my community since I was in my teens, when I went to local gatherings of readers and met writers. I still define myself as a science fiction writer, though I've written plenty of other things. I don't think I've ever met another popular archaeology writer, or if I have, I've forgotten it. But I think of myself as one of the gang in the science fiction world. And have been for sixty years.

Zinos-Amaro: Are there other communities you identify with?

Silverberg: When I was planting the garden here, which occu-pied an enormous amount of my energy in the seventies and early eighties, I got to meet some of the best-known people in the world of California horticulture. Particularly the odd science-fictional end of it that typifies my garden. For a while I was quite in the thick of things.

Zinos-Amaro: No pun intended.

Silverberg: Incidentally, there was an enormous overlap between those people and the science fiction readership. I would go to a spe-cialist nursery that dealt in rare cacti and succulents and a lot of the people running those are not really interested in meeting laymen or having strangers come to their nursery, because they know these peo-

ple don't know what it's all about, and they're impatient with them.
I would go in and purchase some plants, and then I would write a
check or use a credit card and they would say, "Robert Silverberg?"
This would lead to a whole other relationship that would verge on a
different community—the community of horticulturists who are also
science fiction readers.

Zinos-Amaro: Any names that might be familiar to genre readers from this unique intersection?

Silverberg: I don't think the readers would recognize them, and
most of these people are dead now.

The trouble with having lived as long as I have is that most of the
people I've dealt with are dead. I'm trying to remember any editors
I dealt with in my most productive years who are still alive. It's very
hard. Fred Pohl lasted a long time. William L. Hamling is still alive
in his 90s.

Zinos-Amaro: Is community important for a sense of wonder?
It's a very personal experience, obviously. But do you get there on
your own?

Silverberg: I don't think it's related to community. I rarely talk
about science fiction with my colleagues. What I talk about with
them is writing, or the business side of writing. We are not discussing
the miraculous new Earth-like planet that was discovered the other
day, or the flyby of Pluto. That has not been my experience of the
community. Though we're all watching the same things.

Zinos-Amaro: You've talked on occasion about how your curiosity in certain areas has faded over time. Baseball, for example.

Silverberg: I'm not curious about baseball at all now. At one
point I was. Baseball has been so transformed through the corruption

of modern culture that I'm repelled by it. I pay no attention to it. It's not the baseball I knew.

Zinos-Amaro: Was the baseball you knew a source of wonder in any way?

Silverberg: A source of admiration. There's a symmetric and a dramatic inevitability to a lot that goes on in classical baseball. It fascinated me. It could be interpreted in terms of Greek tragedy sometimes; the player committing an act of hubris and being punished immediately. I found that wonderful in the fuller sense of the word. Baseball is a long time ago for me, though. But for the fact that the San Francisco Giants won last year's World Series, I would have no idea who had played in it. I couldn't tell you who won the year before.

Zinos-Amaro: What about science news items, like the ones you just mentioned?

Silverberg: I don't follow science the way I once did because I have no professional need to do it. But I cannot help being stirred by space exploration and the discoveries that come from it.

Zinos-Amaro: It still quickens the blood?

Silverberg: Yeah, the sluggish blood of an octogenarian. Yes, I was reading about this extraterrestrial planet that was in the papers yesterday. I found myself wondering who might live there, just as when I was twelve, reading the stories in *Adventures in Time and Space*, with one wonderful extra-planetary extraterrestrial adventure after another, I wondered what these people were like. And then I wrote about them. That doesn't go away. The intensity with which I follow up the information does, because of the change in my professional attitude. And also because I get tired, and some of the more technical sides of science are now too taxing for me.

Zinos-Amaro: When you say "that doesn't go away"—well, thankfully that's true for you. But it does go away for *some* people. Have you done anything deliberate to preserve it?

Silverberg: No. I am who I am, and this is what I'm like. I am always interested in finding something new and strange to eat; I'm interested in finding a book that I've never read before; going to a city I've never visited; going to a *planet* I've never visited. Just my inherent nature. What other people do is what other people do.

Zinos-Amaro: In the dust jacket of *Empires in the Dust*, it mentions that at the time you had three cats and thirteen goldfish.

Silverberg: Thirteen goldfish? It says that?

Zinos-Amaro: I don't know if you wrote the copy.

Silverberg: This was in 1962. I lived in New York, in a very big house. There was, in the back, a small pond that I did keep goldfish in. I don't remember the count of them. But it proved a problem to get them out of the pond for the New York winter. Eventually they became too much trouble. But I don't remember keeping a census of my goldfish!

I still have cats. There have always been cats around. Any number from one to five.

Zinos-Amaro: Tell me a little more about your relationship with pets. When did it begin, and what other pets have you had?

Silverberg: Remember, I was an only child—still *am* an only child!—and having a playmate in the house was a concern to me. I wanted some company now and then. So I went through the usual childhood pets: a white mouse, a turtle. Cats and dogs were impossible in the circumstances of my childhood. Once, I decided I wanted an eel. I don't remember exactly what was motivating that. I was perhaps eight. I was friendly with a local fish merchant around the corner from us, and I persuaded him to get me a live eel, which I brought home and put in the bathtub. When my mother got home from school, where she taught, she found a live eel in the tub, and this caused a certain amount of upset in my household. But of course you can't keep an eel in the bathtub: there was only one bathtub in the apartment and we needed it. So that's what I did in childhood, the small inconsequential pets. There was a parakeet at one point, long ago.

Then I went to college, where keeping a pet is too complicated. I married right after my graduation, and my wife and I went to visit Robert Lowndes at his suburban home. He was an editor for whom I was already writing stories. His cat had just had kittens and he said, "Would you like a kitten?" My wife and I, who had never discussed this, said, "Well, yeah." That was where the first cat came from, back in 1956. I've never not had a cat since.

I love cats. Wonderful, self-sufficient animals. The only time I was without a cat was in 1980 for a few weeks, when the resident cats of the previous era had just died at a great old age. Most of my cats live to be very old. I was about to leave for the WorldCon on the other side of the country, and it seemed best not to get the new cats, who-ever they might be, until I got back from my trip. So for a period of two or three weeks I lived without a cat. A very strange experience: I would leave doors open! Going downstairs to the basement and leaving the door open was a guilty pleasure. I got the new cats right after the convention and they remained here for a long time. Gradually their replacements arrived. Now I'm down to just one cat for the first time in many years, and we have not rushed to replace the two prior cats, who lived to be twenty-one. We got so accustomed to them that we can't imagine other cats here. But we will get them before long.

As for other pets—dogs, wombats, birds—I've never had any, though I like wombats.

Zinos-Amaro: Any creatures living on the grounds of the mansion?

Silverberg: One day my first wife came home with two gerbils, Twiggy and Copernicus. I don't know who gave them to her. Of course, having small rodents in a house with three cats is not a good idea, evolutionarily speaking—they're not going to last long. But we kept them in a little cage. It was a very big house, and we could have a whole segregated room for the gerbil cage. We waited for them to reproduce, as we understood gerbils did. Finally I took a close look at them and said, "These are both of the same sex." So Twiggy and Copernicus did not reproduce, and that was the end of the gerbil experiment.

Oh, and I had, briefly, an alligator, when I was a boy. Little one.

Zinos-Amaro: No kidding. Bathtub as well?

Silverberg: Yes. Didn't keep it long. They're not good house pets. Caligula.

Zinos-Amaro: Did *you* name it?

Silverberg: Yes. Many years later I wrote a story called "The Calibrated Alligator" and I think there was an alligator named Caligula in it.

Zinos-Amaro: Do you remember how old you were when you had the alligator?

Silverberg: Twelve, maybe.

Zinos-Amaro: Old enough to know some Roman history.

Silverberg: I was a smart little brat. Anyway, Caligula—every boy knows Caligula: it's his hero.

Zinos-Amaro: [laughs] Can you talk a little more about your relationship with cats?

Silverberg: I admire the beauty and the grace of cats. Who doesn't? But also, they're alien beings. I've observed them at close range now for fifty-nine years and I see that though we pretend to understand them we don't remotely know what's going on in their minds. And that's a useful thing to watch. There *are* minds there. It's not like having a pet beetle, or ants.

I've learned a lot from cats about the art of being a cat: how indifferent they are to anything they have no need to get entangled in. The indifference of a cat is a beautiful thing to observe. Their absolute self-centeredness. The present cat is very beautiful but is not in the room. She took herself off and is doing some cat thing and we don't matter at all to her.

Zinos-Amaro: Is there anything besides literature that provides you with a sense of wonder?

Silverberg: You see the plants in the garden. Some of them are quite strange indeed, though they're no longer strange to me. My first encounter with a lot of them was quite remarkable. There's a small succulent native to Madagascar, from the genus of succulents called kalanchoes. I remember seeing a little group of kalanchoes in the National Botanic Garden in Washington. They're indoor plants, of course; because they're subtropical, they're not going to thrive outdoors in the east. I remember thinking that they were utterly weird, *alien* plants. Well, I've had kalanchoes around the house ever since, and I think they're interesting and attractive plants, but I can't find the weirdness of them any more. There's another succulent, the aeonium—I've got perhaps twenty different species of aeoniums scattered around the garden, they do very well in this climate—and Karen, when she came here to live, was fascinated by them. She called them "Martian daisies." They do look mighty weird! You see

that big red thing over there? Doesn't look like your typical gera-
nium.

Zinos-Amaro: You said it's hard to find the weirdness in the kalanchoes now. Does that same concept apply to science fiction works
that may have once evoked a sense of wonder?

Silverberg: I think any sensation becomes anesthetized with repetition. The taste of a particular food, for example. Or sex. I recall the
sex in my earlier years being rather more intense than it became later
on. Not that I lost interest in it, but the impact was different.

Zinos-Amaro: Is it just repetition, or is something else at work
here?

Silverberg: It's familiarity. I can't say familiarity breeds contempt,
in either sex or food or science fiction. But familiarity breeds familiarity. [chuckles] Leads to a lack of strangeness. And wonder requires a
certain amount of strangeness.

I remember the first time I saw the rings of Saturn, in the fascinating, exotic city of Sacramento, California. I was up doing a speaking engagement at a university, and we went on a cold winter night—
and it does get cold at night in Sacramento—to the observatory on
campus. There we looked at Saturn. I had never seen the rings of
Saturn, except in a painting by Chesley Bonestell. I was forty-five
years old at that point; not a boy. I stared in rapture. I've seen the rings
of Saturn since, and while they never fail to stir me with their beauty,
it's not the same as the first time. But there's always a first time for
something else!

Zinos-Amaro: Does your literary sense of the wondrous intersect
with a sense of the uncanny, the bizarre, even the frightening? I know
you've talked about the impact of Lovecraft when you were a boy, and
you were just saying that wonder requires strangeness. What about

writers like Arthur Machen, William Hope Hodgson, or Algernon Blackwood?

Silverberg: Arthur Machen wrote "The Great God Pan," a story I read when I was eleven or so. He wrote a lot about the elder races of the British Isles. There was one story where the protagonist was permitted to see some kind of Walpurgisnacht taking place underground. Of course, I didn't believe that such things happened, but I was able to make the imaginative leap. The story boiled in my mind for years, and I looked for it without success for a long time. Finally found it. I have it marked in the Machen collection I have, so I can easily find it again.

Blackwood's most famous story, I think, is "The Willows." On the face of it, it's about an absolutely mundane event: two young men go boating down the Danube and spend the night on an island in a fairly uninhabited part of the Danube, and the wind in the willows is not in any way cute and cuddly—it's terrifying.

But I don't think of what I got from those people as particularly science fictional. Lovecraft: the stories that most reached me, like "Shadow Out of Time" and "At the Mountains of Madness," those *were* science fiction stories. Hodgson did write a science fiction novel, *The Night Land*, but it's unfortunately unreadable. It does take place in the very distant future and I've made a number of attempts to penetrate it, without success.

Zinos-Amaro: So in your mind this category is distinct from the science fiction stuff?

Silverberg: Yeah. I want a certain science fiction-ness about the stories that are going to light up my imagination. As Damon Knight famously said, "Science fiction is the thing we point to and say, 'This is science fiction.'"

And then there are a lot of writers whose works I admire that cannot achieve or will not achieve that wonder at all. And yet they're perfectly good writers. The prime example is Isaac Asimov, who made the whole universe seem like Manhattan. Every planet in the entire galaxy of *Foundation* seems more or less reachable by subway. Some of it looks like Manhattan, some of it looks like Brooklyn. He had other virtues as a writer, obviously, because we would not hold him in the high esteem that we do if he didn't. But the prosaic nature of the Asimov universe is not what I went to science fiction for.

Zinos-Amaro: Since we're on the subject of weird literature, I wanted to get your thoughts on some writers we haven't discussed, like Robert Aickman.

Silverberg: I hadn't read any of Aickman's work until a couple of years ago, when somebody said something about him that led me to think I would want to know his work. I had a collection of his and I read the stories without pleasure, so I didn't continue. What was said about him was that this was the kind of thing I go to that kind of fiction for. In that case it didn't turn out that way.

Zinos-Amaro: William Sansom?

Silverberg: Sansom? I think of him as a mainstream writer.

Zinos-Amaro: Some of his stories, like "A Woman Seldom Found," have been categorized as weird or supernatural horror.

Silverberg: I don't know that story. What about Robert E. Howard?

Zinos-Amaro: What would you like to say about him?

Silverberg: [laughs] Terrible writer! But yet his vision of the prehistoric world—not prehistoric in the Neanderthal sense, but the world of an inhabited and civilized Europe and Asia before anything we know—fascinated me. I wish that he didn't write the way Robert E. Howard wrote.

Zinos-Amaro: You made him into a character.

Silverberg: Oh, yeah. And I won a Hugo for it, too! But of course he died when he was thirty. Who knows where he would have gone?

Zinos-Amaro: Clark Ashton Smith?

Silverberg: Over the top. Excessive. He's the anti-Asimov.

Zinos-Amaro: Eldritch?

Silverberg: "Eldritch" is an adjective I'll leave with HPL. The heavily overladen prose of Clark Ashton Smith is difficult for me to take seriously, but at least he does provide the color.

Zinos-Amaro: Now and again you enjoy a good ghost story, is that true?

Silverberg: Yes. M. R. James, Oliver Onions.

Zinos-Amaro: William Fryer Harvey?

Silverberg: He wrote a book called *The Beast with Five Fingers*, but I don't know anything about it other than that it exists.

Zinos-Amaro: Sheridan Le Fanu?

Silverberg: At WorldCon last year I met a young woman called Le Fanu. I asked her if she was related to the writer, and she said, "Yes, great-great-granddaughter." I haven't actually read him. [laughs]
Most of what I know about ghost stories comes from a book by

Wise and Fraser, *Great Tales of Terror and the Supernatural*, a huge anthology which is the ghost story equivalent of the famous *Adventures in Time and Space*. It has everything worthwhile in the genre that had been written up to that point. It was published in the '40s but is not hard to find at all. There you will find Blackwood, Onions, and all the other spooky guys. And two great Lovecraft stories, "The Rats in the Walls" and "The Dunwich Horror."

I don't believe in ghosts, you understand, although there have been some odd events right in this house that lead me to tell people that the house is haunted.

Zinos-Amaro: Yes. You wrote a column about that: "Ghost Stories" (*Asimov's*, October/November 2010). I'm wondering how your sense of wonder sits alongside questions of a more existentialist bent. What does "existentialist" mean to you?

Silverberg: I interpret it in a very strict Sartrean sense: existence precedes essence, and we define ourselves by the choices we make. This is how I learned it when I was in college, reading Sartre's essay "Existentialism is a Humanism." However, Norman Mailer took the word and ran with it in sixteen different directions. Everything became an existential issue for him. And now we hear about "existential threats," meaning threats to one's existence. That doesn't have much to do with Sartre.

Words squirrel around too fast for me these days. I'm glad I'm not writing because I would have to learn what they mean to other people. I have a lot of trouble with "edgy," for example. The stories of Arthur Machen make me feel edgy, but they're not considered "edgy" fiction. I see "actionable" used in some new sense now. To me something that is actionable is something that would provoke legal action. But there's some new meaning to it; I don't even know what it is. I barely speak the language any more. So when you ask me about existentialism, I need to know what you mean by it.

Zinos-Amaro: Your definition will do nicely. In the sense you've mentioned, how does existentialism relate to your work? I feel like a lot of your mid-period stuff is strongly existential.

Silverberg: A lot of my characters are creating themselves through their responses to external stimuli, transforming themselves and changing under the impact of their responses. Lester del Rey, a man who I didn't think much of as a writer, but who I thought a very wise man, said to me long ago, "Story is a record of change of character." I took that to heart.

Zinos-Amaro: When you think about the works that have produced the most sense of wonder in you, is it the record of the character's change that has done that, or is it the color, the texture, the landscape?

Silverberg: All of those things have to create the change. If you go through large experiences of that kind, traveling through time and space, and come out unchanged, something's very wrong with you. An example of the most existentialist fiction of mine would be a story called "Trips," which is twelve or thirteen disconnected scenes in which one character travels through a series of alternative universes and eventually returns, apparently, to this world. What nobody else seems to notice is that the world he comes back to is not the one he left from. But he has a series of what I guess Norman Mailer would call existentialist crises as he visits these wildly different worlds. When he comes home, he's somebody else. He comes back to the wrong place. A complicated story.

Zinos-Amaro: But that's not the type of story that would have given you a sense of wonder? Or is it?

Silverberg: Well . . . it is. Some of the worlds he travels through are uninhabited, or have been destroyed in a nuclear holocaust. There's one world where he arrived at the middle of a parade and what's going on is utterly incomprehensible to him (not to those who are taking part in it). I think it's a science fictional equivalent of suddenly finding yourself in a parade in Slovenia not being able to understand a thing of what anyone is saying or what's going on. But this is beyond Slovenia. This is an invented place.

There's another story called "In Entropy's Jaws" that takes place aboard a Faster-than-Light ship. And "Breckenridge and the Continuum," a kind of dream narrative. These and "Trips" are from the same crop. But there's a different kind of strangeness about each of these stories that, had I come to them as a reader, I would have responded to.

I once said that I wrote the stories nobody else had bothered to write for me; the stories I would have wanted to read. In fact, I wrote plenty of stories that I *wouldn't* have wanted to read, stories I was just writing to pay the rent. The ones that mean something to me are all stories I wrote to entertain myself.

Zinos-Amaro: That makes sense. I may have made the unfair leap of associating existentialism with a kind of vertigo, a despair if you will, that is perhaps antithetical to the sense of wonder. I recently interviewed Robert Charles Wilson and he talked about what he called the paradox of the telescope: "What amazing and unprecedented creatures we are, that we can build a telescope and discover what small and insignificant creatures we are. And that's not just a facile irony—I think it's an invitation to awe rather than despair."

Silverberg: But you can look through a telescope on both ends. If you want to feel like a really big person, look through the other end of the telescope at all that small stuff there.

Zinos-Amaro: [laughs] My question to him was prompted by a phrase you once used: the vastness of it and the smallness of us.

Silverberg: It's a *really* big Universe. We are small creatures. And so what? I'm bigger than my cat. I'm not as big as Lebron James. These are simply facts of the universe. When I look up at the night sky I don't feel—as perhaps Franz Kafka might have, though I may do him an injustice—that I want to sink to my knees and bury my head in the ground because it's all so frightening out there. What I think is, "How big. How wondrous. What strange creatures are out there?" I don't expect ever to know the answer. I don't feel any sense of despair at the immensity of the Universe. There was an anecdote about someone who said loudly at a dinner party, "I accept the Universe!" Somebody else said, "By Jove, you better!" I accept the Universe.

I remember the first time I saw the Milky Way. When you grow up in New York you don't get to see a lot of the real night sky because New York is so bright. There I was, in Kenya, out on the great Serengeti plain, and there wasn't any artificial light for miles. I looked up and there was a band of light across the middle of the sky. Ooh, the Milky Way—it's really there. It's made up of millions of stars.

Zinos-Amaro: And you've written about it millions of times.

Silverberg: Millions and millions, as the man said.

Zinos-Amaro: You've written in various places about some of the authors that left deep marks on you. I'm wondering if there are any authors who have inspired you to collect their complete works?

Silverberg: Yes. Most recently Jules Verne. I've been collecting him in his entirety, though I haven't read him in his entirety and probably never will.

Zinos-Amaro: Are there authors by whom you've read everything?

Silverberg: I've read just about all the Lovecraft there is. But there isn't that much Lovecraft. Man died when he was forty-six.

Zinos-Amaro: Have you read his letters?

Silverberg: No. I do try to pursue writers in some detail. I've read a lot of Simenon. I've read nearly all of Dickens—though curiously enough, I've never read *Pickwick Papers*. I have read the great novels several times over. *Bleak House* and *Our Mutual Friend* particularly stand out for me.

Zinos-Amaro: What about Dickens' journalism?

Silverberg: Not a lot of it.

Zinos-Amaro: Other writers, besides Verne, whose complete work you've collected?

Silverberg: I've got a complete Heinlein. I've got a complete Asimov—the science fiction, that is. I've probably read the complete Asimov fiction. I haven't read the complete Heinlein: there are some Heinleins I really don't want to read.

Zinos-Amaro: Have you worked your way through the thirteen volumes of the collected stories of Theodore Sturgeon?

Silverberg: Not systematically. But I read almost all of those stories as they were appearing, with great admiration. I wrote one of the introductions for them, and my price for writing the introduction was copies of the other books, so I have the set. I did read all of the story notes in the back. That always fascinates me.

In my own collected stories you see I have provided that material, not only because it's as close as I will ever come to an autobiography, but because I think it's interesting information that should be set down while I'm here to do it. Sturgeon had to have it done for him. Which is just as well, because Ted—a wonderful man whom I knew very well—was much given to fantasizing. Lord knows what his version of how he came to write any particular story would be. I do try to tell the truth, given the difficulty of reconstructing the past that I spoke of earlier. By my lights I'm telling it as it happened.

Zinos-Amaro: What about the six-volume collected Zelazny?

Silverberg: Yes. Beautiful books, by the way. I have read most of the modern sets that have been assembled. Sheckley, Phil Dick. I have some of the Jack Williamsons, some of the Edmond Hamiltons—the archaeological science fiction. I like to follow a writer's development that way, and I like to have his work conveniently packaged. That's why I'm so delighted that Bill Schafer at Subterranean Press did a collected Silverberg. I made several abortive attempts to get one of those going, and he's actually achieved it. I think it's useful to watch how a writer emerges from his beginnings, although in some cases it's sobering. Sheckley, for example, started right off at the top, and never got any better or worse.

Zinos-Amaro: I read once that at some point Sheckley probably realized he wouldn't be able to write better Sheckley stories than the ones he'd already done, but that he could write imitation Sheckley stories such that no-one could tell the difference, and readers would rather have those than no new Sheckley stories anyway, so that's what he did.

Silverberg: The critic Thomas D. Clareson, dead quite a while now, was a careful student of my work and did essays analyzing my themes and obsessions. When I was writing quite actively in the early '80s and was stuck for a story idea I would go to one of Tom's essays to see what my themes were and I would pick one.

Zinos-Amaro: The observer effect in action!

I'd like to take us on a slightly different track now. In his collection of essays *Keeping an Eye Open*, Julian Barnes recounts how his mother, when young, was "a capable and hopeful pianist. Her playing, however, came to a halt in her early twenties when she found herself faced with a difficult piece of Scriabin. She realized, as she repeatedly failed to master it, that she had reached a certain level which she could never go beyond. She stopped playing, abruptly and finally." Are there any activities you similarly stopped undertaking because you identified some limit in your abilities that called the enterprise into question?

Silverberg: Yes. Riding a bicycle. There were no bicycles available when I was a boy. The war was going on and they weren't being manufactured. Anyway, I lived in a city where it would be dangerous to ride a bike. When I was twenty-five I found myself on a Caribbean island where the best way to get around was by bicycle and just about everybody rode on a bike. My first wife could ride a bike, as most people can. Can you read a bike?

Zinos-Amaro: Yes.

Silverberg: Right. I thought at that time, "Now I'll learn how to ride a bike." Well twenty-five is perhaps a little late for starting. I got on the bike and I could make it go forward but I didn't know how to stop it. It was not a bike with brakes, and I found the whole thing horrifying. Finally what I did was to leap off onto the grassy knoll and said, "This is not included in my skill set. I will not be a bicycle rider." I have never been on a bike since.

But no, I rarely attempt something I don't think I can do well. If I can't do it well, I'd just as soon not do it at all. I studied the clarinet when I was ten or eleven and thought it was a lovely instrument and wanted to make some music with it. But I wasn't very good at it. There was one thing I *could* do, and I did it. And I got better and better at it as I did it. I can't think of anything that I yearned to do, like being a classical pianist, that would have run me into a brick wall, as happened with Barnes' mother. Anyway, I was preoccupied with the one big thing I was doing. Had I planted a garden and everything I planted died, *that* would have been profoundly discouraging! I probably would have moved to an apartment. But that isn't what happened.

Zinos-Amaro: Are there alternative paths you think you could have followed with some success, though? Or was writing the only option that you considered was seriously available to you?

Silverberg: That's a two-pronged question. I could have been a stockbroker, I suppose. I'm fairly good at acquiring the sort of knowledge one needs in the Wall Street life. But I wouldn't have wanted to. I don't know what else was available to me. When I was a boy I thought I wanted to do something scientific, and perhaps something romantically scientific, like becoming an archaeologist, or a paleontologist, even more interesting. What I didn't know at the age of ten or so was how dull most of the daily life of an archaeologist or a paleontologist is, out there under the blazing sun, scraping away with a pickax or a file.

When I was about twelve, a teacher in school said, "I understand that you're thinking of becoming a writer." And I *hadn't* been thinking of becoming a writer. I was doing a lot of writing but the idea of *being* a writer just hadn't occurred to me. I scratched my head and said, "Oh, that's interesting. Being a writer." And yes, apparently I started thinking about it, because I became one. But I was almost always on that track—eerily so.

Digging through the papers in my office, where all kinds of things are haphazardly filed, I came upon the newspaper of the school I went to when I was six. I had written something for it. I always wrote for the school paper, but this was very early. It was a purple, mimeographed thing, and I was quite astounded to find it. I was the editor of my junior high school paper; I was the editor of my high school paper. I published magazines of my own in my teens, fanzines. Writing was what I was going to do, and writing was what I did.

So, alternative professions, no. When I was asked in high school,

"What are you going to do for a living?" I couldn't say, "I'm going to be a science fiction writer," because that sounds preposterous. I said, "I'll probably go into journalism," and that's what I told the interviewer at Columbia when I was applying for admission. I didn't mention science fiction, but that's what I wanted to do. I wanted to do it and thought that perhaps I might even be good at it.

Zinos-Amaro: I want to take us back, for a moment, to the interview with you that was published in Charles Platt's *Dream Makers*. This was 1979.

Silverberg: Yes, he interviewed me at the convention in Brighton.

Zinos-Amaro: You said, "It's very odd to be living all of your own adolescent fantasies." You were forty-four at the time, so you'd already been living some of those fantasies for a while—and my question is, what comes after that? It must be a finite reservoir of experience. I presume you hadn't fantasized decade after decade of hedonistic existence for yourself.

Silverberg: In fact I had "retired" by forty-four. When I was given the Grand Master award in 2004, my acceptance speech began, "There are two things every adolescent boy fantasizes about. You've just given me the other one." Of course adolescent boys' minds are full of hedonistic fantasies. But also I was thinking, "Get published. Write books. Achieve something that will bring you the respect of people whose respect you want to have." I didn't know that I was going to wind up in 2004 in Seattle getting a Grand Master award—the award didn't even exist then—but that would have been the sort of thing I would have thought about at fifteen, just as other boys might think of playing center field for the New York Yankees. They didn't achieve it, most of them; Mickey Mantle did.

I had one adolescent fantasy come to reality in the most remarkable way. A magazine called *Galaxy* published its first issue in the fall of 1950. I was fifteen, writing crude little stories nowhere near publishable level. *Galaxy* announced its policy would be to run three-part serials, three of them a year. Spacing the serials out would be an issue that had no serial. The first serial was by Clifford D. Simak. The second serial was by Isaac Asimov, and there was an issue with no serial. The third serial was by C. M. Kornbluth and Judith Merril. Great magazine. As this policy was announced, I recall lying in bed, going to sleep, thinking, "Someday I'll write the whole year's *Galaxy* serials myself." What a preposterous, mid-teenage, self-aggrandizing fantasy!

Well, it happened, between 1969 and 1972. In the course of those years, *Galaxy*, having gone through many changes, published *Downward to the Earth* (1969-1970), *Tower of Glass* (1970), *A Time of Changes* (1971), *The World Inside* (1970-1971), and *Dying Inside* (1972), virtually in consecutive issues. A pretty good run of books. I'd write a novel, send it in, and the editor— Ejler Jakobsson was his name—would buy it. I'd write another one, and he'd buy it, and then I'd write another one, and he'd run it. I was writing good books then, and he was running them all as serials. I thought, "If I could go back in time and tell my fifteen-year-old self about this!"

Zinos-Amaro: Was it fulfilling?

Silverberg: Yeah. I mean, I thought it was silly in a way. What more preposterous fantasy could I have had than writing all of *Galaxy*'s serials for a year or two? And now I'd done it, and I thought, "Gee, how absurd that you could actually have this happen."

Zinos-Amaro: Some make the case that there's greater joy in anticipating and fantasizing than in the actual living out of a fantasy.

Silverberg: There was no anticipation involved in this case. I didn't seriously expect it to happen. It was just a nice thing to go to sleep thinking about!

Zinos-Amaro: What about other situations? Did the actual event maybe underwhelm?

Silverberg: Most of the times I achieved something I'd fantasized about, I thought, "This is pretty good."

Zinos-Amaro: [laughs] Talk about a lack of despair. Coming back to that same interview, you actually used the word "wonders" near the end of the interview: "I have a feeling that this is a better time for science fiction than even the late-1960s period when I was doing most of my best work, and when everybody else was turning into something strange and wonderful overnight. It's a more settled time, now, and I'm rather a sedate man in some ways. I don't like all those explosions, constantly. I don't like surprises. I like wonders, I like a certain amount of excitement, but moderation, moderation even in excess."

Silverberg: That sounds like me.

Zinos-Amaro: Can you tell me more about moderation as a guiding principle?

Silverberg: Most of the science fiction writers I grew up with as friends—and they were mostly older than I was—were immoderate people. I can think of half a dozen of them who had five wives: Sheckley, Sturgeon, Phil Dick, Fred Pohl, and Ellison, who is not much older than I am. I've had two wives, which is pretty much within the norm for our fractured society. Both of my marriages were quite lengthy ones. I've known a great many alcoholic writers. Though I like to drink a little bit, and have a drink most afternoons, and sometimes with dinner, nobody's ever seen me drunk, and nobody ever will—certainly not now in my eighties. I behaved moderately because that's my temperament. The more uproarious writers had a different temperament. That's the way we are.

Zinos-Amaro: Have you ever been out of control? What does Silverberg out of control look like?

Silverberg: I wouldn't know. I remember in Columbia drinking much too much beer one night and pausing, coming back from wherever I was, to throw up on the street. That's out of control, or at least my digestive tract was out of control. But so far as really uproarious things go, no. I've done some things that might be considered excessive, but I've done them moderately. I try not to get into trouble.

Zinos-Amaro: So the principle of moderation turns out to be more a reflection of your natural temperament than something you use to suppress your natural desires, is that right?

Silverberg: Ah, we're getting back to existentialism now—existence vs. essence. My essence is a moderate one. I'm not physiologically capable of drinking to excess; I get sick, as is evinced by the one anecdote of my throwing up on the street, which until now very few people knew of. Whereas I have seen my colleagues *falling down* in the street. At least in one case I carried a good friend of mine back to a convention. He weighed just about as much as I did and it was rather difficult doing this. If I drank to excess, I'd get sick, and what's the fun of being sick? Other indulgences, like eating, yes, I've overeaten and regretted it. I'm a moderate man because I'm designed to be moderate. I wrote an immoderate amount of fiction.

Zinos-Amaro: *That* was your excess! Returning to the subject of wonder. In his latest collection, Michael Dirda writes that, "Fiction is a house with many stately mansions, but also one in which it is wise, at least sometimes, to swing from the chandeliers." He's talking in part about adventure fiction, and returning to some of the writers he enjoyed when he was young. Do you have swing-from-the-chandeliers writers, and how often do you return to them?

Silverberg: I've gone back to Robert E. Howard, who seemed only to write from the chandeliers.

Zinos-Amaro: What about someone like E. E. Smith? You read him as a boy, right?

Silverberg: As a boy, yeah. But stylistically Smith is to me unreadable. He grates on my inner ear. Most of them do now. A lot of great science fiction doesn't seem so great any more, because of the quality of the prose. I'm talking about classics that are sixty or seventy years old, that I admired greatly before I had quite as highly developed a sense of the rhythms of prose. I regard Verne as a guilty pleasure, for example. He doesn't swing from the chandeliers, but his stories skirt the borders of plausibility. One of the wonderful things of Verne, though, is that he knows that he's skirting the borders of plausibility, and he's doing it brilliantly. It's a lot of fun.

I find it harder and harder to read science fiction in general. Whether this is simply because I've been reading it too long, or because I've *lived* too long, I don't know. But I was very startled when I went to France last month, and I took a few Simenons and *Last Men in London*, one of the few Stapledons I've never read. I couldn't get my way through it. It irritated me and annoyed me and I gave it up. Of course, it's not one of his greatest novels, but after all it's Stapledon. I thought he would open vast vistas for me, but I gave it up.

Zinos-Amaro: You've gone back to *Starmaker* several times, haven't you?

Silverberg: Yes, and *Last and First Men* and *Odd John*. I don't think those have changed for me. But when I try to read something new I often fail.

Right now I'm reading *The Iliad*. That's really gory. Homer will describe where the spear goes in, what organs it passes through, and what happens when it comes out. It makes *Game of Thrones* seem like kid's stuff. Of course, the *Iliad* that I read when I was a boy had been toned down for children.

Zinos-Amaro: I'm going to name some of the armchair adventure titles Dirda mentioned, like *King Solomon's Mines*, and see if they have any meaning for you.

Silverberg: Haggard doesn't swing from the chandeliers! He's a great storyteller. Haggard, Kipling, Dickens—these are storytellers. My favorite Haggard is *She*, rather than *King Solomon's Mines*. But yes, I've read Haggard with pleasure during the last ten years or so.

Zinos-Amaro: What about Robert Louis Stevenson?

Silverberg: I haven't read him in a long time, but I have wanted to. I bought *The Weir of Hermiston* a couple of years ago. An unfinished novel; he died while writing it. Meant to read it, but of course there are a lot of things I mean to read.

Zinos-Amaro: *The Scarlet Pimpernel?*

Silverberg: Saw the movie, both young and old. But never read the book by Baroness Orczy.

Zinos-Amaro: *The Story of the Amulet* by E. Nesbit?

Silverberg: No.

Zinos-Amaro: *The Man Who Was Thursday* by Chesterton?

Silverberg: Yeah. Read that, again, young and old. A clever, charming book. I was able, the second time through, to guess who the secret master was, but I've had a lot of experience figuring things like that out.

Zinos-Amaro: Doyle's *The Lost World*?

Silverberg: Hmm, I suppose I would like it now.

Zinos-Amaro: *Tarzan*?

Silverberg: No. Like "Doc" Smith, Burroughs is a clumsy writer, and I'm very unforgiving in my old age of that kind of prose.

Zinos-Amaro: Kipling's *Kim*?

Silverberg: Sure. But mentioning Burroughs and Kipling in the same sentence seems to me a blasphemy.

Zinos-Amaro: John Buchan's *The Thirty-Nine Steps*?

Silverberg: I don't think I ever read *The Thirty-Nine Steps*. I read a number of Buchan short stories last year and thought they were superb. They almost fit in with Machen and Blackwood. There's an element of the supernatural in them. Fine storyteller. Of course, I saw the movie of *The Thirty-Nine Steps*.

Zinos-Amaro: Here are some titles Dirda mentions as possible candidates for a course in the modern adventure novel: Burrough's *Mars*, Rafael Sabatini's *Captain Blood*, Dashiell Hammett's *The Red Harvest*.

Silverberg: I never read Sabatini. The film adaptation of *Captain Blood* was Errol Flynn kind of stuff. Sabatini was big when I was a boy, but I doubt he's even in print now. I've read Hammett's *The Maltese Falcon*, and a number of his short stories, but I don't remember reading *The Red Harvest*. He tells a fine story. I'm neutral regarding his style. In that genre, Raymond Chandler is a writer I *can't* read, because of the style. It's not entirely Chandler's fault; he's been imitated so much that they turned him retroactively into a cliché.

Zinos-Amaro: Chandleresque.

Silverberg: He's as Chandleresque as they come, so I don't read him.

Zinos-Amaro: Dirda also mentions *Mountains of Madness*, which would intersect with your list.

Silverberg: *Mountains of Madness* and Hammett don't fit in the same universe for me.

Zinos-Amaro: Eric Ambler's *A Coffin for Dimitrios*?

Silverberg: Saw the movie, that's all.

Zinos-Amaro: Bester's *The Stars My Destination*. How *has* Bester aged or not aged for you?

Silverberg: Pretty well. I read the two great Besters within the last decade and thought, "Yes, he was pretty good." However, I did read a couple of the short stories that I admired greatly and they seemed kind of heavy-footed. These were the things he was doing for *F&SF* in the '50s, like "5,271,009," and they let me down a bit. But the two novels are ingenious and fast-moving.

Zinos-Amaro: Chester Himes' *The Real Cool Killers*?

Silverberg: I don't know anything about Himes.

Zinos-Amaro: What about William Goldman's *The Princess Bride*?

Silverberg: Nope.

Zinos-Amaro: We haven't talked much about Edgar Allan Poe.

Silverberg: I've read a great deal of Poe. One of the great bad writers, I think.

Zinos-Amaro: Tell me about the "bad" part of that equation.

Silverberg: Well, like Clark Ashton Smith, he's over the top all the time. But Poe is a genius who could go over the top and have you clapping at its over-the-topness. Smith, no.

Your mention of Poe has reminded me of somebody else I read at school, M. P. Shiel. A most underrated writer, I think. He wrote a novel called *The Purple Cloud* and some very fine short stories. There's a short story of his that takes place in a subterranean, sub-oceanic mansion, in I believe the Arctic Ocean, that astounded me with its inventiveness and its scariness. I think it's called "The House of Sounds." He rewrote it in later years in tighter prose, and I'm not sure which version I prefer.

Zinos-Amaro: Your mention of Shiel makes me think of critical acclaim and awards, about which we haven't talked. Do you find that there's a correlation, for example, between awards you've received and what you think of as your own sense-of-wonder works?

Silverberg: I won a Hugo for the novella "Nightwings," part of a book that worked very hard to develop the kind of exoticism that we mean when we talk about the sense of wonder. On the other hand, *Dying Inside*, which is as mundane in texture as any novel I've written, has won awards all around the world, though not in the United States. It even won an award in Serbia.

Zinos-Amaro: The famous Lazar Komarčić award, right?

Silverberg: The *coveted* Lazar Komarčić award. [chuckles] But *Dying Inside* didn't impress the Hugo voters.

Zinos-Amaro: When I think of your work, *Son of Man* strikes me as extremely far-out and exotic.

Silverberg: *Son of Man* is definitely as colorful and wondrous as I have ever written. But it's not what I would expect to be an award-winner, because its narrative line is so surreal. Science fiction readers are relatively conservative and you don't find the far-out stuff winning awards very often. Harlan Ellison managed to win some awards for very unusual stories, but mostly they don't win.

Zinos-Amaro: Nebulas have a better history of recognizing experimentation?

Silverberg: Yes, writers are a little more open to experimentation than readers. "Sailing to Byzantium" is an award-winner that I would say has some color to it.

Zinos-Amaro: *Star of Gypsies*, I thought, was very colorful.

Silverberg: Nobody seemed to notice that one. It came and went. I invented a new planet on about every other page. In fact, if I were still writing, I would probably be cannibalizing *Star of Gypsies* for all the things I left lying around unused.

Zinos-Amaro: You received a Hugo for "Gilgamesh in the Outback."

Silverberg: There are some strange creatures in it, but that's about it.

Zinos-Amaro: "Born with the Dead" won a Nebula, and "Enter a Soldier. Later Enter Another" won a Hugo. The latter was mostly dialogue.

Silverberg: But don't you think it's wonderful that Socrates and Pizarro are having an argument?

Zinos-Amaro: I do think it's wonderful. But I'm not sure how *wondrous* it is.

Silverberg: [laughs] The answer is that I think there's no correlation.

Zinos-Amaro: Let's say there's no correlation in the case of your work. What about other writers?

And I'm curious, did you ever use awards as a way of discovering the kinds of books you enjoyed? "Here's the latest Hugo winner, it may tickle the senses." Did awards have any significance for you as a reader?

Silverberg: I never used the awards as a guide to anything. They didn't begin until 1953, by which time I was a younger reader, but I was also on the edge of my career. The first Hugo went to *The Demolished Man*, which is a fascinating book, but not quite like *Son of Man* in its texture. The second Hugo went to a novel nobody remembers, *They'd Rather Be Right* by Frank Riley and Mark Clifton. The only thing I paid attention to about the Hugos was trying to figure out what sort of thing won Hugos, because though I don't think my career strategy has been particularly awards-driven, it's better to win them than not to. It feels good and has some commercial value. Not winning them can be quite destructive. I can tell you about several deserving writers who never won any award and were quite bitter about it.

I began, actually, to feel the pressure of that. I had a run of creativity between 1966 and 1972, beginning with *Thorns* and ending with *Dying Inside* and *The Book of Skulls*. I did something like fifteen novels in that period, many of which were, I think, outstanding work. None of them won Hugos. Eventually I wondered: "What more do the readers expect of me?"

One of those novels won a Nebula. But if none of those works—
The Man in the Maze, Tower of Glass, Downward to the Earth, A Time of Changes, The World Inside, and so on—was good enough for a Hugo in any year at all, then what was the expectation for my work? And this led, in large measure, to my giving up writing after *The Stochastic Man* in 1974. I thought, "I'm very tired. I've worked extremely hard. And the readers don't seem to be on my wavelength. Why should I bother?" That's not entirely similar to my current retirement, which is just a matter of my reaching a considerable age and thinking that I don't need to work any more, and I'd rather not. It's not an angry retirement of the kind that I had in the '70s. That's what I mean about the awards being destructive.

Zinos-Amaro: But you've deconstructed that anger, haven't you?

Silverberg: Yes. When I got the Grand Master award, I thought, "This cancels out all the Hugos I lost, because it puts me in a very select group of writers whom I admire." I don't admire all the Hugo winners. In fact, a number of them strike me as astonishingly not-good books. But to be chosen to join a group that began with Heinlein and went on through Williamson, Simak, Bester, Bradbury, Clarke, Vance, Asimov, that was good company. I didn't win the Hugo any particular year for whatever reason: each year there could be some explanation that had to do with some other book that struck some nerve. Here I was, plodding along, each year writing a Hugo nominee and never winning. None of that mattered any more, because I had been recognized for the *totality* of the achievement.

Zinos-Amaro: Did that award also close the loop on "Most Promising New Author?" That was quite an arc you followed.

Silverberg: [laughs] Actually, it closed it in a number of ways. The two other candidates for most promising new author were Harlan Ellison and Frank Herbert. Harlan hadn't published anything of any note then, and didn't really deserve to be on the ballot. Herbert had published a splendid novel, *Under Pressure*, later called *The Dragon in the Sea*. But that was all. I had had dozens of stories everywhere in sight. So I exploded into the field in a very conspicuous way and I got the award that year. I don't think Harlan was expecting to win it, but he would have preferred to. At the other end, when I got the Grand Master, Harlan presented it to me. Though he did say when he'd heard I won, "You really should decline it in my honor, because I'm older than you are, and I want it first." I said, "Tough." He was not serious and, of course, he got it himself a couple of years later.

Zinos-Amaro: Did you ever talk about that early Hugo with Frank Herbert?

Silverberg: I knew Frank very well but we didn't discuss it. I don't think he paid too much attention to awards. *Dune* won the Hugo in 1966, and the Nebula. I don't think he won any other awards.

Zinos-Amaro: By the way, do you consider *Dune* to have the kind of color we were talking about?

Silverberg: *Dune* is one of those novels whose style I find off-putting. I can't get into the experience. What I did find wondrous about the Dune universe: an academic called Willis E. McNelly did a Dune encyclopedia, which covers all manner of things that I don't think are in the Dune books themselves. I think it's an expansion of Frank Herbert's universe. It was a group effort, where for example Frank would talk about a dynasty and the contributor to the encyclopedia would invent the names of the dynasty. I found that encyclopedia fascinating and wondrous. It opened up a whole universe of the imagination. The novel itself was not my cup of spice.

Awards often elude big, bestselling writers. Anne McCaffrey, who was the first woman ever to win a Hugo, won it for one of her early Dragon stories, before the books had been published. She never won another one.

Zinos-Amaro: That was for "Weyr Search" in 1968.

Silverberg: Yes, I handed it to her, right here in Berkeley, California.

Zinos-Amaro: Do you think her other non-wins were canceled out by her Grand Master Award in 2005?

Silverberg: I think they were canceled out by the millions and millions of dollars she made from writing one bestseller after another. George R. R. Martin has won plenty of awards, but he hasn't been getting them for the *Game of Thrones* books. Much to everybody's surprise, Jo Walton beat him with *Among Others*, the book about reading science fiction.

Zinos-Amaro: George has been winning Hugos in a way, in the dramatic presentation category.

Silverberg: The dramatic awards, the blogging and podcast awards, those come mostly from a secondary voting group. The hardcore readers seem to shy away from the bestsellers.

Zinos-Amaro: In fact, that's one of the things that led to this year's very unique voting situation. Some people felt that popular, bestselling science fiction works tend to be excluded from the ballot. But analysis shows that a number of nominees have been bestsellers, and some winners too, like Harry Potter, or John Scalzi, or Neil Gaiman.

Silverberg: Gaiman became one of those writers who exercised a stranglehold on the award. He could win for anything after a while.

Just as Michael Whelan for years automatically won the best artist award. There have been others who seemed to win a decade at a time.

Zinos-Amaro: You've mentioned associating a sense of wonder with your childhood books, which were mythological, fantastical, science fiction, and so on.

Silverberg: In fact relatively few of them are science fiction. My first science fiction childhood books were *The Time Machine* and *20,000 Leagues Under the Sea*. There was wonder in both of those, of different kinds. Wells opened up the very far future, and Verne depicted the underwater world. The Norse myths I read, *The Odyssey*, Walter de la Mare's *The Three Mulla-Mulgars*. That last one is the great unknown fantasy book of my childhood.

Zinos-Amaro: Have you read other works by de la Mare? Dirda spends some time discussing *The Return* in one of the pieces in *Browsings*.

Silverberg: I've read some of his short stories, which are ghost stories, mostly. I don't think he ever hit that note again. I have two of his novels, *The Return* and another one, but I haven't read them. I did of course pursue that kind of magic in my early reading. John Taine's *Before the Dawn* was a great dinosaur novel; Lovecraft's *Shadow Out of Time*; Stapledon's *Odd John* left me dazed. These were in the same book, the *Portable Library Novels of Science* volume. The Wells in that book is *The First Men in the Moon*, which I think is one of his weaker novels. And there was also David Lindsay's *Voyage to Arcturus*, which I haven't read in decades, though it had a big influence on *Son of Man*, its color. When I think of *Voyage to Arcturus* I think of forests in which the trees have different colors on every leaf, even if it's not in the book.

Zinos-Amaro: *The World Below?*

Silverberg: That's another one. I did reread that recently. It didn't transport me the way it did in 1953, but what would?

The Worm Ouroboros I think may be the greatest fantasy novel of them all. I have read it many times, enjoying the size of it. I don't mean the words—I mean the world.

On the subject of fantasy, I'll say I've never read Tolkien. Couldn't get past the opening chapters. I recall a character named Tom Bombadil. I thought, "I don't want to spend much time with this guy." Put it back on the shelf and never went back to it.

The trilogy school of fantasy requires a big commitment of time. I don't think the trilogy form itself has anything inherently wrong with it. *The Divine Comedy* is a trilogy, and I have read that, even the second and third parts that aren't much read these days. But the trilogy concept, the notion that nothing is complete by itself and when you begin a book you're committed to thousands of pages—I don't dare do it.

Zinos-Amaro: In terms of fantasy, you've written about Lewis Carroll.

Silverberg: When I was seven or eight, I was given *The Complete Works of Lewis Carroll*, the Modern Library edition. I think you've seen the book, and how thick it is. Though it's got the two Wonderland books in it, it has some things that nobody else reads, like *Sylvia* and *Bruno*. Very mysterious. I never figured out what those books were about, but I loved wandering through them! Almost surreal.

Zinos-Amaro: Is there any author that does that for you now—you can't figure out the work but you love wandering through it nonetheless?

Silverberg: No. I don't like being baffled any more. [laughs]

I've been reading a lot of Simenon lately. And he's not a writer of wonder at all. I tend now to shy away from the fantastic in most of what I read. I will occasionally go back to something like *The Moun-*

tains of Madness. But when I think of the things I've been reading lately, they don't have much wonder. *Buddenbrooks* by Thomas Mann, for example. *The Iliad.* Herodotus—there is a certain amount of fantasy in Herodotus, and play of the imagination, but he's an historian.

Zinos-Amaro: Why do you think you no longer have that appetite for the baffling or surreal?

Silverberg: I have a powerful sense of time running out. Maybe I have fifteen years of reading left, maybe three weeks. Every day is a novelty when you're past eighty. And my interests have largely turned back towards my college years. I first read *Buddenbrooks* when I was in college. That was when I studied Mann, Faulkner, Lawrence, that crowd. Reading them now, with a long contemplative life behind me, I wonder how much I understood of what I was reading then. I suppose I understood enough.

Zinos-Amaro: Have you gone back to Faulkner too?

Silverberg: No. I meant to last year and then somehow got distracted. I wanted to read the three Snopes books again, though I don't think they're the greatest of Faulkner. I wanted to reread *Light in August*, which is a book I don't think I did justice to the first time I read it. There's so much to read.

Zinos-Amaro: Will *As I Lay Dying* be added to your Faulkner reread?

Silverberg: Not only have I read *As I Lay Dying* many times, I've rewritten it once. [chuckles]

Zinos-Amaro: In this particular scenario, where you're going back to reread, say, *Buddenbrooks*, is there a different sense of wonder, not inherently in the text, but in you thinking about how you were different back then from how you are now, in thinking about how the text changes as you change? Or is it just an intellectual experience?

Silverberg: Not wondrous. I've had a long and complicated life, but a fairly predictable one. I've done the things I wanted to do, and was surprised I was able to do so many of them. But it isn't as though there had been zigzag changes in my course that completely reevaluate everything I did before.

Zinos-Amaro: Maybe the fact that you're rereading *Buddenbrooks* is almost a proof of that predictability!

Silverberg: I'm going back to these books in part because in many cases it's more than sixty years since I've read them, and they're not fresh in my mind. Or they *are* fresh in my mind and I want to have that experience again. Herodotus, Rabelais. I'd like to get back to *The Magic Mountain*. But these are long books, and time is short. That's why I find reading the latest science fiction magazine kind of hard to fit in. I stopped reading science fiction regularly sometime around 1975.

Zinos-Amaro: Or long fantasy novels.

Silverberg: Well, case in point is George Martin's series. I read the first volume with great admiration. I think George is a wonderful writer. And yet I never continued with it, in part because there's so much of it, in part because it's unfinished, and I'd rather know where the journey ends. I've had a different and interesting problem with the television show. I watched the first two seasons almost through to the end and I found I'm too squeamish now. I don't want to see all that bloodshed. I was warned that there's a big gory event about to happen, and I didn't watch it, and haven't gone back to it, even though I admire a lot of the acting. Peter Dinklage, particularly, does a splendid job. I gave up watching the show out of dismay at the graphic violence.

Zinos-Amaro: Would that not have bothered you when you were younger?

Silverberg: It would have bothered me some, but not as much. I've never been one for scary stuff on the screen. I remember when I was a kid and my playmates would go off to see *Frankenstein Meets the Wolfman* and things like that, I would never go. I think I've become unwilling to have these images in my mind now. I've heard about some of them and they're pretty horrendous.

CHAPTER 5
Libraries

Alvaro Zinos-Amaro. I'd like to talk about libraries today: ones you've visited, and your own personal collection.

Robert Silverberg. "Everyman, I will go with thee, and be thy guide…"

Zinos-Amaro: That sets the stage nicely. What were some of the public libraries of significance when you were young? Harold Bloom, for example, has written about his fond childhood memories of the Melrose branch of the New York Public Library, as well as the Fordham Road Library, and then of course the central New York Public Library on Fifth Avenue.

Silverberg: The Melrose branch? He must have grown up in a different part of the city from me.

I had two libraries when I was a boy. I lived almost equidistant between them. There was my local branch, and then there was the main Brooklyn Public Library in Grand Army Plaza, I think in New York second only to the Fifth Avenue library in Manhattan, which is one of a kind. Both of these were within walking distance for me from the time I was seven or eight years old, and I frequently went to them. I was allowed to take out an astonishing number of books at a time—I don't think they had a limit, and I would come home with as many as I could carry. Because this was in the 1940s, these libraries had books going back to the turn of the century, which wasn't that far in the past. I had access then to all of the great 19th-century children's classics, with their wonderful illustrations, particularly in the main Brooklyn branch, which had a separate children's library that was a major library in its own. Many, many years later I went back to Brooklyn and I went to the children's library to see if I could find any of the books of my childhood, but they'd all been thrown out, of course, and replaced with the skinny picture books that are children's books now.

I was allowed great privileges at those libraries. The local branch, the Schenectady Avenue branch, had a complete Oxford English Dictionary. It was, I don't know, ten or fifteen volumes, whatever the full print edition was at that point, but it took up a vast shelf behind the librarian's desk; it wasn't on public access. I said to her, "Is that a dictionary? It's so big! Could I look at it?" She handed me a volume of it and I sat down and looked at the OED. I was ten years old.

There was in that library a bound file of *St. Nicholas Magazine*, a now totally forgotten children's magazine that went back into the 1870s. Even the 1870s weren't that far away in 1944. It's comparable now to 1945, which seems like yesterday to me: I remember the day Roosevelt died and the dropping of the atomic bomb very clearly. Well, that's how far back these magazines went then. But I didn't go to the library primarily to look at the OED or *St. Nicholas Magazine*. What I was going there for was essentially fantasy: the collections of myths, the retelling of the Greek and Norse myths, the *Iliad*, the *Odyssey*. Padraic Colum did a wonderful book called *The Children's Homer* in which he wove the *Iliad* and the *Odyssey* together in one story. That's what I went there to look for. I didn't know I was looking for fantasy, I was just looking for good stories.

I treasured all those books. Eventually, in late life, I've acquired all those books for my own library. I reconstructed the books I used to go to the library for. When I buy them on the Internet, I specify that I want an edition published somewhere between 1920 and 1940, and then I know I will get the very book—with the very fingerprints [chuckles]—I had back then.

When I was thirteen and beginning to read science fiction, I would go to the main part of the main library, the adult section, where they had science fiction books. I would look in the catalog for them. There were hardcover science fiction books then: H. G. Wells, John Taine, the occasional small press post-War real science fiction category fiction book, the Heinleins and whatnot. They had them in the card catalog listed as "pseudo-scientific literature." That was the term. It took me a while to figure that out.

Zinos-Amaro: That's almost as bad as "scientifiction."

Silverberg: "Scientifiction" was a very esoteric, in-joke kind of term. That was just Hugo Gernsback's coinage. They called these books "pseudo-scientific literature," and I could never find those books, I think, because there were high-school boys always a step ahead of me, finding them and taking them out.

Zinos-Amaro: How often would you go to the library in those days?

Silverberg: Once a week. I'd probably go on Saturday morning. I did have school to go to. I'd come home with an armload or a double-armload of books, and I'd read them all during the week. Then the next week I'd go back and do it all over again. I had a pretty good private library of my own, and I still have many of my books. My parents and my aunts and uncles were very good about buying books for me.

Zinos-Amaro: How would you pick what you wanted to be bought?

Silverberg: They knew what I should be getting.

Zinos-Amaro: Ah, so they decided for you.

Silverberg: Well, they made the right decisions. I still have many of those books. *The Complete Works of Lewis Carroll* bears an inscription from my Aunt Sylvie, for my birthday of 1944. I think they had a sense of what was appropriate for me, and they were usually right.

Zinos-Amaro: How did your access to or use of these libraries change when you went to high school and then college?

Silverberg: I stopped going to the Schenectady Avenue branch of the Brooklyn Public Library somewhere in my high school years, because I was off at high school, which was at a considerable distance from that library. My high school had a splendid library of its own. Erasmus Hall was the premier public high school of Brooklyn at that time. I don't think it has that reputation any more, but it's still in the same building, a huge Gothic fortress of a building four stories high, around a quadrangle. Immense building. The library was on the top floor of one wing of the quadrangle, with red leather banquettes. I didn't really have a delightful adolescence, and I recall retreating up there after class and hanging out until they would close the school. I would sit on one of those banquettes, reading through the library.

At Columbia—now we're talking about one of the great universities, and of course the Columbia University Library is a great library—you could not normally roam the shelves the way you would at your local branch library. You had to request books using slips. But my roommate at college found a way to get access to the stacks. He told me about it, and I applied for a stack pass in my sophomore year and got one. I don't know what pretext I used. Undergraduates were not supposed to be going in there. I would wander through this cavernous building, maybe ten or twelve stories high, and every hundred feet or so there would be a little study alcove, with a desk and a light, and usually some graduate student would have a stack of books piled up.

That was a life-changing experience, because I had all the scholarship of the world available to me. I had my own classes, but I recall looking for collateral reading for all literature courses, and finding academic journals and translations, rare books. I learned how to do research, which served me in good stead when I began writing the non-fiction books seven or eight years later. I don't believe you were allowed to take books out from the stacks. You had to leave them on the premises. But I'm not clear about that. Anyway, that was like discovering the Library of Alexandria. I had access to everything.

Zinos-Amaro: Would you go there on the weekends?

Silverberg: I'd go there anytime. I had a fairly light academic schedule. The system at Columbia then—probably totally transformed now—put heavy academic weight on certain courses. You had to take a certain number of points per year, but some of the more esoteric courses carried enormous amounts of points with them. Most of mine did. And so I had the proper complement of points and graduated in the proper way, but I didn't have a lot of *hours* of classes a week. I'd have an evening class, called Colloquium, limited to fifteen students, with a great professor at each end of the table. I don't know how many points Colloquium carried, but I'd go one evening a week and racked them up. So I had plenty of time to go to the library.

Zinos-Amaro: Did you just happen to pick those courses that carried a lot of points because the subject matter interested you, or did you deliberately seek out high-point courses?

Silverberg: I wasn't doing it by points, I was doing it by the subject. Since Colloquium was *the* major discussion of the great books, anybody who was a literature major wanted to get into it. It was a two-year course.

Zinos-Amaro: How were the fifteen students selected?

Silverberg: By application only. That included an interview. The course had a flabbergasting reading list. We would be handed the complete Sophocles to read one week, and *The Red and the Black* the next. A giant amount of reading. An Ivy League college—they didn't make it easy.

So all through, from the Schenectady Avenue branch of the Brooklyn Public Library to my various school libraries—and I always took advantage of those—to the wonderfully sheltering high school library with the red leather banquettes, where I'd sit near a stained-glass window high above the quadrangle, to Columbia, libraries were always important to me. But when I became a professional writer I needed the time to work. I couldn't spend my time commuting to libraries, especially as I got more and more remote from the nearest good library. I lived in Upper Manhattan, near Columbia, but I no longer had the stack pass, because I was no longer a student. Then I moved to a suburb where there was no library.

I built my own library and didn't have to leave the house to do my research.

Zinos-Amaro: This would be in the 1960s.

Silverberg: Yes. I bought the big house in Riverdale in 1961, and that had infinite bookshelf space.

Zinos-Amaro: To come back to your high school library for a moment, do you remember any specific books you discovered there?

Silverberg: No. I graduated from high school sixty-three years ago! Longish time. I do remember in junior high school reading a book called *Tros of Samothrace* by Talbot Mundy, which is valued by connoisseurs of fantasy. It's set in ancient Rome, but it has some fantastic elements to it. A nine-hundred page book. I found that on

the shelf of the junior high school library and now I have two copies of it. I have thought for many years of reading *Tros of Samothrace*
again, but haven't done it.

Zinos-Amaro: Were you systematic about reading your way
through certain sections of the library, or did you just grab the books
that seemed most interesting for whatever reason?

Silverberg: I read whatever took my fancy at the time. In junior
high school I was for a while a passionate baseball fan. The Dodgers
were in their glory run and I was eleven or twelve years old. I discovered in the junior high school library the novels of John R. Tunis, a
sports fiction novelist for boys who wrote stories about the Brooklyn
Dodgers. The protagonist was an invented character, but the others
were the real Dodgers, not of my time, of course, but from the 1920s
and '30s. I recall reading through the whole shelf of John R. Tunis.
Recently, i.e. in the last ten years, I bought a Tunis book. Good stuff.

I would read persistently in any one area that I was following. I
was interested in following up on what I was reading to a point, and
then I would get deviated off onto something else. I read all the science fiction I could find, but there wasn't much available then.

Zinos-Amaro: You read a lot of the mythology and fantasy.

Silverberg: I read all of it.

Zinos-Amaro: When did you first read any non-fiction, particularly archaeology or history? Did that discovery happen at a library?

Silverberg: Probably not. In our first conversation I mentioned a
book called *Lost Worlds*, by Anne Terry White, which was a family gift
when I was quite young. I have it in the next room; let's take a look.

[We walk over to the main library.]

Here it is. "January 15th, 1945. Happy Birthday Robert, from

Aunt Sylvie and Uncle Lou." Here's the grave of Agammenon, Assyria, and all the things I later wrote about myself.

Zinos-Amaro: You were ten years old.

Silverberg: Yes. I may have gone off to the library to see what collateral reading I could find, but there we are. There was another book, one about Egypt by Tom Prideaux, called *Never to Die: Egyptians in their Own Words*. Here it is, right in front of me. I didn't own this book—this one was a library book. Now I own it because I went and got it. Someone called Lucille Morrison had it in 1945; I have no idea who she was. This is a book I would read in the library, and ultimately in adult life I bought my own copy.

Zinos-Amaro: Ancient Egypt is another subject you would write about, in *Before the Sphinx*.

Silverberg: Well, these were great subjects.

Zinos-Amaro: I wonder, when you travel, do you seek out some of the great libraries?

Silverberg: Sometimes. I recall last time I was in Oxford going to the Bodleian. I have connections with Oxford: my high school girlfriend became an Oxford don and lives there. Has a British accent now. Her husband, a famous classicist, is also in Oxford. So when I visited—I re-established contact with her many years after high school—we went over to the Bodleian with them, which meant we had insider guides.

What I like seeing in Europe is the great library architecture, the wonderful buildings with the shelves going up and up, and the golden pillars and all of that. The one that comes to mind instantly is in Portugal, in Coimbra; a splendid, splendid building, one of the great sites of that university town. And of course I go to the British Museum, and when they had the British Library there I used to go to look at the displays of books. I like looking at the fine bindings, but I don't do research in libraries now. I stopped doing that a long time ago.

Zinos-Amaro: Have you ever been to the Library of Congress?

Silverberg: I don't recall going to the Library of Congress, but I suppose I have. I haven't spent a lot of time in Washington. It's not a city I particularly like. But maybe on one of my early visits there, in the '60s, I did go.

Zinos-Amaro: The Massachusetts Harvard University Library?

Silverberg: I did visit that once. I don't recall much about the experience; it was in the '60s.

The Vatican Library I've been to. Fifteenth-century books. They don't really let you touch anything, you just stare.

Of course, there's the Morgan Library in New York, and I've been there many times.

Zinos-Amaro: What about the Bibliothèque Nationale de France?

Silverberg: Yes, I've been there. Again, I had some insider connections, and was shown around very nicely by the curator of Numismatics.

Zinos-Amaro: I remember being taken to the Library of Escorial, in Spain, when I was a kid.

Silverberg: I've only been to Madrid once, and the weather was very hot. I went to the Prado and was glad to get out of town.

Zinos-Amaro: I know you've spent some time in Germany and

Austria. Have you visited any libraries there, like maybe Frankfurt's German National Library?

Silverberg: I've been to Vienna, and I've spent a fair amount of time in Berlin, and some in Munich, but I don't recall visiting any libraries there.

Zinos-Amaro: The Bavarian State Library in Munich is where I discovered science fiction, thanks to my dad, who checked out a copy of Isaac Asimov's *Foundation's Edge*, thinking I might like it. He sure turned out to be right. I was in high school at the time.

Outside of the personal significance of libraries, I'm curious if you've ever become interested in the history of libraries?

Silverberg: The only library whose history I've studied with great care is that of Alexandria, because it's a lost library. It turns up frequently in my stories, as a time traveler goes back there to ransack it for lost plays. I have several books about what might have been in the Library of Alexandria and what happened to it. You know, whenever a ship docked at Alexandria that had books aboard, the captain was required to turn his books in at the library so that they could be copied. Nothing passed through Alexandria that didn't remain on shelves there. Then it was all burned, several times. The Romans burned it; the Arabs, bless them, got rid of it.

Zinos-Amaro: Apparently some of those burnings took a long time, too.

Silverberg: Well, you have to heat it to Fahrenheit 451.

I haven't studied the history of libraries in great measure. One other library that did interest me is right here in the Bay Area, the Bancroft Library. H. H. Bancroft was a California businessman who during the boom times of the Gold Rush became inordinately wealthy and began to collect manuscripts dealing with the history of California, and then the entire West. Bancroft hired an army of ghostwriters, impecunious scholars who worked with his enormous manuscript collection and extracted from it information that was turned into *The Complete Works of H. H. Bancroft*, which is in the next room. Fifteen or twenty giant volumes of the history of the Western States. When he died his enormous collection was left to the University of California, so the Bancroft Library is now over here. I do recall consulting it for something, early in my California life.

His granddaughter-in-law—I believe that's what she is—has a wonderful garden. She's a hundred-and-three years old. The Bancroft garden is about twenty minutes east of here and has rare succulents— it's quite a sight. She, until recent years, could be seen actually tottering around in the garden. I think she's the widow of Bancroft's grandson. But anyway, the Bancroft is a local library of note. It is *the* great collection of Western Americana, and it's just down the road and across the street from where we had dinner last night.

Zinos-Amaro: I have a few follow up questions about the creation of your personal library. You have all of this shelf space in the LaGuardia spot in 1961, and you have the income to buy whatever books you want. What criteria do you use at that time to decide, "This will be a reference book I own, but this one won't"?

Silverberg: Some of them I had consulted at public libraries. I was in New York at the time, so I had the 42nd Street Library. I had the Library of the American Geographical Society in Upper Manhattan, which I used for the books on exploration. I'm capable of reading a bibliography, and forming my notion of what I should have at hand permanently. It was a wonderful time for forming a great library, because books were relatively cheap—certainly absurdly cheap by today's standards, but even then, there was not much interest in the annals of exploration, for example. I formed connections with British book dealers, like Maggs Brothers, and Bernard Quaritch, and lot of others, and I would see their catalogs and buy books for five or ten pounds that are now exceedingly rare.

There was a bookshop of Orientalia in New York in the east fifties, called Paragon Book Service, a descendant of which is still functioning, I think, in Chicago. I recall going there and buying, circa 1963, a two-volume, early 18th-century folio of explorations and travels. It was $55 for the two volumes. The proprietor said, "You know, it's a very good investment." I wasn't buying it as an investment, but the last time I saw a quote on it, it was $3,000 or something like that. The point is not that the books have increased in value, or that the currency has diminished in value, both of which have happened, but that I was able build to a really splendid library quickly with the help of some inspired booksellers—I don't know if we have that kind of bookseller any more—and at a reasonable price.

Zinos-Amaro: After several years of doing this, by the mid-'60s let's say, how many books do you think you had?

Silverberg: No idea. I don't even know how many books I've written, let alone how many I own!

Zinos-Amaro: How were the books spread throughout the twenty rooms of that house?

Silverberg: My office was on the third floor of the building. The fourth floor was a finished attic completely lined with bookshelves. That was the part that burned, incidentally. So the entire length of the house on the fourth floor was a library. On the third floor I had a three-room office. The biggest room was the one in which I worked, and that had a wall of books. That was where I kept most of the science fiction books. In the adjacent room I kept all of the science fiction magazines. So we already have the attic and two thirds of the third floor. The second floor was the living space. It had our bedroom and an empty room that had bookshelves, a guest room, and then a room where the cats lived, so just one book room on the second floor.

On the first floor there was a living room with some book space—and a library! It was a room about the size of the one you're sitting in now, a two-story room. Up there, in what was just about the upper reaches, there was the second story, with a catwalk of sorts, and a rolling ladder to reach the upper shelves. There was room for *a lot* of books.

Then I moved to California. It's a somewhat smaller house, but there's the library in the main house, one in the basement, that alcove full of books over there, and then I have the other building, which as you know, is full of books. It was my fate to marry a book acquirer the second time. That's caused a bit of a problem because the place was already full when she got here.

Zinos-Amaro: You just mentioned science fiction magazines. They're a huge part of your collection. When did you begin acquiring those? At some point you must have decided to become methodical about it and to go back to earlier issues.

Silverberg: I bought my first science fiction magazines on the newsstand in 1948. There weren't many of them then, but I began buying them, and buying them, and buying them. By early 1950 I started prowling the second-hand bookshops of Manhattan, of which there were many. There was a district on Fourth Avenue that was all bookstores for about ten blocks, culminating at the lower end in Stephen's Book Service, which was a science fiction shop, presided over by Stephen Takacs. Stephen was a very voluble Hungarian who, as long as I knew him, was finding business terrible, couldn't understand how he was staying in business. But every year he was there. I bought all the science fiction magazines there were in three or four years, back to the beginning. I eventually formed a nearly complete collection of the American and most of the British science fiction magazines. It was quite easy to find them.

Zinos-Amaro: Did your parents frown at any time, as you were bringing in all of these magazines?

Silverberg: Oh, to some extent. At that point I kept them in a closet in my bedroom, but they began to exfoliate from there. But as my parents saw that I was actually writing the stuff and I tended to be pretty serious about that they complained less about it. And then I moved out. I was already gone by the time I was seventeen, although I left the magazines behind while I was at college.

I said I formed a *nearly* complete collection of magazines. There was one I couldn't find: the very first Hugo Gernsback magazine, the April 1926 issue of *Amazing Stories*. One day, probably in the late '50s, maybe in the early '60s, Forrest J. Ackerman came to New York and stopped off to visit me. Of course he was a great collector; he had a house in Los Angeles even larger than my New York house, with every nook and cranny stuffed with collectible science fiction. I took him on a tour of my library and he was pretty impressed. For a kid half his age I'd put together a great library of science fiction. But I said, "I don't have the first issue of *Amazing Stories*. I've never been able to find it." He said, "I'm so sorry to hear that." A week later I got a package from him: he sent me one.

Zinos-Amaro: How wonderful! So at that point it became a complete run.

Silverberg: Yes. It is now a complete run of the standard science fiction print magazines of which there are now, I think, only three left: *Asimov's*, *Analog* and *F&SF*. At any given time it's fluctuated. I remember in 1953 there were there thirty-nine being published at various times. I do not keep up with the contemporary desktop magazines. Every now and then somebody hands me a copy at a convention, but I don't pretend to be collecting them with the assiduity of the others. I don't read the three classic magazines, but I do still get them. The idea of *not* having the latest issue is appalling to me, although I look at it only very quickly and put it on the shelf.

One magazine I didn't collect particularly seriously was *Weird Tales*, because I regarded that as an inferior life form: it wasn't science fiction, and science fiction was what Jim Blish used to call the True Quill. But later on I began collecting *Weird Tales* too. Again, the first issue presented difficulties. That first issue is now worth thousands of dollars, by the way. Robert Lowndes, an editor I've mentioned before, and also a collector of science fiction—he was a fan before he was an editor—got tired of his first issue of *Weird Tales* and gave it to me one day! "I don't want this any more," he said. So these two great rarities were both given to me by veterans of the field.

Zinos-Amaro: And these are the same copies you have today?

Silverberg: Yes, they survived the fire.

Gradually I thought I would collect *Weird Tales* too. A lot of interesting stuff in it, a lot of great Lovecraft, and some science fiction. So I have all but two issues now. My friend Malcolm Edwards, the British publisher, also collects *Weird Tales*, and I think he's missing two issues too, and we each have the issues that the other is missing.

Zinos-Amaro: Collectively you have a complete run.

Silverberg: Yeah. We do it in a very non-competitive way. When he hears that early issues are for sale, he lets me know, and I do the same. I bid once for him in an American auction on some issues.

Zinos-Amaro: Have you acquired any of your own books and magazines through auctions?

Silverberg: I got those *Weird Tales* issues that way, but generally I work in close relationship with book dealers. The books on archaeology and exploration largely came from England, from Maggs Brothers, whom I mentioned, and there were others, like Blackwell's up in Oxford. The science fiction, well, I formed it from all over the place. I still buy the occasional science fiction book, and I usually get those from Lloyd Currey, a specialist dealer. But now, with the Internet, buying books is all too simple.

Zinos-Amaro: To take us in a slightly different direction now, but still related to the subject of libraries, I'm going to recount a short anecdote. Apparently Christian writers in Rome, between the second and fifth centuries, were concerned about pagan literature being in their libraries. Jerome, in the fifth century AD, describes a troubling dream he had in which a heavenly judge asked him what religion he was, to which Jerome replied, "I am a Christian."

And the judge said, "You lie: You are not a Christian, you are a Ciceronian."

I thought that was a telling story about having things in your library which perhaps push up against the limits of your personal comfort. Do you have anything like that?

Silverberg: [chuckles] No. I don't have to worry about transgressing against my religious beliefs, because I have none.

Zinos-Amaro: What about ethical beliefs, perhaps?

Silverberg: I'm not politically correct, Alvaro. I'm a cultural relativist. I believe that mores have changed with time and we need not condemn books that disagree with the received political truths of the moment, many of which I don't care about myself. I'll tell you a story about purging a library.

When I was nine or ten, there was a comic book called *Picture Stories from the Bible*, which illustrated all the great tales of both the Old and New Testaments. I found these great stories—I regard them as stories, you understand. Yes, I would read the set of comics that told about Moses' adventures in the desert, but I'd also read the New Testament ones about Jesus chasing the moneylenders out of the temple. They were all stories. I was sitting on the stoop, as we called it in Brooklyn, the front step of a house of a friend of mine, not a very intelligent friend of mine. He had taken my copy of *Picture Stories from the Bible*, the one I happened to have on me at the moment, and he was leafing through it. It was a New Testament volume. Suddenly his father appeared, his enormous father. I can see the man to this day, nine feet tall. He looked down, saw *Picture Stories from the Bible*, a Jesus volume in his son's hands, and he seized it and ripped it to shreds. I said, "Wait a minute, that's my comic." I was pretty indignant. That may have been my first encounter with bigotry. He would not allow his son to experience this story, and most dramatically let his wishes be known. He was a large, probably tyrannical father, but it was *my* book. I think I got a dime from him.

On another occasion, I was standing across the street from my house—now I'm twelve or so—with a classmate who is holding a group of books. One of them is his Hebrew grammar text, because he's studying for his bar mitzvah, which is not relevant to my life. For some reason he handed me his books, and for some reason—perhaps there were too many—I let the Hebrew grammar book drop. I picked it up and handed it back to him, and he said, "Kiss that book." I said, "It's a grammar book. This is not Holy Scripture." Again he said, "Kiss that book!" Well, of course I didn't. But that too told on me, because it's now sixty-eight years later, and I remember it quite vividly, that slender red book and him saying, "Kiss that book!"

What I learned from these two episodes, unfortunately both Jewish episodes, was that Jews could be just as dumb as goyim. The dogmatic self-limitation, intellectual closing of doors, I hate. I hate it when I encounter it among feminists, or among blacks, or among Christians, or among Jews, where, for what seem to them good and profound reasons, they want to block out anything they disagree with, not only for them, but block it out for *everybody*.

Zinos-Amaro: When you were writing non-fiction you wrote a book about the Marquis de Sade, so I assume there wasn't much you were unable to deal with.

Silverberg: No, but there were a lot of things that the Marquis de Sade did that I would like neither to do nor to watch. I have my limitations. I'm a squeamish guy; I don't like to watch violence. I told you earlier that I stopped watching *Game of Thrones* because it was too gory.

Zinos-Amaro: Were there books you stopped reading, because they were too gory, or authors you stopped reading because their work was excessive in some way?

Silverberg: I don't think so. I read and wrote about the Marquis de Sade, and he was pretty excessive. There are books I've stopped reading because they bored me. That's different.

Zinos-Amaro: Have you ever had the sense of being weighed down by your vast collection of books? I'll add to that a quote by Timon of Phlius, a 3rd-century Greek skeptic, who called the Library of Alexandria a "bird-cage of the Muses." Do you ever feel you have too much?

Silverberg: Not really. Keeping everything in order is a problem, and keeping everything tidy is a serious problem, because I'm a much neater man than my life allows me to be. I've acquired so much that things are scattered all over the place and it would take me twenty-eight hours a day to do all the tidying that I would like to do, so eventually I don't do any of it. But no, I've never fretted about having too many books, or I'd get rid of them. I lose books *in the house*. I have fairly good filing systems but now and then I don't remember what category I considered a particular book to be part of and then I can't find it. In the wonderful world of the Internet, sometimes now after a prolonged search, I just buy another copy. I figure I'm not going to run out of money, and I want that book, and I *am* going to run out of time before I find that book.

What I do feel weighed down with—and this will startle almost anybody who hears it—is the immensity of my own output. I've written an awful lot, and I can't find my way around in it all the time. People like you ask me to discuss my own books, and sometimes I can't remember them. In my office there are thousands of copies of books that I've written: the many editions, translations, whatever. Sometimes I go up there, to the upper story, which you helped me put in order—but things don't stay in order because new things keep arriving—and I feel a great fatigue come over me as I look over all this stuff. "You wrote all that," I think. And I remind myself, "You wrote it one word at a time. You didn't write it all last week." So it's not the pressure of other people's books in the house that upsets me. Sometimes, of course, I feel the pressure of unread books, and I wish I had time to read them all, but everybody feels that. No, it's the pressure of my own oeuvre that weighs on me in a way that I think is impossible for anyone who hasn't written as much as me to understand. But I wouldn't un-write any of it.

Zinos-Amaro: Have you known writers or fans that were perhaps consumed, physically or psychically, by their collections? Preoccupied with their collections to an unhealthy degree?

Silverberg: Oh, I think any kind of collecting is unhealthy. Accumulation, acquisition, becoming attached to things—it's all wrong. But it's too late for me!

Zinos-Amaro: You sound deeply unrepentant. [laughs] You talked about misplacing books. Any book-related serendipities?

Silverberg: Happens all the time. I would frequently say to Karen, "I can't find X," as though she knows where it is. How would she know where I keep anything in my office, when I barely know myself? What Karen usually says in these cases, when I can't find X, is "Look for Y." And she's right. Very often, as I'm looking for something else, I suddenly look down and say, "There's *that*."

Walter De La Mare's *The Three Mulla-Mulgars* is an example. I talked about it with you, and then looked for my copy and couldn't find it. I know where I keep all the books of that sort, the books that shaped me as a reader when I was young, they're all on one bookshelf in my office. After not finding it, which upset me greatly, I bought another copy on the Internet. When that was slow in arriving, I was so impatient that I bought yet another! And then, looking through that area of childhood books one day for something else, I said, "Oh, there's *The Three Mulla-Mulgars*."

Zinos-Amaro: So now it's more like the three *Three Mulla-Mulgars*.

Silverberg: In fact I now have *four* copies. The spine lettering had worn off. The book was precisely where it ought to have been, but as I scanned those shelves over and over I didn't see it.

Zinos-Amaro: What are some of the best science fiction libraries, either private or open for research, that you're acquainted with?

Silverberg: I've known who the great collectors of yore were. A physician in Ohio, Dr. C. L. Barrett, who evidently had a very lucrative practice, could be seen at conventions of the '50s and '60s buying the great rarities. There was a man named Darrell Richardson in one of the southern States who was a collector of pulps and a scholar who wrote some bibliographical works. I knew Doc Barrett; I never met Richardson. Ackerman, of course; I did visit his astounding accumulation of stuff. There was a man in some remote part of Montana named Walter A. Coslet. These are all collectors of decades ago. I don't know who's forming collections now, if anybody.

Zinos-Amaro: Charlie Brown had a pretty sizable collection.

Silverberg: Yeah, Charlie had a great book collection. He had the magazines somewhere, in some subterranean part of his house. I never saw his magazine collection.

Zinos-Amaro: Really?

Silverberg: And I was over at the house all the time. Same with Harlan Ellison. I know he's got a magazine collection, but it's not accessible.

Zinos-Amaro: He also has a considerable comics collection.

Silverberg: Well, I don't care about the comic books.

Zinos-Amaro: What about libraries?

Silverberg: The only library that I can think of with a science fiction collection that I've actually visited is the Williamson Library in New Mexico. Jack Williamson left what was evidently one of the great collections to the Library and they have it all in wonderfully impeccable glass cases. They've got a great collection. I was out in New Mexico for Jack Williamson's 96th birthday, and I was shown the Williamson Library and *would* that I had a library like that, everything immaculate and a staff of thousands!

Zinos-Amaro: There's one at Riverside too, isn't there?

Silverberg: There is, at U. C. Riverside, but I have not been there. I was to have been there about a month from now, to collect a lifetime achievement award, but they've run into some problems at their library and they canceled the shindig.

Zinos-Amaro: Does your library reflect, to borrow a phrase from Alberto Manguel, a "plurality of identities?"

Silverberg: There's a plurality of books here—but they're all my books. I contain multitudes. As for Manguel, he wrote a charming book about his own reading, and he's edited some fantasy anthologies too, two volumes of fantasy short stories that I have in my office; he's one of us.

Zinos-Amaro: Within your library, what are some of the books that have the most personal meaning for you? You showed me a book with an inscription from your aunt before. I'm wondering if you have other inscribed books of personal value.

Silverberg: Aunt Sylvie, who was the most intelligent of my relatives, would give me books frequently, and would always inscribe them. I told you about the Lewis Carroll, and I showed you the archaeology book. There are others. I have never been much of an autograph collector, despite my access to my colleagues. Somehow it has never occurred to me to take advantage of that access. But I do have at least two autographed science fiction objects.

When I was fifteen I went to a small convention in Manhattan, at which John W. Campbell and Will Jenkins were speakers. I thought I should get their autographs, and I had the latest issue of *Astounding* with me, and I had a pencil. I went up to them and they scrawled their names, in pencil, in the March 1950 issue of *Astounding*, which is over there in the office. I treasure it, even though within five years I was selling stories to John W. Campbell, let alone collecting his autographs. There was the wonderful episode where Will Jenkins was in Campbell's office when I brought a story in that Campbell didn't want to buy, and Jenkins read it on the spot and told me how to rewrite it. I had no idea that *that* was coming when I got their autographs in 1950.

The other autograph: I was at a WorldCon and there was a Jack Williamson book for sale that I wanted at one of the dealer's tables. I think it was a first edition of *The Humanoids*. I bought it, and discovered Jack Williamson right by my elbow. "I just bought your book,

Jack, would you sign it?" I never do this, but what the hell—Jack Williamson! And he wrote such a magnificent inscription, in praise of *my* work, in his book, that surely Karen can live for years on the proceeds of the sale of that.

Those are the only two autographed science fiction books that I can remember asking for. I have a lot of signed books that I accidentally bought. My copy of S. Fowler Wright's *The World Below* is signed by S. Fowler Wright, though I simply bought it from the publisher. I wonder if he signed an entire edition.

Zinos-Amaro: Any books that were gifted to you by colleagues? I don't know, maybe Sturgeon dedicated a book to you, and signed it and gave it to you, or something like that.

Silverberg: There are. Not Sturgeon, though. He never dedicated a book to me, and he wouldn't have given me a book because he never had a spare anything around.

Yes, of course, writers have sent me copies of their books. I thought of one in a very odd context just the other day. After the fire in 1968 I had to replace some books. I mentioned to Alexei Panshin, who lived in my area then and with whom I was friendly, that I had lost my copy of Zelazny's *Lord of Light*. So Alex very kindly sent me a copy of the Doubleday edition, now very rare, of *Lord of Light*, and inscribed it to me: "Here, Bob, is *Lord of Light*, the best science fiction novel of 1968." *Lord of Light* had just beaten out a book of mine for the Nebula by about three votes, and I thought, "This is a very uncouth inscription. He's rubbing my face in it, without even knowing what he's doing."

Zinos-Amaro: Uncouth indeed.

Silverberg: There was a book of mine published by Gnome Press called *Starman's Quest*, and Charlie Brown had me autograph it. Charlie was a fanatic autograph hound. You couldn't step into his house without him giving you a stack of things to sign. So I autographed *Starman's Quest* for Charlie—and then lost my own copy in the fire. He gave it back to me, and said, "Here, Bob. Now you've got an autographed copy of your own book." People may wonder in the future, if they go through my books, "Why would he sign his own book?"

Zinos-Amaro: Have you ever considered, since you have such an amazing collection of science fiction magazines, opening it up to the public in some limited way, as a resource?

Silverberg: What a strange idea. About as far I'll go in the direction of opening anything up to the public is letting you and Rebecca periodically come into the house.

Zinos-Amaro: [laughs]

Rebecca Fowler: [laughs] We're representative members of the public.

Zinos-Amaro: Yes, we're just delegates from the outside world.

Silverberg: Do you really think I want strangers marching through here to consult my delicate copies of 1946 *Thrilling Wonder Stories*? No. I duck the public; I keep them at bay.

Zinos-Amaro: Within your science fiction collection, what are some of your most prized books? The ones you'd never part with, even when forced to give up most of what you own?

Silverberg: That's not a question I can answer. I do have items of particular sentimental value, like the first copy of *Amazing Stories* that I bought in 1948, for example. I bought a *Weird Tales* around the same time. It had a story by Edmond Hamilton about the Norse gods. 1948 was not very far from my obsession with Odin and Thor back there in

1944 or so. So even though *Weird Tales* was not a magazine that I particularly liked, and it was going through a period of real mediocrity, I did buy that 1948 issue and feel very tender toward it.

Any part of the collection . . . I have an association with the acquisition or the reading of it.

Zinos-Amaro: What about non science fiction items; any tender feelings there? Did you ever, say, run into John Updike and maybe he signed a book for you?

Silverberg: No, I never ran into John Updike. These emotions are focused on science fiction only.

Zinos-Amaro: Do you have any additional curious stories about how you came to possess certain books or magazines? You mentioned a couple with those first magazine issues.

Silverberg: There were some curious stories.

In 1950 I used to write letters to the magazines of the day, saying, "I'm interested in acquiring old magazines." One day I got a letter from a collector who said, "I have a lot of old science fiction magazines that I'd like to get rid of. If you have any science fiction books that I haven't read, I'll trade you on a basis of cover price." A lot of science fiction and fantasy books at that time were being remaindered for 29 cents at stores in Manhattan. I sent him a batch of them, and he sent me, for each three-dollar book—that was the cover price—twelve 25-cent science fiction magazines. What he was sending me, in return for these 29-cent remainders, was 1943 issues of *Unknown Worlds* that were *already* unobtainable. I remember one of the books I sent him was a novel called *Zotz!* by Walter Karig about some superweapon. Every remainder house had tables and tables of this book and I remember telling a friend that I traded a copy of *Zotz!* for twelve copies of *Unknown Worlds*—it caused quite a stir. This was the nucleus of my old magazine collection. He sent me package after package of magazines. I think he just felt we ought to trade *something*; he didn't care, he wanted to get rid of the magazines. *Unknown* was really the most desirable magazine of the time, a wonderful magazine, and there were no copies around.

My best acquisition story I told in *Asimov's*, in a column called "Aladdin's Lamp." I wandered into a junk shop and found everything going back to the first issue of *Astounding*, at 50 cents apiece. The seller was delighted that *I* was so delighted by this stuff. I was happy to take them away. That file of *Astounding* has an interesting scar on it. The Clayton *Astounding*, the first publisher, was a file two-and-a-half to three feet long and was not harmed by the fire. But the water splashed from one end of the file to another, and you can see a dark stain on the spines running from about July 1931 to October 1933.

Zinos-Amaro: That's a very slow-moving splash; it took two years to get across.

Silverberg: [laughs] I'm reminded of the fire every time I see that stain.

Zinos-Amaro: And the items that were actually burned in the fire, you eventually reacquired?

Silverberg: Yes, one way or another. Most of the collection was untouched, but my file of my own published work, which was in a different place, was completely lost. I mentioned the Zelazny book with the churlish inscription. A few days after the fire Anne McCaffrey showed up at the house with a huge carton of science fiction magazines with stories by me in them, from her library. It was an act of absolute empathy and love.

Zinos-Amaro: And these remain in the collection today.

Silverberg: Yes. But they've been filtered in with all the others, so I'd be hard-pressed to identify them now.

Zinos-Amaro: You mean she didn't sign them?

Silverberg: Charlie Brown went down to Heinlein's place one time and hauled away tons of foreign editions of Heinlein books, and made him sign every one of them. I have a German edition of a Heinlein book that I got from Charlie somehow that has a Heinlein autograph in it.

Zinos-Amaro: I should bring German editions of your work here for you to sign. This discussion on the value of books makes me wonder, what are the most rare books in your library?

Silverberg: There was an illustrated book called *The Ship That Sailed to Mars*, with a kind of fantasy narrative strung loosely through, and it has thirty or forty lovely colored plates. The book was published in the early '20s. It is legendary among science fiction collectors. Ten or fifteen years ago I came upon a copy at a San Francisco antiquary book fair. I don't know what it had been selling for—if you bring up ABE you can see the current price—but this copy was maybe four or five hundred dollars. It was not an impeccable copy. I thought, "I never expected to own this book, but I do have four or five hundred dollars," or whatever it cost. Then, later, it was reissued in a very crisp but not nearly as attractive edition. They were trying to make it as close to the original as possible, and they did a nice job, but a facsimile is a facsimile. Karen reviewed the new edition for *Locus*. With the luxury of the original on hand, she was able to make a few points about how the original was finer.

Zinos-Amaro: It looks like some of the art prints are being sold individually. The book itself is selling for hefty sums.

Silverberg: I've got some rare books, but these days everybody has some rare books.

I've sometimes been queasy about expenditures for no rational reason. Ballantine Books in its early years used to do hardcover editions of the paperbacks, small runs of these hardcovers, and most of them are quite rare. The rarest of all at this time was a book called *The Green Odyssey* by Philip José Farmer. It came out for $2.95 but by the time I thought I should own it, because I liked the Ballantine hardcovers, it was already up to between two and three hundred dollars. I thought, "That's a ridiculous price for a book I could have bought for three dollars." So I didn't buy it, and didn't buy it, and the price kept going up. Finally I was at a convention and there was a copy, now for seven hundred dollars. I said to Karen, "You know, I've been watching this thing go up for twenty-five years without buying it." And she said, "Well, why don't you buy it?" I told her, "It's crazy to pay seven hundred dollars for a book I could have bought for three dollars." But of course the price was never going to bounce back. So I bought it.

The recent Jules Verne acquisitions aren't cheap. In an earlier era, when I had to deal with real-world economics, I didn't buy such expensive books. With the books I buy today, the cost is irrelevant. I'm not saving for my old age, and I'm not leaving Karen impoverished. And I'm not going to be here that much longer.

CHAPTER 6
Potpourri

Alvaro Zinos-Amaro. I have some questions for you that were submitted to me by email or via Facebook. The first one is from Matthias Belz. He says: "There is no official bibliography, alas, and the unofficial ones are all incomplete. This means there are a lot of Silverberg stories out there that no one knows about." He quotes a few specific examples where this causes difficulties, and goes on to say, "I have the impression that Mr. Silverberg doesn't attach too much importance to this, but in my opinion, a comprehensive bibliography would be an important part of his literary legacy."

Robert Silverberg. He's wrong and right. I attach enormous importance to my bibliography—how else am I ever going to find my way around my own work? There *are* official bibliographies. There was one that was published in 1981, done by Thomas D. Clareson. Clareson came here one day and sat on that couch. Unfortunately he didn't ask to go into my office and do bibliographical research, which I would have been willing to let him do. He did compile a thorough bibliography: the science fiction is not hard to find. But the peripheral stuff *is*, and I have a big file of it, miles and miles of it.

Zinos-Amaro: So Clareson's bibliography annotates some but not all of the pseudonymous fiction and non-fiction. I think Matthias' point is that there is no *comprehensive* official bibliography.

Silverberg: Right. That's as comprehensive as anyone did, in terms of a real bibliography published as a separate book. Phil Stephensen-Payne also compiled a Silverberg bibliography, which is apparently out there somewhere online. I don't think he's published it, but I have a copy. There are many international ones. I have a German bibliography, a French one, an Italian one.

Harlan Ellison, who has also written a lot, though not quite as much, says that a new bibliography of his is in the works. But there is an existing Ellison bibliography.

I'm certainly willing to have a new bibliography done, but it's an unthinkably big job. Like I said, there have been several attempts. I would not create obstacles, but I don't want someone coming and pitching a tent on my lawn, and going through all the magazines for weeks on end.

Zinos-Amaro: I think that's what it would take, though, to do the full job.

Silverberg: I'm sure Graham Greene didn't have someone pitch a tent on his lawn.

Zinos-Amaro: Do you think he wrote as many erotic stories, for example, as you did?

Silverberg: No, he didn't write as much of anything as I did. But he wrote quite a lot. There's a tabulation of all of his letters in the bibliography, for example. But that was not a matter of going to visit Graham Greene; it was a matter of going to the special collections.

Zinos-Amaro: In the case of your work, Matthias says he's having trouble finding out about the adventure stories specifically. He mentions that you reference publishing stories in *True Men Adventures* in *To The Dark Star*, but he hasn't found any of those.

Silverberg: Yes, that's what Clareson failed to look through when he was here. I would have shown them to him.

Zinos-Amaro: Another detail Matthias includes concerns the novel *Lesbian Love*, published in 1960 by Nightstand Books. The Majipoor.com website says it's by you, writing as Maureen Longman, but a website about Greenleaf Classics associates that byline with Marion Zimmer Bradley.

Silverberg: Greenleaf was very casual about sticking bylines on things. When they saw that Don Elliot sold better than other names, everything of mine started getting a Don Elliot byline. Marion did write some lesbian books for them. In fact, looking at the reference lists, I see that I wrote the first Marlene Longman book, *Sin Girls*, and Marion wrote the next one, *Lesbian Love*.

In connection with the erotic books, I'll mention that the F.B.I. came to talk to me one day. They came to my Fiorello La Guardia house because somehow they had linked me to pornographic books, though the word "pornography" was never mentioned. The two gentlemen in suits and ties came in and I received them in the paneled library. And they said, "Mr. Silverberg, we understand you're a writer." I said, "Yes, that's true. Here are some of my latest books." I showed them a few recent books on archaeology and science for young readers I had written—books I just happened to have close at hand. And they looked with great interest. And then they said, "Have you ever heard of a company called Reed Enterprises?" Well, Reed Enterprises was one of the dummy corporations through which the checks to the writers came. But it so happened that my checks came from Blake Pharmaceutical Corporation instead, a different dummy corporation, and the nice F.B.I. men had gotten things mixed up. I, who do not tell lies, said, "No sir, never heard of them." The F.B.I. went away and didn't bother me again.

Zinos-Amaro: Who said being a writer wasn't risky business?

The following question is from Eric del Carlo. He'd like to know if there was a single watershed story that you see as your graduation from the plot-heavy, John W. Campbell era stories to your more sophisticated, character-intensive brand of fiction? One story of yours which broke that ground for you.

Silverberg: There were several. *Thorns* was a deliberate attempt at new ground. And "To See the Invisible Man," which was earlier than *Thorns*.

Zinos-Amaro: What about the story "A Man of Talent," about a poet, which you wrote after the first Milford Science Fiction Writers' Conference? I remember you saying that you were inspired by that meeting.

Silverberg: Yes, that was a story I did for Bob Lowndes in the '50s. That was earlier than the two I just mentioned, and I still wrote a lot of pulp stuff after that.

It depended on what they would let me do. Lowndes would let me do anything, so I wrote "The Songs of Summer" with nine different narrators, and things like that. But mostly it was a very conservative field, and I wrote what they wanted to buy.

Zinos-Amaro: Was there any particular magazine that you remember being more restrictive than others?

Silverberg: The most restrictive was *Astounding* at the time that I dealt with it, although of course it was very different in the '40s, but I was not writing then. A number of magazines were quite liberal-minded. There was one called *Venture* that lasted for about ten issues and allowed for considerable intensity of characterization. And Lowndes' various magazines, and Larry Shaw's *Infinity*. All these magazines died quickly.

Zinos-Amaro: Speaking of the '50s, Jack Skillingstead was wondering if you'd say a little about the early days in NYC when you lived in the same building as Harlan Ellison and another science fiction writer. You were young and writing short stories at breakneck speed—did you see yourself as being in competition with these other writers?

Silverberg: The other writer in the building was Randall Garret. Garrett and I were not only not competitive, we were collaborators. We worked together.

Harlan and I had a certain inevitable competitive situation because we had come up as professionals at virtually the same time. Everybody was watching us, and the year I received the Hugo for most promising new writer, he was one of the other names on the ballot, so that is inherently competitive. But we did not put obstacles in each other's way. When new magazines started, we told each other, "There's a new market." It's only the competition of two contemporaries of the same age who happened to be running on parallel tracks. But we looked after each other.

Zinos-Amaro: So how *did* the three of you come to live in the same building?

Silverberg: I was living there, across the street from Columbia University. Harlan had a very brief college career, about three months, and then came to New York to seek fame and fortune. He knew me and he came up to see me. He looked at the building where I lived and said, "I'll rent a room down the hall," and he did. Garrett, a rather roguish sort, and eight years older than me, had been living in Peoria as the guest of well-known science fiction writer of the era who threw him out after a while, because of his roguish behavior. And Garrett thought, "Well, it's time to go to the Big Apple and crack the barriers there." He came to New York, and virtually the only person he knew in New York at that time was Harlan. So he came up to visit Harlan, and rented a room on the second floor with the rest of us. But they

202   Alvaro Zinos-Amaro

were not compatible personally. And Harlan also was at that point rather undeveloped as a writer. Garrett needed the spur of a collaborator. He was a very good writer, a very skillful storyteller and very good with science fiction ideas—but an alcoholic, and he couldn't finish much of his work. I was a capable writer for my age, a pro, and *not* an alcoholic. And so I could make him work.

Zinos-Amaro: How did that collaborative situation come about? He brought it up in conversation one day, inviting the possibility?

Silverberg: It just seemed like the logical thing to do. I was not very different from what I am now. I was methodical and disciplined and in those days hard-working. Garrett was the opposite in every way and he saw that there was an attraction of opposites. He said, "Let's go down to John Campbell's office and propose a novel to him. And then we'll write a novel together!" I thought, "This is madness. I'm twenty years old and I'm proposing to sell a novel to John Campbell?" But why not?

We went down to Campbell's office. John was fascinated by me. Bright young Jewish boys; well, there had been Asimov fifteen years before me, and he thought he might find another one of those. Randy and I told John the idea we had laboriously worked out, and John said, "That's very interesting . . . but let's do it this way." He proceeded to turn it inside out and upside down. We had a story about, of course, a Scotsman—because John knew that the Scots were the highest form of life—who goes to some other planet and disrupts its governmental system for its own benefit. John said, "Fine, that's a wonderful idea—but tell it from the point of view of the aliens. And don't do it as a novel, do it as a series of novelettes." We went home and wrote a 12,000-word story together. We talked it out, and he wrote some of it and I wrote some of it.

Zinos-Amaro: Did you work in shifts?

Silverberg: Yes. Generally I did the final draft, because even then I was a smoother stylist, but he was a good idea man, and also he had a background in chemistry. I was a college kid, what did I know? We took it down to Campbell and he read it right on the spot.

Zinos-Amaro: All 12,000 words? That must have taken a while. You guys were just sitting there in his office the whole time?

Silverberg: Yes, we sat there, sweating bullets. He made one small editorial change and bought it. He wouldn't have read it on the spot if he were not already predisposed to buy it. He knew Garrett's work, had published half a dozen of his stories. Substantial stories. And he was hoping he'd find another Asimov in me. Which on several levels he did. This was the summer of 1955. I went home and thought, "I sold a story to John Campbell. Imagine that." I couldn't sleep all night.

Then of course he wanted two sequels. We wrote the two sequels. Then he said, "Now go home and write a novel." And that's how it became a three-part serial: "The Chosen People," "The Promised Land," and "False Prophet." These became *The Shrouded Planet*, followed by *The Dawning Light*. We finished *The Dawning Light* in the summer of '56. It's now a year since we'd pitched the first thing. I had just graduated from Columbia in June and I got married in August, and we made this $3,000 sale to a top market. Then I went off to the WorldCon the following week, with a honeymoon in between, and got a Hugo. Good start to a career!

Zinos-Amaro: When you started writing these stories with Randall Garrett, did it change the dynamic with Harlan?

Silverberg: Very severely. They came almost to blows. They couldn't get along at all, although in earlier times they had met at conventions and apparently had some kind of friendship. Harlan was struggling. He was writing stories and he'd get them back the day before he submitted them. Here I am, not only selling reams and reams of stuff, but now with this collaborator, whom I've stolen from Harlan, essentially, I'm selling to *Astounding*, and on my own to *Galaxy*, and a little while later to *F&SF*. I'm running a major career right off the bat. He's not. He's able to sell a few stories here and there to subsidiary markets, but he wasn't doing well. Later, in '58 or '59, things got very different for him, but this is '55 and '56. So of course things were very tense.

Zinos-Amaro: Did it affect your relationship with him?

Silverberg: Not particularly. It wasn't my fault that I was selling stories. And who would not have taken advantage of the collaborative opportunity? *They* could never have collaborated, though.

Zinos-Amaro: Any comments on the "breakneck speed" part of Jack's question?

Silverberg: I knew how to type, I knew how to tell a story. There was one year that I wrote and sold two million words of fiction. At 50,000 words a book, that's 40 novels—in 52 weeks. I'd call that a breakneck speed!

Zinos-Amaro: You wrote so much fiction under so many different names, too; particularly later on, with the erotic books.

Silverberg: I even wrote a Western once. The writer Jonas Ward wrote Westerns about a character named Buchanan. When he died he left half a novel behind, and I wrote the other half. It's called *Buchanan On the Prod*—my only Western novel.

Zinos-Amaro: Never heard of it. How did you become involved in the project, through your agent?

Silverberg: Through my agent, yes. He called up and said, "Want to finish a Western, Bob?" And why not? It was just work. I wrote all sorts of stuff.

Zinos-Amaro: This next question is from Jim Long: Have you ever had an experience where a character seems to develop a life of his or her own and resists doing what you had planned?

Silverberg: They generally develop lives of their own because I'm creating them as I go and getting to know them better. The main instance of resistance came not from a character exactly. When I was writing *Up the Line*, which as you know is a complicated time paradox novel, I had a certain ending in mind—I always have a certain ending in mind. I was perhaps midway through the book when I realized that under the rules that I had set up for time travel here I could not get to the ending that I wanted to get to. I had to stop and re-plot the novel at that point. I did get to my ending, but I had to change the rules along the way. This was a lot harder to do in the days before computers. You can't just create a block of material and mortar it into place. You have to rip out pages and retype and all that. I did it, the book was published, and is still in print.

That was the chief resistance. I've never had a character, that I recall, say to me, "No, I'm not going to do what you want me to do. *I'm* the boss."

Zinos-Amaro: What about more subtly pushing the narrative in a different direction?

Silverberg: That may have happened. But it's been a long career, Alvaro. Lots of books, and I don't remember it all clearly.

Zinos-Amaro: Fair enough. This next question is a very specific one from Dave Creek. He's from Louisville, KY, and says that the local papers years ago asserted that you'd visited Louisville and that the sight of the "800 Building" was the inspiration for your novel *The*

World Inside. It mentioned the repetitive nature of the air conditioning units on the outside of the building. Any insights there?

Silverberg: No. I've never been to Louisville.

Zinos-Amaro: You've written about the influence of the Italian
architect Paolo Soleri on the novel, particularly Soleri's concept of
"arcologies." So the novel was not inspired by travel, was it?

Silverberg: No, though I did eventually visit Soleri's headquarters
in Arizona, but that was years later. I heard about Soleri's theories and
had, more or less simultaneously, been thinking, "Gee, if we keep on
reproducing and pave the whole planet, where are we going to grow
the vegetables?" These came together in *The World Inside*.

Zinos-Amaro: The next question is from Wichael Tellez. He
asks, "What is the #1 thing you would say to young wannabe writers
trying to get published?"

Silverberg: Write. Write and read.

Zinos-Amaro: In a 2011 interview, you were asked a similar
question, and back then you replied: "Read as much as you can. Write
as much as you can, and show it to editors. Live as much as you can.
And try to be patient."

Silverberg: That's what I would have said to you just now, except
that I've said all that before! What I might also say is, "Don't quit your
day job." I don't think it's possible to do now what I did when I was
twenty. You'd need to work at such velocity . . . Jay Lake was doing
it for a while. I was capable of writing two stories a day and selling
them. You need the markets. Well, there are a lot of markets. I don't
know their names any more, but there's a lot of online stuff, desktop
publishing. That capability to write a story on demand, though, which

I doubt I would have now—but I'm quite old now—is the first step. It's a low-paying field now. It's much more of a low-paying field than it was when I was starting out. We thought we were being scandalously underpaid by the magazines of the day. Two and three cents a word didn't sound right. But in terms of purchasing power, a short story sold to one of the top magazines would get you $150; that for me was a month's rent at my elegant, five-room apartment. The equivalent rent today would be between three and five thousand dollars a month, and you can't get that for a science fiction short story today. I was getting it back in the '80s, when we had *Playboy* and *Penthouse* going, but they're not doing it any more.

So it's not possible to have the sort of career that I had unless you can immediately leap in with some fantasy series that is going to captivate millions of readers. I don't mean *Game of Thrones*. George R. R. Martin was not an overnight success. Actually, George had some struggling to do along the way. But there have been the occasional writers who in their twenties write some kind of fantasy trilogy that was the quintessence of their adolescent dreams—they'd been living this fantasy world, would write it and sell it and it would catch on. That happens maybe once every five or eight years. For the rest of them, I think it's very difficult to make a living. It always has been.

Zinos-Amaro: It seems that these days we also have the phenomenon of writers who self-publish, sometimes just in e-book format, and at times strike great success.

Silverberg: Some of the most successful books of our time—not science fiction—like *Fifty Shades of Grey* or *Twilight* began as self-published books. But you can't *organize* that. You can't generate it. It's not a matter of will. It's something that happens like a lightning strike. I'm sure that for each *Fifty Shades of Grey* there are fifty or five hundred other authors writing similar stuff that are unknown. What I did was to tell myself, "I want to be a professional science fiction writer. I want to be a full-time science fiction writer and earn a living doing only that." And I did. There were many markets, in terms of purchasing power the pay was very good, and I had the gift that Jack called "breakneck speed" before. That's not waiting to be struck by lightning after self-publishing your book. That's organizing a career and making it happen.

I benefitted greatly from being in New York, and from being taken around to the editors by Randall Garrett, by being able at a very early age to make myself part of the New York professional scene, so that editors would call me when I was twenty-two years old and say, "Bob, I need a 10,000-word story by Tuesday." That's not easy to duplicate now.

Zinos-Amaro: Thanks for the perspective. Given how much you've published, the next question from Sharon Joss seems appropriate. She writes: "Long time fan, here. I just bought a (signed!) copy of *A Time of Changes*, and I am very much looking forward to reading it. Given you are such a prolific writer, I wondered which of your novels are your particular favorites?"

Related to this question, I've brought a copy of Mike Ashley's *The Illustrated Book of Science Fiction Lists* with me, because you answered a similar question in that book. There's a list titled, "Robert Silverberg's Ten Favorites of His Own Books."

Silverberg: [laughs] That says something about the kind of writer I was. "What are your favorites?" "Well, the *ten* that come to mind are…" Let's see. This book was published in 1982. It's still a pretty good list. It consists of: *Dying Inside*, *The Book of Skulls*, *Born with the Dead*, *The World Inside*, *Son of Man*, *Tower of Glass*, "Capricorn Games," "Sundance," *Nightwings*, and *Downward to the Earth*. Of these I think *Son of Man* was the most interesting writing experience I've ever had, tapping straight into the unconscious on every page.

If I were doing this today, I'd add "Sailing to Byzantium" to replace something there. "The Secret Sharer" is another story I'm pleased with, and the novella "We Are for the Dark" that nobody ever noticed.

Zinos-Amaro: Would you consider *Tom O'Bedlam* among your favorites?

Silverberg: I think it's a good book. I liked writing it. Not sure I would place it in the top ten. Some of them were a great strain to write. *At Winter's End*, such a huge book that it was painful to write. *Tom O'Bedlam* just danced along.

Zinos-Amaro: Next we have a question from Greg Benford. What are your thoughts on "hard science fiction," particularly in contrast with the more literary science fiction books you are best known for, such as *Dying Inside*?

Silverberg: I'm not trained in physics or mathematics so I don't regard myself as deeply enmeshed in the world of "hard" science as Greg understands it. I have a small background in chemistry and a considerable one in archaeology and history, social sciences, I suppose. But I don't have much of an answer . . .

Zinos-Amaro: As a science fiction reader, are there any books you enjoyed that are considered "hard" sf?

Silverberg: I think highly of Hal Clement's *Mission of Gravity*. But if you ask me, "What are your favorite hard sf books?" the answer is that I don't think in that category. Is *The Time Machine* hard science fiction? Or complete fantasy? I've often said that science fiction is a branch of fantasy. And why I shy away from hard science fiction as a concept is that it is an attempt to paper over the basic improbability of science fiction.

Zinos-Amaro: So why does, say, *Mission of Gravity* succeed for you?

Silverberg: *Mission of Gravity* succeeds because it defines an unusual planet where the gravity varies rapidly with latitude and then extracts the narrative power from that situation. But I believe *any* good science fiction story does that. Does *The World Inside* qualify as hard science fiction? I attempted to design those buildings in a plausible architectural way. *The World Inside* begins with a fantastic situation—800-story high apartment houses—and then extracts all the narrative juice that can be extracted. But the reason I don't think of things as hard or soft science fiction is that I prefer to think of them as *good* science fiction and *bad* science fiction. The bad science fiction is the story that fumbles its own premise. The good science fiction is the one that follows its own premise to its logical conclusion. In that mindset, *X*, *Y* and *Z* space operas might well become bad science fiction.

As a writer, I can only write about things I understand, and my knowledge of physics is a shallow one. So I didn't plunge deeply into the implications of the physical universe, because I didn't have that type of education.

Zinos-Amaro: I wonder if something like Joe Haldeman's *The Forever War* is potentially hard science fiction? I certainly think it's good science fiction. There's rigor to the extrapolation and there's narrative power.

Silverberg: There's certainly narrative power there. Whether there's technological rigor, I don't remember—I haven't read that story in forty years.

Zinos-Amaro: I was thinking of the relativistic aspects of space travel.

Silverberg: Well any of us could get *that* right.

Zinos-Amaro: [laughs]

Silverberg: Like I said, the whole hard/soft dichotomy is of little interest to me. Good/bad, that's the dichotomy that I want to work on.

Zinos-Amaro: Moving on to a question inspired by something you said a moment ago: You mentioned the physical universe and its implications. Do you believe in anything supernatural?

Silverberg: I don't believe in the supernatural in the sense of angels or God or ghosts.

Zinos-Amaro: What about telepathy? Or telekinesis?

Silverberg: Those aren't necessarily supernatural—but not yet demonstrated. I believe telepathy is not inherently impossible. I don't think there have been any demonstrated examples of it, and plenty of fraud. But it's very different to talk about believing in telepathy and believing that God manifested himself to Moses in the form of a burning bush. One of those is at least possible to me.

Zinos-Amaro: So psychic abilities and extra-sensory perception would be potentially possible?

Silverberg: Yes, *potentially* possible.

Zinos-Amaro: As long as they don't violate any physical mechanisms.

Silverberg: They don't violate any physical laws because they don't seem to operate *in* any physical laws!
I have my doubts about time travel as a scientific reality. That didn't stop me from writing plenty of it.

Zinos-Amaro: What about the soul? Spiritual existence after the body has passed, all that type of stuff?

Silverberg: Not proven. I think inherently not provable.

Zinos-Amaro: Implausible?

Silverberg: Well, most people seem to believe it, so it must have some superficial plausibility. Not for me. For me, we turn the light switch, and the light goes out. But I can't prove non-existence after death; and I can't disprove it. I know what I think, but that's just a hypothesis.

Zinos-Amaro: You wrote a column about your house being haunted, which we talked a little about in Chapter 4.

Silverberg: Inexplicable things have happened here. But there's a lot that's inexplicable to me. Playing the piano and doing different things with different hands—I can't explain that. I don't know how people do that; I can't. But I know it's done. I've seen it done. I've been married to people who can do it.

Zinos-Amaro: Some of your answers to readers' questions have made me think of Nietzsche's ideas about artists. For him the greatness of an artist is not measured by the fine sentiments that he excites, but rather, as he writes in *The Will To Power*, in the ability "to become master of the chaos that one is; to compel one's chaos to become form: logical, simple, unequivocal; to become mathematics, law—that is the grand ambition here." What do you make of this, besides the Nietzsche hyperbole?

Silverberg: Yes, hyperbole. I think he's making a false dichotomy. I don't think the greatness of an artist is measured by the sentiments he creates, but measured by the works of art that he creates, which are not necessarily sentimental. Michelangelo's *David* creates no sentiment; it's merely a block of stone. The late quartets of Beethoven are simply patterns of sound; there's no sentiment there. You can pretend there is, but there's not; it's just abstract sound. As for the other half of his dichotomy, the business of mastering the chaos within, of course Nietzsche was a disturbed man who ended up in an insane asylum. I think what you have to master as an artist is the material that you are struggling with, which is in the beginning without form. Even God looked upon the face of the waters without form. Then you impose form on them. That's what an artist does. And Nietzsche overstates the case by talking about the chaos. I don't think a novel that is in the process of gestation is emerging from chaos, I think it's emerging from nothingness. That's not the same thing. By a process of selection and compression, the artist produces, in whatever art he practices, a work of art.

I haven't read Nietzsche in fifty or sixty years and I have no plans to, since he's not an important figure in my mental artillery.

Zinos-Amaro: In my same reading I hit on something else I wanted to bring up, and this has more to do with my interest in your life choices than your technical abilities as an artist. It has to do with the work of the Spanish philosopher and writer Miguel de Unamuno on the concept of suffering. It seems that, unlike Buddhists, who in a way see suffering as a problem to be overcome by practicing detachment, for Unamuno it's essential that we face our own suffering so we can truly love other suffering beings. Where do you stand in terms of detachment and experiencing suffering?

Silverberg: I try to be as detached from my suffering as I can be. [chuckles] Interesting that you bring up Unamuno because I haven't read him since my college days, but when you said "the Spanish philosopher" the name Unamuno was already in my mind. I suppose it might as easily have been Santayana...

Zinos-Amaro: Or Ortega y Gasset.

Silverberg: Yeah. But Unamuno came up immediately. However, I

can't remember my readings of his work. As for suffering and detachment, I've tried to live as un-turbulent a life as the world will allow.
When you wake up at three in the morning with your house on fire,
you are not in what Sartre would call an existential position: you've
made no choice, it's just been thrust upon you. And that happened
to me. But you shape fiction out of suffering, conflict, and the shaper
needs a certain detachment from what he's shaping if he's going to
maintain control over the Nietzschean chaos that he's working with.

So one avoids suffering—that's merely a rational decision, and
I'm a rational person—but one marches forward *through* it. One experiences it out, as somebody once said. And out of that you make your
fiction. David Selig suffered, but comes to some kind of acceptance of
the suffering at the end. That is what fiction normally does: comes to
an epiphany and healing, or destruction, it makes no difference.

Zinos-Amaro: I think we can push a little harder on the concept
of detachment.

Silverberg: I'm a rather more detached person than most. I have
chosen an almost solitary life, although I've been married all my adult
life. But I have not worked out in public. I prefer to be within the
walls of my own house. And I'm quite capable of being alone for a
good chunk of each day.

Zinos-Amaro: Is that really detachment?

Silverberg: You're stepping back from the world. There are people
who are frantically attached, always volunteering for things. I don't
think it's a good idea to volunteer. I will occasionally affiliate myself
with something. I was president of many of the organizations that I
belonged to, but I don't push forward. I'm not a self-promoter, I'm not
a joiner, because I have the life that I have chosen, which involves solitude, reflection, and for a long time creation. These are things done—
well, solitude *especially* you have to do alone.

Zinos-Amaro: [laughs] That's a great line. Do cats count?

Silverberg: Yes, cats do count. You notice I don't have any dogs. Dogs are extremely demanding, interactive animals. They come at you, they woof, they jump up and down. I have one cat right now and love her dearly. She comes over and I stroke her fur, and she may say something to me, or she may not, and then she'll walk away. That's what cats are like. And I much prefer the company of cats to dogs or, for that matter, to most people.

*

Zinos-Amaro: In your anthology *Worlds of Wonder*, which was republished as *Science Fiction 101*, you analyze the technical merits of several excellent short stories, and you go into some detail. What I was hoping you could do now is to pick three or four works of literature and discuss their openings; but I'd like you to select at least one whose prose doesn't work for you, and explain why.

In fact, I'm going to suggest we start with Thomas Hardy's *Jude the Obscure*. We've exchanged emails about it and I know you find the prose off-putting.

Silverberg: In fact, Hardy is so off-putting that I've never actually read an entire novel of his.

Zinos-Amaro: Here's my copy of *Jude the Obscure*.

Silverberg: I forget which Hardy I made my most recent attempt at. It may have been *Jude*. I couldn't penetrate its style. This is less of a problem for writers who are not known for their styles.

Zinos-Amaro: Right!

Silverberg: Let's take a look at the opening of *Jude*:

"The schoolmaster was leaving the village, and everybody seemed sorry. The miller at Cresscombe lent him the small white tilted cart and horse to carry his goods to the city of his destination, about twenty miles off, such a vehicle proving of quite sufficient size for the departing teacher's effects. For the schoolhouse had been partly furnished by the managers, and the only cumbersome article possessed by the master, in addition to the packing-case of books, was a cottage piano that he had bought at an auction during the year in which he thought of learning instrumental music. But the enthusiasm having waned he had never acquired any skill in playing, and the purchased article had been a perpetual trouble to him ever since in moving house.

The rector had gone away for the day, being a man who disliked the sight of changes. He did not mean to return till the evening, when the new school-teacher would have arrived and settled in, and everything would be smooth again."

It doesn't seem too terrible. But it is *ponderous*, clumsy. For example in this line: *"The rector had gone away for the day, being a man who disliked the sight of changes."* That's not how I would hear it: *"The rector was a man who disliked the sight of changes. He'd gone away for the day."*

But reading this I wonder which passage it was that so annoyed me. I see, incidentally, that the introduction objects not to the style, but to the story. People were apparently not put off by the style.

Zinos-Amaro: You used the words "ponderous" and "clumsy." Where does this come from? Is it the grammatical construction of the sentences? The assembling of sentences into paragraphs?

Silverberg: The sentence I chose as an example—it just doesn't seem to me to be the most efficient way to communicate the material. The second clause, "being a man who disliked the changes," modifies the rector, but there's a lot between the rector and the "being." Changing the order to "*The rector, being a man who disliked the changes, had gone away for the day*" sounds much better to me. It doesn't matter at all to people who are not sensitive to style. What I rewrote, I rewrote in a very simple way, but simply moving the clause around is an improvement over what's here.

Zinos-Amaro: What about the description in the first paragraph?

Silverberg: "*The schoolmaster was leaving the village, and everybody seemed sorry.*" That's a nice opening line. Then we have: "*The miller at Cresscombe lent him the small white tilted cart and horse to carry his goods to the city of his destination, about twenty miles off, such a vehicle proving of quite sufficient size for the departing teacher's effects.*" He's using the same type of modifying clause as in the other example, and using a participle where I think an indicative verb would be more direct. This is followed by two more sentences that have a lot of words. The "purchased article"… The line that begins with "*For the schoolhouse had been partly furnished by the managers*" is in the passive voice and I would recommend changing it to active: "*The managers had partly furnished the schoolhouse.*" The rest, which is also in the passive, could become: "*The master's only cumbersome article was a piano that he bought at action.*" Wherever you poke it, it's too much. It's not effective prose. Plenty of people have read Hardy, but I don't know who reads him any more. What he does here is put a screen between the reader and the events. He's creating a veil by not phrasing things in the most immediate way.

I flipped to another page at random and was met by this sentence: "*It did not occur for a moment to the schoolmaster and recluse that Jude's ardour in promoting the arrangement arose from any other feelings towards Sue than the instinct of co-operation common among members of the same family.*" There's surely a better way of saying whatever he's saying than that! Because he says it in a negative way: "*it* didn't *occur to him that his ardour could have possibly arisen from any other thing…*" Well, a whole book of that, I found indigestible. Also, where he writes "the schoolmaster and recluse," is that a way of cramming information into the sentence? It's presumably the same person. Then why not, "the reclusive schoolmaster"?

But I'm not sure I want to continue to deliver a sermon on bad prose. I'd rather discuss good prose.

Zinos-Amaro: I am interested in the things you're sensitive to in prose that you find disagreeable.

Silverberg: I value lucidity in prose.

Zinos-Amaro: Have you read *Robinson Crusoe*? I wonder what you think of its prose. Though admittedly we're going farther back with that.

Silverberg: The last time I read *Robinson Crusoe* I was ten, and I couldn't tell you anything about it. Daniel Defoe is a seventeenth-century writer, and we've had some changes in prose. But there are some seventeenth-century writers like Dryden whose prose is remarkably lucid.

Now let me pick out a couple of books I'd like to praise. I've selected, almost at random, Ernest Hemingway and Graham Greene. I believe in, and have always practiced, the notion that the opening page of a book should draw the reader in by generating some sense of the theme and some sense of the conflict. This is what we call the narrative hook. I don't think it's absolutely required, but it's a good idea.

I'll give you an example of how I don't think it's absolutely required by citing two novels of Hemingway, a writer I do admire but don't particularly imitate. His two early novels, *The Sun Also Rises* and *A Farewell to Arms*, are both considered great novels, without much disagreement, but they open in very different ways. Here's the opening of *A Farewell to Arms*, the later novel:

"In the late summer of that year we lived in a house in a village that

looked across the river and the plain to the mountains. In the bed of the river there were pebbles and boulders, dry and white in the sun, and the water was clear and swiftly moving and blue in the channels. Troops went by the house and down the road and the dust they raised powdered the leaves of the trees. The trunks of the trees too were dusty and the leaves fell early that year and we saw the troops marching along the road and the dust rising and leaves, stirred by the breeze, falling and the soldiers marching and afterward the road bare and white except for the leaves."

Very simple prose, although when you look at it closely you see it's very mannered prose also. He does set the stage very vividly. You see the river, the plain, the pebbles; troops are going by the house. There's trouble somewhere. And this is all in the first ten lines.

Zinos-Amaro: You get the sense of nature being contaminated too.

Silverberg: Yes. That I think is a superb opening paragraph to a superb novel.

The Sun Also Rises is a very different novel, because it's not about wartime, but decadence after the war. Here's how it opens:

"Robert Cohn was once middleweight boxing champion of Princeton. Do not think that I am very much impressed by that as a boxing title, but it meant a lot to Cohn. He cared nothing for boxing, in fact he disliked it, but he learned it painfully and thoroughly to counteract the feeling of inferiority and shyness he had felt on being treated as a Jew at Princeton. There was a certain inner comfort in knowing he could knock down anybody who was snooty to him, although, being very shy and a thoroughly nice boy, he never fought except in the gym."

And so on. It's clear Hemingway prose, but this book is not about Robert Cohn. It opens with him for one full, long paragraph, but it's narrated in the first person by somebody else. It goes on:

"*I mistrust all frank and simple people, especially when their stories hold together. I always had a suspicion that perhaps Robert Cohn had never been middleweight champion and that perhaps a horse had stepped on his face or perhaps his mother had been frightened or something.*"

What Hemingway is doing here is opening with something that seems irrelevant and then bringing in the narrator to indicate what the narrator is like. The narrator is immediately contradicting what we've been told about Robert Cohn. It is a funny way to open a book, though, if you believe that it should open with the drama, especially since he goes on to talk about Robert Cohn for quite a while. I think the older Hemingway would not have done this. But eventually Robert Cohn moves into the background and Jake Barnes takes over the book. And of course it ends in that wonderful way:

"'*Oh, Jake,*' *Brett said,* '*we could have had such a damned good time together.*'
Ahead was a mounted policeman in khaki directing traffic. He raised his baton. The car slowed suddenly pressing Brett against me.
'*Yes,*' *I said.* '*Isn't it pretty to think so?*'"

This is one of the best endings of a novel imaginable, especially if you know what these two characters have been through. Here's a writer in his twenties—he's already Hemingway, though I am not comfortable with his opening. The other one, *A Farewell to Arms*, has a perfect introduction, leading you in. You're in some dusty, probably Mediterranean place—in fact, you'll find out you're in Italy—and the soldiers are marching by.

Zinos-Amaro: You used the word "mannered" in connection with the opening to *A Farewell to Arms*. Do you think that creates distance for the reader?

Silverberg: It can. The distance is created in this case if you get caught up in the fact that Hemingway is playing with his sentences, instead of getting caught up in what the sentences are telling you. "*. . . we saw the troops marching along the road and the dust rising and leaves, stirred by the breeze, falling and the soldiers marching and afterward the road bare and white except for the leaves.*" It's deliberately incantatory. And you might, if you're impatient, say, "Come on Hemingway, get on with it." I don't ask that of Hemingway. But by the time you get to *For Whom the Bell Tolls* the mannerisms *have* begun to swamp the narrative, although that's still a very gripping book.

Here's a book by a writer whose mannerisms never took over. This is *The Power and the Glory*, though the American edition is called *The Labyrinthine Ways*, somebody's very bad idea.

"*Mr. Tench went out to look for his ether cylinder: out into the blazing Mexican sun and the bleaching dust. A few buzzards looked down from the roof with shabby indifference: he wasn't carrion yet. A faint feeling of rebellion stirred in Mr. Tench's heart, and he wrenched up a piece of the road with splintering finger-nails and tossed it feebly up at them. One of them rose and flapped across the town: over the tiny plaza, over the bust of an ex-president, ex-general, ex-human being, over the two stalls which sold mineral water, towards the river and the sea. It wouldn't find anything there: the sharks looked after the carrion on that side. Mr. Tench went on across the plaza.*"

This book isn't about Mr. Tench, either. But we have the blazing Mexican sun, we have the buzzards, we have the hint of political upheavals. There's a *big* political upheaval going on in the subtext of this book.

Zinos-Amaro: The phrase you used before, narrative hook, gets kicked around a lot these days. In the case of the Hemingway novel that opens with Cohn rather than Barnes, is there a narrative hook in the traditional sense?

Silverberg: There's a narrative hook—in the *un*traditional sense. What Hemingway has given us is Robert Cohn, a secondary character, though he'll figure in it fairly extensively. But then in the second paragraph he gives us Jake Barnes' dismissive view of Robert Cohn, which *is* important to the narrative, because Cohn is a bit of a phony and Barnes is not, and they are going to be companions through the story. So it does launch the story, but in a very subtle and complex way that is not the ordinary kind of narrative hook. In *A Farewell to Arms* you don't get any characters in the first paragraph, you get the description. There is a "we" in "we lived in a house," but who is it? Then we get more description, and the soldiers. A certain tone is being established. There's a war going on and he's not in it, but he'll be affected by it. He's telling it in a very rugged, individual way, and before very long you cannot help but read.

In this case we don't know who Mr. Tench is, though we'll find out pretty quickly.

Zinos-Amaro: I wanted to ask about this. Do you think that deliberately concealing him, or not providing information about him, is one of the things that pulls you in as a reader?

Silverberg: Absolutely. If what else you're seeing is sufficiently interesting, you will wait to find out who Mr. Tench is. You'll discover that Tench is a minor character, and it's the priest that matters here.

Zinos-Amaro: This almost seems like the antithesis of what Hardy was doing. When he introduces his characters, like the schoolmaster, he gives information about who they are.

Silverberg: Yes, and it's not only that he was giving the information, but the way he was giving the information. Greene is withholding almost everything. We don't know what Mr. Tench is doing in Mexico, though we start finding out pretty quickly, right in the next few lines: "*He said 'Buenos días' to a man with a gun who sat in a small* *patch of shade against a wall. But it wasn't like England: the man said nothing at all, just stared malevolently up at Mr. Tench, as if he had never had any dealings with the foreigner, as if Mr. Tench were not responsible for his two gold bicuspid teeth.*" Now we know that Mr. Tench is an Englishman, a dentist, in Mexico.

"*Mr. Tench went sweating by, past the Treasury which had once been a church, towards the quay.*" Why is the church converted into a public building?

"*Half-way across he suddenly forgot what he had come out for—a glass of mineral water? That was all there was to drink in this prohibition state—except beer, but that was a government monopoly and too expensive except on special occasions.*" You're already learning that the times are out of joint. And you're only two paragraphs into the story.

Zinos-Amaro: I notice as you're reading through it that a lot of these beats are generating questions, and reading on gives us some answers. Same with the Hemingway. In the Hardy there were few questions. What we were told, we were told fully.

Silverberg: People do read Hardy, but not me. Now, at what point do we lose Mr. Tench? He's going to set up a dental practice here and meet the priest. This is very early for Greene, not his first book but within the first decade of his career.

Zinos-Amaro: Happens to be the only Graham Greene novel I've read.

Silverberg: It's a good one. I remember now that with Hardy it was *Tess of the d'Urbervilles* that I struck out on. In *Jude* the schoolmaster is moving; we're told that he's got all these books and things; the rector has gone away. It goes on, "*The blacksmith, the farm bailiff, and the schoolmaster himself were standing in perplexed attitudes in the parlor before the instrument.*" You're outside the characters. "*The master had remarked that even if he got it into the cart he should not know what* *to do with it on his arrival at Christminster, the city he was bound for, since he was only going into temporary lodgings just at first.*" He may be telling a compelling story, but he's telling it with his elbows.

Zinos-Amaro: I've pulled up the opening of *Tess*. "*On an evening in the latter part of May a middle-aged man was walking homeward from Shaston to the village of Marlott, in the adjoining Vale of Blakemore, or Blackmoor. The pair of legs that carried him were rickety, and there was a bias in his gait which inclined him somewhat to the left of a straight line.*"

Silverberg: "*The pair of legs that carried him*"!

Zinos-Amaro: "*He occasionally gave a smart nod, as if in confirmation of some opinion, though he was not thinking of anything in particular. An empty egg-basket was slung upon his arm, the nap of his hat was ruffled, a patch being quite worn away at its brim where his thumb came in taking it off.*"

Silverberg: This is not, for me, effective prose.

Zinos-Amaro: You being someone who doesn't admire this prose. I see what you mean. We have the same type of convolutions, the participles and so on.

Silverberg: Also, there's nothing going on in the character's mind. We haven't established anything. Mr. Tench is crossing a blazing plaza and there's a man with a gun sitting on the other side of it. This fellow who is a middle-aged man, we don't even know his name, whose legs are not quite right and who's tilting off to one side, is not thinking of anything. In fact, nothing much is happening. People still publish Hardy, but they probably don't read him.

Zinos-Amaro: Only because they have to, perhaps.

Silverberg: We're not talking about captive audiences here, we're talking about willing, eager audiences, palpitating to buy the book.

Zinos-Amaro: I want to go back to the end of *The Sun Also Rises* for a moment, to this line: "*The car slowed suddenly pressing Brett against me.*" It seems that some writers are very sensitive to adverbs these days, in particular something like "suddenly." The idea is that if you want to convey suddenness, you can do so by picking a better verb that does it for you, without then having to modify it. To be more elegant in the word choice and make the adverb unnecessary.

Silverberg: I don't see anything wrong with "suddenly." I object to finding different ways to say, "he said." But "suddenly"?

Look, there's some people who'll tell you that you shouldn't use adverbs at all. Or that you shouldn't use adjectives at all. Whatever works. Whatever Hardy is doing, it doesn't work for me. Hemingway works. A random page of *Jude* I just turned to:

"*Jude Fawley, with the self-conceit, effrontery, and aplomb of a strong-brained fellow in liquor, threw in his remarks somewhat peremptorily; and his aims having been what they were for so many years, everything the others said turned upon his tongue, by a sort of mechanical craze, to the subject of scholarship and study, the extent of his own learning being dwelt upon with an insistence that would have appeared pitiable to himself in his sane hours.*"

You might say that there have been prose changes since 1895, but Dickens wrote fifty years before that and you don't pick up Dickens and say, "How boring. How congested." Whatever story is unfolding beneath the clumsiness in Hardy is obscured for me by the tortuous nature of the prose.

Graham Greene maintained his control all throughout. He knew how to tell a story; he told it directly and with great suppleness.

Hemingway eventually becomes so Hemingway-esque that you

start chuckling when you read his prose, and that's bad too. But that was many years after these two books. I'll get my copy of *Across the River and Into the Trees*, from 1950. This is how it begins:

> *"They started two hours before daylight, and at first, it was not necessary to break the ice across the canal as other boats had gone on ahead. In each boat, in the darkness, so you could not see, but only hear him, the poler stood in the stern, with his long oar. The shooter sat on a shooting stool fastened to the top of a box that contained his lunch and shells, and the shooter's two, or more, guns were propped against the load of wooden decoys. Somewhere, in each boat, there was a sack with one or two live mallard hens, or a hen and a drake, and in each boat there was a dog who shifted and shivered uneasily at the sound of the wings of the ducks that passed overhead in the darkness."*

And so on, and so on, for quite a way. Then you get a conversation between the guy pushing the pole and the one holding the gun.

Zinos-Amaro: To go back to your comment from before, we don't know anything about the minds of the characters. There's not much of a narrative hook.

Silverberg: There *are* no characters at first. And you're not even sure where you are. Eventually you meet the characters—and you don't like them. This book got him laughed to scorn.

Zinos-Amaro: I wonder if with the Hardy and this example of Hemingway pacing is an issue too. But Proust wrote long sentences and told a very slow-moving story. Would you say that on the level of sentences Proust is still conveying more information, and more directly, to the reader, even if it is about the nature of conscious thought, for example?

Silverberg: Proust writes very convoluted paragraphs. He's a difficult writer. But he's not clumsy in the way that Hardy is. With Proust it's sometimes difficult to remember by the time you get to the end of a paragraph, where it began.

Zinos-Amaro: That can happen with Henry James too.

Silverberg: Well, you have different Jameses. We discussed James a little in Chapter 2. The sly critical remark is that there's James the First, James the Second, and the Old Pretender. Early James is quite lucid and accessible. Middle James, like *The Portrait of a Lady*, is very strong narrative. By the time you get to *The Ambassadors* it's a struggle to read him. By now he's dictating his books—and it made a difference. The words flowing on and on and on and on. *The Wings of the Dove* is good, but long-winded. *The Portrait of a Lady* is an unforgettable, marvelous novel. So we know he could do it. He just changed his notion of what he wanted to do.

In science fiction, though, for the most part people just tell the stories. Except for X, Y and Z, of course.

CHAPTER 7
After the Myths Went Home

Alvaro Zinos-Amaro. In this final chapter I'd like to discuss your perspective on age, and on what it's like to look back on a professional writing career that's lasted over six decades. I'm going to start with a quote from your book *Other Spaces, Other Times*, which gathers previously published autobiographical material. There's a piece in which you describe your teenage mind, and you say: "I had a superb memory and a quick wit, but I lacked depth, originality, and consistency; my mind was like a hummingbird, darting erratically over surfaces. I wanted to encompass too much, and mastered nothing." How does that compare with how you perceive your own mind now?

Robert Silverberg. I still leap around a lot. But I've had sixty-odd years to learn a few things. One difference between the writer I was then and the writer I became is that he was a kid. Though I was technically quite precocious, and was able to assemble stories that looked like professional stories, I was competing against the likes of Alfred Bester and Robert A. Heinlein and Phil Klass and Robert Sheckley and such. These were people who had been in the war, had been through divorces, who had experienced all the turbulence of adult life—and I was a kid. So it was difficult to compete with them, and I had to wait a few years until I'd done a little living. The leaping from place to place, part of it was an attempt to learn everything at once, and part of it was simply the nature of being an adolescent, which is what I was when I began my career.

Zinos-Amaro: How much of the change, I'm wondering, was deliberate, and how much was informed by these more turbulent experiences beyond your direct control?

Silverberg: You can't avoid turbulent experiences, short of sequestering yourself in a monastery; turbulent experiences will come and get *you*. I've had my share of them. I've been able to insulate myself against some of the worst ones. I know little about poverty and would like to keep it that way. But I had a marriage fall apart. I uprooted myself from the city of my birth and moved to the other end of the country, and that was not without its trauma. Each of these is what we call in California a "learning experience." [chuckles] But some of it is simply the process of living, the deepening of the synapses that comes as you continue to read and think and travel and experience. You don't need problems to learn. There are other ways to learn—I hope.

Zinos-Amaro: Was there ever a conscious moment of you thinking to yourself that your mind was too erratic, and taking deliberate action to make it less so?

Silverberg: No. What I told myself at the beginning is, "I'm a bright guy, but I've led a sheltered life. I haven't had the experiences of the world that the older writers have had. But I will continue to study. I will go to college. I will read sequentially." I learned at college to follow a course. I went to a very good college and had some wonderful professors. This was not a process of deliberately repairing myself—it was a process of growing up.

Remember, I started very young. So did Asimov, so did Bradbury. And though Bradbury, by the time he was twenty-five or so, was writing some remarkable things, the stuff he was doing at nineteen was not Bradbury. Asimov at twenty-one wrote "Nightfall"! That was unusual to the point where for years thereafter people would say to him, "Why don't you write something as good as 'Nightfall' again?" You can imagine how he found that.

Zinos-Amaro: Speaking of starting soon, I want to bring up a piece I mentioned right at the beginning of these conversations: "Starting Too Soon." There you quoted Stendhal: "We learn everything in solitude except character." How much do you believe that to be true? Clearly character informs the things we do in life.

Silverberg: You get out into the world, as far out into the world as you're willing to go, and you encounter the world and it changes you. This is a process that's called growing up. Some people never do it.

Zinos-Amaro: Even though they have the experiences.

Silverberg: They have the experiences, but they don't grow up. What I had that confused everybody was that precocious technical skill that allowed me to write stories with beginnings, middles and ends, with dialogue and exposition, but I was still writing without a solid grounding in life.

Zinos-Amaro: You mentioned Asimov a few moments ago. Writing about the three stories of his that you expanded into novels, you said, "I needed to absorb and replicate Isaac's own literary style. His prose always was simple, lucid, straightforward. My own tone, somewhat more baroque, had to be suppressed. His narrative method relied almost entirely on dialogue and bare-bones exposition; he had little interest in evoking sensory images, particularly visual ones, whereas I have always strived toward rich descriptive impact." Where does that comparative baroqueness, that heightened interest in sensory impact, come from? Is it a response to your conception of science fiction as a visionary literature, or the result of your reading influences, perhaps as a child?

Silverberg: It was more a matter of the things I was reading as an adult. Isaac; a great conceptual mind. He was, of course, a scientist, and a teacher of science. Not a literary man, though certainly he did produce an *amount* of writing. But not literary writing. He wrote basic narrative. I, though I read all manner of pulp magazines, was also reading Joyce and Mann and Kafka and Faulkner and Conrad, and was seeing what the possibilities of the narrative art were. I think it was Heinlein, in an irreverent mood, who said something like, "The Sears catalog is worth more literarily than the entire works of James Joyce." I think that's approximately what he said. Well, that was Heinlein being a provocateur. I don't think he really believed that—I hope he didn't. But nevertheless he and Isaac were not what I would call *conscious* literary artists, and had not, in fact, read the great books.

The only science fiction writers before me who seemed acquainted with anything other than pulp fiction were Sturgeon, Bradbury, Vance, Blish, Kuttner, maybe a few others. Most of the rest were straightforward storytellers. I tried to do both. This led to the somewhat schizoid career that I had. At one point I was writing bang-bang space opera, at another point I was writing imitation Faulkner.

Zinos-Amaro: My next set of questions were inspired by a reading of Malcolm Cowley's *The View from 80*, written, as the title suggests, when he turned eighty. Early in the book he talks about the "pleasures of the body, of the mind, that are enjoyed by a greater number of older persons." He goes on to write: "Those pleasures include some that younger people find hard to appreciate. One of them is simply sitting still, like a snake on a sun-warmed stone, with a delicious feeling of indolence that was seldom attained in earlier years."

Silverberg: Perhaps I'll get there some day—but I'm only eighty! I'm not at all good at sitting still.

Zinos-Amaro: "A leaf flutters down; a cloud moves by inches across the horizon. At such moments the older person, completely relaxed, has become a part of nature—and a living part, with blood coursing through his veins. The future does not exist for him. He thinks, if he thinks at all, that life for younger persons is still a battle royal of each against each, but that now he has nothing more to win or lose." Do you ever find yourself experiencing this contemplative state?

Silverberg: I do experience that sense of having nothing more to win or lose. That's why I don't write any more. There's nothing I want to achieve; I don't want to write a best-selling trilogy, I don't want to write an award-winning work, I don't want to write a masterpiece, I don't want to write anything at all. I did it.

So on that level, yes, I look back at the young people madly tweeting and blogging and Facebooking and running around from convention to convention and pushing themselves into the face of the public and I think, "I don't need to do that. I don't want to do that. I'm not going to do that." I don't do that.

As for what Cowley writes about sitting like a lizard on a stone, I'm a restless, high-strung guy and that is not changing even with considerable old age. As I sit here talking I'm also tapping my foot and playing with my cat. The *cat* knows a lot about sitting still but I'm not a cat.

Zinos-Amaro: Have you found pleasures that you think it would be hard for younger people to enjoy, maybe even a younger version of yourself?

Silverberg: No. The pleasures diminish with age; that's one of the definitions of age. I like to eat and I go to a lot of fine restaurants. But I'm cautious now about what I eat and the speed with which I eat it, because my body is in decline. That's what age is. The other physical pleasures, like the pleasure of over-exerting oneself, for example, taking a ten-mile hike; no, I won't do that. I can't. I think everything gradually shuts down in age. And I'm quite philosophical about that.

I certainly don't want to be running marathons. I know there are a few unusual seniors who do unusual things but although in my small way I was an athletic young man, I was not prodigious. Here in old age I'm not going to challenge mortality by over-exerting myself.

There is one thing about old age that does connect with what Cowley is saying. You dispense with a great deal that a younger person might care about. I get three newspapers, the *San Francisco Chronicle*, which is a dreadful paper, the *New York Times*, which is a splendid paper, and the *Wall Street Journal*, which is useful to me in a number of ways. Three newspapers a day is a lot of newspaper input. But I edit my reading. I look at a headline and know I don't need to read about it. I abolish much of the content of the newspaper and only read that which has some relationship to the quieter, closed-in life of an old man.

Zinos-Amaro: And you read newspaper articles more broadly when you were thirty or forty?

Silverberg: As an active writer I wanted to know everything, and took in all the information I could suck up. I'm not an active writer now, and there's a lot I just don't need to know. I don't need to know what Quentin Tarantino's new movie is about, because I know I'm not going to see it. In the past, even though I wasn't going to see the movie, I might have wanted to be informed about it. So one aspect of the Cowley kind of age is closing off things that a younger man would deliberately pursue. There isn't time to pursue everything. How long did Cowley last after turning eighty?

Zinos-Amaro: Great question. He made it to ninety. So he had a full decade after writing his book on old age.

Silverberg: That's pretty good. Of course, Jack Vance was ninety-six, but I don't think Jack was accomplishing very much in the final five years.

Zinos-Amaro: At the beginning of Chapter 2 of Cowley's book, this struck me as interesting: "One's 80th birthday is a time for thinking about the future, not the past."

Silverberg: Contemplating how much future there is.

Zinos-Amaro: Exactly. Is that something you found yourself doing?

Silverberg: Oh yes. I want to read Gibbon again. It's three huge volumes in my edition and I do ask myself, "Do I have time to read Gibbon again? And if I do, what am I passing up?" You have to calibrate the reading time available against the lifespan that's available. I don't think I thought much about that when I was forty or forty-five. But it's certainly plausible . . . I'm in good health now; my guess is I have five to ten years left. I might surprise everybody and last another fifteen, or I might not make it to the morning. I don't know. But if *you* felt that you had five to ten years left at your age, you'd live very differently. Actually, you would be indignant, because you are expecting to live another fifty years or more. And you probably will. I know I won't—I'm not even sure I would want to. So you accept the finite nature of your life, but then you make the adjustments. Will I read Gibbon? I think I probably will. If I've got ten years left, there's time to read Gibbon. It'll take about four months.

Zinos-Amaro: Another thing I found interesting is that Cowley spends a little bit of time talking about vitalism, this idea that somehow as you live you're exhausting some vital reserve of energy. He acknowledges that the idea is medically discredited, but he wonders whether "each of us is born with a smaller or larger store of energy. Of course the store isn't constant; it can be renewed or diminished by circumstances; but each of us may have some voice in determining how fast the energy will be spent." He then provides two examples. One of them is Elihu Root.

Silverberg: Root was a diplomat during the Theodore Roosevelt era.

Zinos-Amaro: Cowley says that Elihu "decided at the age of 47 to last a long time." He apparently shared this with one of his doctors. "From that day forward he watched his diet and refrained from activities that would strain his heart, such, for instance, as running for office (though he consented to serve as secretary of state and later as U.S. senator, in the days when senators were still appointed). He was always the wise counselor, not the harassed executive, and he lived to be just short of 92."

The other example he gives is John D. Rockefeller, Sr. "He appears to have made a similar decision at 58, after he had amassed his fortune; thenceforth he devoted himself to golf and philanthropy. [...] he had given away $530 million before he died at 97."

What do you think about this? Did you ever make a similar decision, which maybe in part has led to your longevity?

Silverberg: I have lived a long time, so clearly I did it right. But I haven't done anything specific. I am by nature a man of moderate habits. A drink or two a day; I eat until I'm not hungry and then I stop. I eat regular hours. I sleep regular hours. This is simply the way I am, not the way I've designed myself to be. I don't like irregularity. I don't like staying up until three in the morning of a given day and then sleeping till noon, and then the next day going to bed at nine and getting up at two a.m. That's not what I do. So the innate programming of my body has been beneficial to me, without my working at it.

And also my palette does not incline me towards unhealthy things. I don't eat forty-ounce steaks; I don't eat anything sugary particularly, like soft drinks; I've never smoked. This was not an excess of virtue, simply my body choosing for me. Where I *have* made a few decisions is when they've been forced on me. In my mid-seventies I began having cardiac problems, which, if we did not have modern technology, probably would have killed me. The only medication I take is a cholesterol-lowering one, because after having a couple of arteries plugged up I'm willing to concede the possibility that lowering cholesterol extends your life. I don't take other medications because I don't have other ailments, like diabetes or high blood pressure. I don't even wear glasses. But this is a matter of luck and constitution, not choice.

Zinos-Amaro: As might be expected, Cowley talks about people who were productive well into old age, and others who burned out a lot younger. Examples of artists—painters and sculptors, specifically—who had very long productive lives are Goya, Titian, Michelangelo, Monet, Matisse, Chagall and Picasso. When he shifts the discussion to novelists Cowley references E. M. Forster, Somerset Maugham and P. G. Woodehouse, who lived into their nineties.

Silverberg: Not as productive writers.

Zinos-Amaro: Not as productive writers perhaps, but he contrasts them with Balzac and Dickens, whose example he says must have been followed by others who likewise "shortened their time on earth by living hypertensively in their imaginations." That's a curious turn of phrase.

Silverberg: Yes, but it's nonsense. Balzac shortened his time on earth by drinking sixteen or more cups of coffee a day. Another thing that I don't do—I don't drink any coffee. Balzac drank it all day long by the gallon and died at fifty. He was also constantly in debt. When he earned money, and he earned a good deal of it, he would spend it as fast as he could make it. He created a stressful existence for himself and it killed him at fifty.

Dickens lasted to fifty-eight. He was a hard-working man who launched into an extramarital affair in his fifties, which required enhancing his income. He went on a profoundly stressful lecture tour that wore him out. Here in my eighties, I've skipped extramarital affairs *and* lecture tours both.

Elihu Root talked about avoiding the stress of running for office. Writing, I found, was stressful, though I did plenty of it. I did it at high velocity and with great intensity. I got very tired by the end of my working day, but the next day I'd go right back and start again. I wound it down. I don't think it would kill me to continue writing. But it would certainly consume energy that I don't want to devote to giving the world more science fiction. Very few novelists have achieved much after sixty. Hemingway was already dead at sixty-two, but he hadn't written anything significant in years. Faulkner lived to be sixty-seven and he too had sloped off. Philip Roth is an example of a writer who continued writing until about eighty, and then he said, "I'm done. I'm going to stop." His last couple of books, whatever he may have thought of them, were not well-received. Saul Bellow did write a book in his eighties and was roundly drubbed for it, whereas Picasso was painting right to the last day of his life. Maybe painting is easier! I don't know.

Zinos-Amaro: Cowley writes about wealth and age, as well, a topic we've touched on. He says: "Wealth becomes less important in age, except as a symbol of power and security. Things harder to measure—health, temperament, education, esteem, and self-esteem—contribute more to one's life. Thus, intellectual poverty proves to be as bad as material poverty." Do you think that's true?

Silverberg: I'm careful with money, and have invested wisely, and I earned a good living from the beginning of my career, because I was productive and disciplined, so I don't know much about poverty. I *have* had periods of financial stress, like when my house burned in 1968 and I had suddenly to lay out the equivalent of half a million dollars in twenty-first century money before the insurance started coming in. I had some problems. When my first marriage broke up and I had to buy my way out of it, that created some financial stress.

But basically I've had enough money to get me through. I don't see wealth as a symbol of anything. I don't go strutting around saying, "I'm richer than you."

Zinos-Amaro: Surely some people do.

Silverberg: No doubt. There are people who do the most amazing things.

Wealth *is* a unit of security for me. I know that even though I'm not writing now, I'm not going to be forced back to writing at the age of eighty-seven because I can't pay my mortgage. I think one of the factors that drove me to the vast prolificity of my early career was the sense that the more I earned and the faster I earned it, the better I could keep the world at bay. And now I literally live behind a wall.

Also, money is useful. I travel widely and I really don't want to stay in Motel Six when I go to France, for example. Money makes for a quieter life, and I'm not interested in turbulence. So I don't agree with a lot of what Cowley is saying there. But he was a literary critic, and I'm a creator.

Zinos-Amaro: The disagreement is of interest to me. You just spoke of security. Cowley writes about fears and old age. He says that he suspects that many old people are "haunted by fears that they prefer not to talk about. One of the fears—I wonder how many have suffered from it—is that of declining into simplified versions of themselves, of being reduced from the complexity of adult life into a single characteristic." He goes on to give several examples.

Silverberg: Such as?

Zinos-Amaro: "If they had always insisted on having their way, in age they become . . . tyrants without a toady. If they had always been dissatisfied, they become whiners and scolds, the terror of nursing homes. [. . .] the chatterbox, the fussbudget, the invalid, the hag, the hermit, the Langley Collyer, the secret drinker, the miser, the frightened soul, the bottom pincher, the maiden aunt, or the bachelor auntie." He says that it's "frightening to think that one might end as a caricature of oneself." Have you seen this happen to any of your peers who were long-lived in science fiction?

Silverberg: One of our famous Grand Masters was a notorious bottom pincher.

But a caricature of oneself? No. Fred Pohl lived to be ninety-three, and though physically he was pretty much of a wreck the last few years, his mind remained alert and questing. His personality, which was an assiduous one, remained assiduous but not cranky.

Jack Vance did deteriorate in his mid-nineties. He was blind and I would regard that as a horrific thing to happen to me. He began to recycle himself. He did not move forward in life; he retold old stories and relived old memories. I can't say that I worry about becoming a caricature of myself. I'm still the person I was at sixty, at forty, at twenty. I'm actually very similar to those people! I don't spend a lot of time worrying about the deterioration of the body, which I have very gradually experienced over eighty years. Gradually. I've made an underlined point of saying I don't wear glasses. Mostly I function as a younger man would, but more slowly, more carefully, and with limitations. I would not like to go blind, and I would not like to enter dementia, but I'm not doing those things, and to spend time worrying about them is foolish. I *will* eventually die. I know people who can't believe that, that they will die. But I do, because so far everybody who has ever walked the earth has died, and I don't see why I would be an exception. But I do expect to live a while longer. I feel pretty good, and so it saddens me to think I might get two-thirds of the way through Gibbon and not get through the fall of Constantinople this time around, but it's not something I lose sleep over.

Zinos-Amaro: What about "the fear of being as dependent as a young child"?

Silverberg: Vance was blind and housebound. Jack Williamson was pretty functional to a great old age. He had a great support system around him in the small town where he lived. I have a considerably younger wife, and she has taken over many of the burdens because I tire. It was Karen who did the hard work when the cat got sick in November and had to be taken down to the emergency hospital and visited. But I don't see myself on the verge of doddering. Harlan Ellison, whom I've known now for more than sixty years, had a stroke. I haven't seen him since the stroke. Though he sounds strong and confident and unbowed, I know that he can't move around very well. I don't lose sleep fearing this, but I wouldn't like it. Who would?

These points that Cowley is making are the points of a man who worries about different things. I worry about earthquakes. I live two blocks from the Hayward fault. I've had a house burn, and I worry about the destruction and the chaos that an earthquake would visit on me. I worry about burglars, about vandals. But not about becoming physically helpless. If I do become physically helpless—well, that's what the money is for. That's why we buy security.

Zinos-Amaro: I have one more Cowley-inspired question. He says in Chapter 4 that "every old person needs a work project if he wants to keep himself more alive. It should be big enough to demand his best efforts, yet not so big as to dishearten him and let him fall back into apathy." What accomplishes this for you?

Silverberg: My work project is cleaning up my office, getting everything in order so that when I want to find a given book, I can find it [chuckles]. I don't fall back into apathy when it doesn't work out well, but I'm never going to succeed at this; the input is too great, the daily rush of mail, and now email and whatnot. That's a very trivial goal, compared with somebody who wants to create a unified field theory. But I'm not interested in creating a unified field theory, and I probably wouldn't do it right anyway! I hope to clean up my office.

There are periods when it has been tidy. This sounds funny, but I'm serious.

Zinos-Amaro: When you say, "clean up my office," in point of fact that includes managing reprint requests, foreign rights requests, many things besides the physical tidying up. You're also continuing to write a monthly column, and you're editing an anthology at present.

Silverberg: Yeah. I do go to the office every day, and I'm over there for about an hour. If I'm writing a column, well, that's what I do; if I'm assembling an anthology, I do that. Otherwise I work on filing; I try to get the stuff off the floor and get it organized. I maintain contact with publishers by email. I have new editions of old things. I do interview questions. In fact, I'm now negotiating for another essay collection. This will be the non-*Asimov's* essays, going back a long period of time. I said to the representative of the publisher, "It'll be interesting to see whether I still agree with some of the things I said back then. If I don't, I'll do footnotes." So that's a kind of work. But it's not what I consider work, because I wrote *Thorns* in ten days— *that's* work.

It's the battle against entropy that I will never win, but I will never cease. That's my project, and it's been my project for a long time.

*

Zinos-Amaro: I'd like to continue today exploring the subjects of ageing and perspective, this time with a set of questions inspired by reading Penelope Lively's memoir *Dancing Fish and Ammonites*. Have you read it, by the way?

Silverberg: No. Karen has read a lot of Lively's work, but I haven't.

Zinos-Amaro: By way of context, I'll say that there's a few things you and Penelope Lively seem to have in common.

Silverberg: We're old?

Zinos-Amaro: Besides being old. She likes history and archaeology, and she has traveled broadly. And she's an avid gardener. Early in the book she says, "An addiction to gardening is genetic, I believe." That makes me wonder if your parents had any interest in gardening?

Silverberg: None at all. And I don't think there are addictions to gardening. I'm not sure that there are any genetically transmitted addictions at all, though of course exposure to addictive substances through the placenta could pass on an addiction.

Conan Doyle, whose biography I'm reading, was the son of an alcoholic, and he worried about whether he'd be an alcoholic. But he wasn't, and he drank heartily all his life, and he lived to the ripe old age of seventy.

My parents were apartment house dwellers, and though they knew that I, from an early age, was very interested in plants, they themselves were not, and could not have gardened. But I had potted plants.

Zinos-Amaro: How old were you?

Silverberg: Nine. My teacher in the fifth grade, Mrs. Truelsen, was very interested in botany and brought in dried leaves to show us, beautiful autumn leaves that she collected, and she got me quite interested. I would go to the local botanic garden. She was a ferocious old battle-axe, but a great teacher.

Zinos-Amaro: I'm not sure that I remember all my teachers. From the early ones in Spain I remember only some, but I do remember all my high school teachers from Germany.

Silverberg: That's terrible, Alvaro—it was merely twenty-five years ago! I remember all my teachers. I got a letter from one of my high school teachers about twenty years ago. He was, of course, long retired, but he had noticed that my adolescent interests in science fiction had actually stayed with me and become something.

Zinos-Amaro: Lively goes on to say: "Gardening defies time; your labor today is in the interests of tomorrow; you think in seasons to come, cutting down the border this autumn but with next spring in your mind's eye." Does gardening have that same effect on you?

Silverberg: Oh, absolutely. You garden for the future. You plant things in 1975 in the hope that they will still be here in 2010 and that you will be here to appreciate their full growth. I'm living in a garden that I began establishing essentially in 1973, so I've watched it for forty-two years, through a couple of freezes and droughts. There are things that I put in as tiny seedlings that are now huge trees. We had a big freeze here in December of '72 that wiped out much of the existing plantings. Some of them, I never even knew what they were. I'd been here for a short time and hadn't had time to learn them. Anyway, I replaced them.

Zinos-Amaro: The question of what "old" means—whether for plants or humans—is an interesting one. Lively references a UK survey that found that "most believe that old age starts at fifty-nine while youth ends at forty-one. People over eighty, on the other hand, believe sixty-eight to herald old age, while fifty-two is the end of youth." Where do you place the cut-off between youth and old age or middle age?

Silverberg: Old age for me is certainly eighty! That's a very *loud* number. I suppose I would peg the start of old age for me at seventy-five. When I was building the garden, and aware that it was going to become more work than I could handle, I would tell myself—I was perhaps fifty-five then—"I'll have to hire somebody to help me when I'm seventy-five." So I guess I defined that as the age beyond which I would no longer have the vigor of middle age.

Actually, I didn't seriously begin cutting back on my gardening until I was about seventy-eight. I had a heart attack at seventy-eight, and now I tend to avoid really strenuous stuff. Some of the climbing around the roof that I used to do I have to do when Karen's not looking, because otherwise she gets very queasy about it. I don't, of course, do anything that would endanger myself. I'm not that sort of person. But there's some things I just *can't* do any more. For example, my thumbs have developed some kind of arthritis. It's the only arthritic symptom I have. This doesn't affect my typing, because what do you do with your thumb? You hit the spacebar, and I can still do that. But it does affect using pruning shears. I need to be able to close my hand firmly and it hurts. So I've had to modify some of my pruning techniques because of the deterioration of the thumbs.

Zinos-Amaro: In this same scheme, where is the end of youth and the start of middle age?

Silverberg: Oh . . . thirty-six, Alvaro.

Zinos-Amaro: [chuckles] Can we make it thirty-seven please?

Silverberg: I never drew much of a distinction between youth and middle age. I suppose the fifties is the official start of middle age but I slid right along, living the way I lived: a fairly active, vigorous life. I was fifty when Karen came to live with me—a much younger woman, and she still is—and I didn't regard myself as her elderly husband, or even her middle-aged husband, just her husband. These are not important distinctions for me. The one distinction I will concede: eighty is old. I take precautions now that I wouldn't have taken even five years ago.

I get tired. We went to San Francisco for Christmas dinner. San Francisco is a city with hills, and after dinner we walked back from the restaurant to Karen's brother's apartment, and it was a steep uphill and I paused to catch my breath. I wanted and I needed to. I'm not big on denial. If I'm walking uphill, and short on breath, I stop. He waited for me; he's fifty-six.

Zinos-Amaro: This makes me think of something else Lively speculates about: "Perhaps there is some benign mechanism that aligns diminished capacity with diminished desire."

Silverberg: Well, that's called acceptance. Resignation. You accept reality. I accept the diminished capacity of age. It would be silly not to. I'm glad that it's not diminishing any faster than it *has*. I would rather not be using a walker now. Or a wheelchair. But it's the real thing. It happens at a constant rate from the age of eighteen on.

Zinos-Amaro: "You get used to it. And that surprises me. You get used to diminishment, to a body that is stalled, an impediment? Well, yes, you do. [. . .] Acceptance has set in, somehow, has crept up on you, which is just as well, because the alternative—perpetual rage and resentment—would not help matters. [. . .] you have to come to terms with a different incarnation."

Silverberg: "Diminishment?"—Does she say that?

Zinos-Amaro: Yes.

Silverberg: Remember what the poet said: "Rage, rage, against the dying of the light." I said a moment ago it happens at a constant rate from the age of eighteen on. You get used to it. It's not even a matter of getting used to it. You live with it. It's called life. I said yesterday, when we were talking about how my writing matured as the years went along, that that was called "growing up." The steady decline of the physical abilities is called "growing old." And you're doing that from the beginning on.

Zinos-Amaro: For a long time you don't really think of yourself as growing old, do you, though? When you're twenty, say, do you think of yourself as being old compared to nineteen?

Silverberg: That's too gradual. When you're forty you don't do some things that you might have done when you were eighteen. And you may perceive, as you plunge into the future at a rate of one second per second, that things have changed. I remember, when I was fifty-two or so, I was in New York with Karen visiting a friend, and I left something behind in a restaurant. We had walked back to his apartment before I remembered that I had left it. It was five or six blocks, some modest distance. And I ran the whole way, because the thing I had left behind I felt some anxiety about, and I didn't want to waste any time getting back there to look for it. I simply ran through the city streets of Manhattan, between five and eight blocks. I wouldn't dream of doing that now. I probably wouldn't have done it ten years ago. But I was fifty-two and I had no problem with it.

At the WorldCon that was held in Anaheim in 1984 a few of us actually went to Disneyland, which was close by the convention. There were buses to take us back to the convention afterwards. I was with Julius Schwartz, the grand, old-time comic book editor and literary agent before that. Julie said, "The bus is about to leave. Let's run." And so we ran, side by side, across the immense Disneyland parking lot, to the bus. In 1984 I was forty-nine years old, and we got to the bus and neither of us was out of breath. I looked at Julie and said, "How old are you?" I knew he'd been a big figure in the '30s. He was then sixty-nine and he had run right alongside me. I thought, "Good for you. I hope I'm like that when I'm your age." He was very vigorous right to the end. He died at eighty-eight, very suddenly. But I will not forget running with "that old man."

Zinos-Amaro: I think that one time by email you may have mentioned you started to notice a decline in your energy in your forties, whereas I guess some people feel that starting in their mid-thirties.

Silverberg: I'm ageing slowly. People are always amazed to find that I'm eighty. "You don't look eighty," they say. But I sure *feel* it. I've been aware of declining energy steadily. The process is gradual but continuous; only when you choose two fairly distant comparison points do you perceive just how extreme the decline has been. I don't think I'm particularly less vigorous than I was a year ago. But I probably am.

Zinos-Amaro: Lively talks about ageing in terms of different selves. For example, she says, "There is this interesting accretion—the varieties of ourselves—and the puzzling thing in old age is to find yourself out there as the culmination of all these, knowing that they are you, but that you are also now this someone else." Later she adds, "My attitude towards these earlier selves—varieties of myself—is peculiar, I find. It is kindly, indulgent—as though towards a younger relative, sometimes impatient (you idiot), occasionally grateful. I'm grateful for all that work done—a bunch of other people wrote my books, it can seem." Given how prolific you were, do you ever have that sense?

Silverberg: I'm certainly grateful that I wrote all those books, the income from which I'm still enjoying. And sometimes, in a rather ironic way, I'll think, "I'm glad he did all that work for me." But I regard myself as a continuum. I don't see myself as a group of separate selves.

I've certainly changed. I was, for example, at the age of six or seven, a very extroverted little boy, and then became a shy boy later on, as some of my extroversion got me in trouble with my classmates, and I learned to keep quiet. And the persona that I projected was quite different at six or seven and at ten or eleven. Later on I was younger than most of my classmates during adolescence, because I'd been rushed through school so fast. And when you get into adolescence, with all the complexities that that creates, and you are a year or a year and a half younger than the girls around you and you are not a girl, again certain attitudes control you; social attitudes. The difficulties that I had as a young heterosexual adolescent because the girls of my education level were older than I was, and the girls of my age were still children—well, I survived that too, and moved along. These different phases produce different responses to the world, and make you appear to be a somewhat different person. But I don't share Penelope Lively's view that I'm an accretion of different people. I'm the same guy.

Zinos-Amaro: You mentioned experiences that got you in trouble with your schoolmates when you were six or even. What were they?

Silverberg: I was a bright kid. I could read when I was three and a half and that got me skipped through a lot of things. But it made me something of a showoff. I would get impatient with a classmate who couldn't seem to understand something and I would help him—out loud!

Zinos-Amaro: In front of others.

Silverberg: Yes. Or I would talk with adults without any recognition of the fact that I was a small child. There are certain ways in which you're not supposed to do that. And of course we're talking about the vastly different culture of 1942 or thereabouts.

As I left the sheltered world of the progressive school that I was in, and was thrust, somewhat to my surprise and dismay, into a public school with young ruffians, the young ruffians were not in any way amused by my behavior.

Zinos-Amaro: When did that move happen?

Silverberg: 1943. I was suddenly put into the fourth grade in a public school. I'd barely been to school at all. I'd skipped the second grade and I'd skipped kindergarten. Luckily for me, I made a friend in that class: Saul Diskin. He came from that rough, working-class world that I knew nothing about, and he told me, "You can't behave that way." He didn't say it that way, because we were eight years old, but he said, "This isn't a good way to do things." And I learned from him where I was rubbing my classmates wrong. After all, I had no siblings, nobody to tell me anything. As a precocious child I was applauded for all my showing off. Well, I learned not to do it. But that made me very quiet. As for Saul, we remained friends right through life. He died last year. He remembered very vividly my entry into his class.

Curiously, a few months ago I tracked down a girl from that class, who had gone all through school with me. I had dated her briefly in high school, and then we lost touch right after we graduated from high school. I was curious about what had become of her; I liked her. Someone in my chat group did the Internet trace on her and found her. We had a correspondence. She's now eighty years old and a grandmother. I was afraid, when I wrote to her, that she would say, "Who is this guy?" After all, it was sixty-two years since we last had any contact! Or, since we had dated briefly and I had moved on to the girl who I eventually married, that she would say, "I don't want to hear from him." But she was delighted to hear from me. She said, "I remember you very well. You were one of the *nice* boys in the class. Most of them were very rough."

She had been rather timid and gentle and enjoyed my company. It was quite strange to get that parallax effect, after all this time. She clearly remembers what we were like at age ten and twelve and sixteen. I had often thought of her over the subsequent years because we did have a nice friendship, and then when I went to college she stayed in Brooklyn and it was just too difficult to maintain the relationship, and I began dating someone else. But what if I had married her? It would *not* have been a good idea. She has four children that she had almost immediately after getting married. And I was never inclined to be a reproducer. So there would have been impossible conflict right away. In fact, I traced her through her oldest son, who's a doctor in New Jersey. I said, "I think your mother was X, who I went to school with." And he said, "Yes, and this is her email address."

Zinos-Amaro: When you knew you guys were going to be separated because you were going to college, did you consider staying in touch through correspondence?

Silverberg: No, I never had any contact with her again. You know, you don't marry everybody you date in high school. And I went off to Columbia and I had a long subway ride to get to school. She was back there in our old neighborhood in Brooklyn. Logistically it was impossible. Then I moved up to Columbia in the second year and met Barbara. But I remembered her fondly and over quite a long period of time.

Zinos-Amaro: Did you ever wish you had a sibling?

Silverberg: I don't think so. I rather enjoyed being an only child, doing whatever I wanted to do without negotiating. It would have been very good to have an older brother to tell me what not to do, or an older sister to explain girls to me. But I didn't, and I got quite used to the idea of being an only child early on.

My experience of other people with siblings has been that it was not always the most wonderful thing. Karen has a splendid relationship with her brother, who is a fine fellow and lives in San Francisco, and they're close as can be. But I know people with sisters and brothers who just seem like useless baggage, and sometimes there's great hostility between them. I lived my life as an only child and I don't think I regretted it. As for being childless, that was a matter of choice, which being an only child was not. Occasionally, in late life, I have said and, and I may have even said it to you, "It would be nice to have someone to push around the wheelchair." But I'm not yet in the wheelchair.

Zinos-Amaro: There's a part of Lively's book where she hits on something similar to what Cowley was saying about dozing in the sun. "With those old consuming vigors now muted, something else comes into its own—an almost luxurious appreciation of the world you are still in . . . The small pleasures have bloomed into points of relish in the day—food, opening the newspaper, a shower, the comfort of bed." Is this the case for you?

Silverberg: In part. Opening the newspaper is never a pleasure for me—always a horror!

Zinos-Amaro: [laughs]

Silverberg: The times are out of joint. *The Times* itself is not out of joint, but the times are. My own local newspaper is politically so alien and remote that I'm offended by almost everything it writes about! I make sure to *get* the newspaper, though. The papers are delivered to the door at 6:15 am, when my neighbors are deep in unconsciousness, and I'm out there looking for my *Wall Street Journal*, in the dark and in the cold.

But there's certainly a great pleasure in taking a shower. I like to be clean, and it's relaxing. I don't think it has anything to do with age. I've taken a shower every day of my adult life. It's not a small pleasure that has bloomed into a point of relish—it's a constant.

Getting into bed, yes, I do welcome that. But I can't think of a time when I didn't.

I don't really agree with either Cowley or Lively with old age as a time for basking in the sun. When there's sun, I *do* bask in it, but it's not idle basking. I haven't turned into a lizard. I'm always conscious of the ticking of the clock. I don't waste my time. When you stepped away just now and came back into the room, you saw that I was reading something. Not sitting there, thinking, "Glorious old age, eventually he'll go away and I can take a nap!"

Zinos-Amaro: Right! Now, Lively does include food in her catalog, and I'm wondering if maybe that has become more of a daily highlight for you. Or are there restrictions in place?

Silverberg: I've tried, since the heart attack, to eat less red meat than I used to, but basically I eat whatever I please. The restrictions are those imposed upon me by my metabolism. I'm not a glutton, or a gourmand, in the strict sense of that word's meaning, and I'm not a heavy drinker. But I've always, since childhood really, regarded food with great interest. I remember in the progressive private school I went to, before I was thrust into the real world, we would have lunch every day and I would use condiments very freely, as I still do. I like highly seasoned food. I recall somebody at my table at the lunchroom saying to somebody else, "Robert puts too much salt on his food!" I was six years old.

When I left home to live at Columbia, and I had my choice of restaurants in Manhattan, I made a point of going to the ethnic restaurants all around Columbia and finding out what Vietnamese food was like. We had one Vietnamese restaurant back then, although the bulk of them came in after the war. I had Italian food besides spaghetti and meatballs, Japanese food, and so on. I was nineteen. There is a difference in age, though. The body doesn't process food as capably as it once did. I will sometimes, after a particularly robust meal, feel some discomfort in the night that I wouldn't have done at the age of fifty-five or so. That's life, is what they say.

Zinos-Amaro: Lively observes that our perception of the passage of time changes: ". . . time accelerates, it has broken into a gallop by the time you are old—a day then has nothing of the remembered pace of childhood days, which inched ahead, stood still at points, ambled from lunchtime to teatime. [. . .] What has happened to time, that it whisks away like this?"

Silverberg: Again, I don't agree. Of course time moves much more slowly when you're young: you haven't lived many days, and suddenly you're living another one, and it's adding a great percentage to what you've already lived. But now, especially when I don't devote three or four hours a day to writing, which was a very intense experience—I wrote in a kind of trance, and the time flew by—I devote those hours to other things, some of which are not very interesting, like book-keeping, and the day sometimes seems quite long to me.

Zinos-Amaro: By the way, it's kind of comforting to hear you disagree with some of these statements. Reading these books I was beginning to get a little worried about what's in store for me!

Silverberg: Well, you *don't* know what's in store for you. That's one of the unnerving things about being thirty-six. You have all that time ahead, full of question marks. I don't. I know what was in store for me; I've lived through it. But although I don't object to the length of the day, sometimes, particularly when we've chosen the restaurant for the night and I know where I'm going to be at seven thirty, but it's only four thirty, I think, "That's a long way to go before the *foie gras*."

Zinos-Amaro: So it's almost the opposite of what she's saying there: time isn't whisking away for you, it's moving slowly. It's drag-ging?

Silverberg: Well, it doesn't drag; my days are full. There's a lot to do. You see the stacks of books and magazines, my reading, in the liv-ing room here. And as I said yesterday, I'm constantly in combat with entropy, so there's always something to tidy up somewhere. I don't worry about where the time has gone. And I don't ever find myself wondering, "What am I going to do next?" for lack of things to do. It's mostly, "Which of these five things am I going to do next?" [chuckles] The day itself, though it doesn't drag, does seem quite extensive in its time, even as it did when I was a child.

Zinos-Amaro: Speaking of reading, she says: "I think that a writer's reading experience does not so much determine how they will write, as what they feel about writing; you do not want to write like the person you admire, even if you were capable of it—you want to do justice to the very activity, you want to give it your own best, whatever that may be. A standard has been set."

Silverberg: She's saying a bunch of different things in a bunch of different directions, and I'm not sure I follow it all. And of course I'm not a writer now, I'm a *former* writer. When I was an active writer I had to be careful in what I read when there was a project underway because some other writers' voices are too compelling. I didn't have to worry about reading Shakespeare because there was no risk that I would suddenly begin writing in iambic pentameter. But Faulkner, for example, was a writer I learned to avoid when I was working on something, because his voice is impossibly compelling to me, and I don't want to sound like Faulkner. I'm very happy that *Faulkner* sounds like Faulkner. And then of course you have to be careful not to read something that conforms in theme with what you're writing, so that it will bend your own next day's work.

Zinos-Amaro: When did you first notice this was a risk for you?

Silverberg: Right away. I'm sensitive to style and a good mimic. That's why I was able to write Asimov novels, a parallel story to C. L. Moore's "Vintage Season," a Zelazny story, and so on, though I prefer to write Silverberg when I'm allowed to. I always noticed the danger of trying to imitate. At the beginning I *wanted* to imitate because I was a beginner and I wanted to imitate the successful writers because I wanted to be successful. But after a point, when I had become Robert Silverberg, I just wanted to write like him and didn't want to be drawn into writing like somebody else.

There was one other interesting reading effect. I called it the Sunday night effect. I almost never have worked on weekends; only when there's some kind of emergency, otherwise Monday to Friday has been my working habit all through my career. I'd spend the weekend doing whatever I did on the weekend, but it didn't include sitting at the typewriter. Sunday night, the weekend is over, I'm relaxing, I'm reading something, and I found—this going back into the '50s and '60s—that I would be reading a science fiction story, and I'd think, "Ooh, that's easy to do. I can't wait to get to work tomorrow morning and get back to my story, because look, it's just one word after another, and there's nothing to it!" And though I wrote relatively easily and very prolifically, there was never a point at which it *wasn't* work. So I'd get to my desk Monday morning, remembering the Sunday night effect, and wondering where it went! Here I am, faced with the next sentence of whatever I'd left unfinished, and I have to pick it up and get it going and then *keep* it going for the next three and a half or four hours. It was all so much easier Sunday night . . .

Zinos-Amaro: What do you think of her statement about wanting to give it your best? To me that's almost more about character than a particular activity.

Silverberg: I can't see wanting to do anything badly. What's the point? You *will* do some things badly because you just aren't good enough.

Zinos-Amaro: But you'll still do your personal best.

Silverberg: Yeah. I wrote a lot of hackwork in the '50s and early '60s, and it was the very best hackwork I could do. It was the work of a craftsman. The fact that I was writing a story that I wouldn't myself want to read had nothing to do with it. I was manufacturing an object, and doing it with all the skill at my command. The publishers of this hackwork were aware of that and solicited my work. I had more work than I could possibly handle because I was one of the best hacks around. After a while I stopped doing that stuff because I had enough work that *wasn't* hackwork.

Zinos-Amaro: Have you ever coasted? Knowingly given less than you knew you were capable of?

Silverberg: No. You become a terrible hack if you do that. A *bad* hack. And if you're going to do hackwork, you don't want to do bad hackwork.

Zinos-Amaro: What about outside of writing?

Silverberg: No coasting. There are some things that I know if I did I would do badly, and I get somebody else to do them for me. We have a plumbing problem right now in my shower. I'm not going to try to fix it myself. I'm not a plumber and would make a mess of it. That has nothing to do with coasting, but it has to do with attempting something you know you would do badly. I have certain skills and then there are certain areas where I have no ability whatever.

In junior high school, what they now call middle school, I think, you were required to take shop courses, God knows why. We had one in electrical wiring and one in carpentry. This somehow was thought to be part of a liberal arts education. I was also being taught Latin, so it was a very odd mixture of things. Anyway, I was terrible in the shop courses. I do not have the skills of manual dexterity. I could not figure out electrical wiring. I can think my way through an instruction manual but I'm not comfortable doing it and can't do precision work. I haven't been raised from childhood as a mechanic; there are people with innate mechanical skills, they can do the wiring, and I'll do the novel-writing. I have *that* skill. Or I had it, anyway.

Zinos-Amaro: These comments make me think about learning, and how it may or may not change with age. Here are two contrasting views. The French composer Rameau said, "After sixty one cannot change. Experience points plainly enough the best course, but the mind refuses to obey."

On the other hand, at eighty Goya drew an ancient man propped on two sticks, with a mass of white hair and beard hiding his face, and inscribed it with the famous line, "I am still learning." How much is there of Rameau versus Goya in Silverberg at eighty?

Silverberg: Not much of either. Rameau was a great composer and probably said this without meaning it. If experience shows a great composer what the best course is, and he says, "No, I'm not going to do that," he's just being silly and cantankerous. Rameau worked at a time when the arts were ritually formularized and if it had suddenly occurred to Rameau in 1753 to write twelve-tone music he probably would have resisted, because had he not resisted that impulse he would have been locked up.

As for Goya, well, yes, maybe he *was* still learning at eighty, I don't know. Picasso went on painting until he was ninety-something, and his work changed; it became more hasty. That's an odd word to use for a man who was the fastest painter in the universe, but he didn't bother filling in the details at ninety-two. And this is very common among elderly artists. They stipulate, "Yes, that's there, but I'm not going to bother doing it, and you know I can do it." Goya, I forget what he was doing at eighty; I knew his work pretty well, but not in sequence. But if he felt he was still growing at eighty, more power to him.

Verdi, the classic example of genius in old age, wrote two op- eras in his eighties that were far beyond anything he had done in his prime. Masterpieces. *Otello* does sound a little bit like the rumpty- dump Verdi of *Il trovatore* or *Aida*, but *Falstaff* sounds like nothing but *Falstaff*; he was eighty-one.

Zinos-Amaro: Despite your claim, you continue to learn, par- ticularly in connection with technology. I've seen you learn how to use devices that weren't around just a few years ago.

Silverberg: Well, if you don't, you're obliterated! There's a lot, though, that in the Rameau fashion I resist. I have no idea how to use a cell phone, for example. I have no doubt that if I bought a cell phone, within half an hour I would understand at least the basics of how to turn it on and make a telephone call. It's not an inability on my part, it's a decision. It's a thing that I have not learned. I can't speak Aramaic either. There are some things I *can't* learn. How to play an organ, for example. I don't think I could do that even if I devoted all my heart and soul to it now. All right, well, we have Helmut Walcha to play organ for us, on twelve CDs.

I don't think that I'm continuing to learn very much. I continue to read. My memory has begun to get a little porous. Just yesterday I was reading the Conan Doyle biography and an individual was mentioned and I wondered, "Where did *he* come from?" I looked him up on the index and he came from the previous page! But this is where I'm in tune with Cowley and Lively: I don't ask of myself at eighty a lot of things that I might have asked of myself back then, because I don't see any point to it. I do try, when I set out to cross the street, to look in both directions—and to get to the other side. I do ask of myself that. This reminds me, I saw my mother at seventy-five or so drift into the street without looking anywhere.

Zinos-Amaro: Oh my.

Silverberg: Karen thinks she was suffering from the obliviousness that comes from being a complete narcissist; my mother was in the midst of telling me some story and so she wasn't really paying attention to the fact that she'd gotten out of the car and was wandering into the street. I think a narcissist should have enough self-interest to keep from getting run over. The truth is, she was getting old. It struck me as a dim-witted thing, but she did not actually enter any kind of dementia. She died at eighty-one. I never thought she had a keen mind.

Zinos-Amaro: It doesn't seem like you were close with your parents.

Silverberg: I wasn't.

Zinos-Amaro: What course did that relationship follow?

Silverberg: My father understood me pretty well, and was proud of what I was achieving and what I was going to achieve.

Zinos-Amaro: Did he read science fiction?

Silverberg: No. There were some books around the house, and he read the newspaper, but I can't recall his ever reading a book. He was an intelligent man who went on to get a professional degree when immigrants weren't doing that kind of thing, so he must have read some books at some point, but I never *saw* him reading a book.

Of course I only lived with him until I was sixteen or seventeen. We didn't discuss books. We discussed current events. He did buy me books constantly, and I still have many of them. He knew that I was something special and that I was going to be something special and he saw to it that I had the opportunities that were appropriate: museums, libraries, college. But he was a difficult, angry, embittered man, and not easy to get close to. And I didn't try, particularly.

Late in his life—he died at seventy-five—when I was living in the mansion and making a lot of money, well, of course it was easy for us to get along. There was no stress in the relationship. He did my tax return at that time and saw what I was earning. But in school, when I was fourteen or fifteen, and I thought it was more important for me to read the new issue of *Astounding* and study what was being published there, he wondered whether I was paying sufficient attention to my studies. He thought for a long time that science fiction was a great waste of time, until suddenly I began selling it all over the place at the age of nineteen.

Zinos-Amaro: Why do you think he was embittered and angry? Where did that come from?

Silverberg: He didn't like his work; he didn't like his wife very much; he didn't like his wife's relatives; didn't like a lot of the things that people around him did and said. He was quite an alienated character. He was born in London and moved to the States almost immediately because his parents were on their way here. So they were immigrants and that can't have been easy, even if they managed fairly well for immigrants. I can see where there might have been some embittering experiences there. Karen believes that he was in part alienated by his intelligence.

Zinos-Amaro: Have you traced your ancestors through this London line?

Silverberg: He was born in London just by accident. The family was on the way from Russia. They stopped in London just long enough for him to be born. I like to say that I'm the son of an Englishman, but in fact he's hardly even an immigrant; he was six months old when came to the United States.

My mother's grandfather was a rabbi, by the way. I never knew him. He was a rabbi in the non-congregational sense; he stayed home and studied the scriptures.

Zinos-Amaro: Did you know your father's parents?

Silverberg: My father's father died before I was born. I never knew even his first name until my mother unearthed a bunch of documents and sent them to me. One of them was my father's birth certificate, with his father's name. I knew my maternal grandparents very well.

Zinos-Amaro: Tell me more about your mom.

Silverberg: She was a schoolteacher, third grade. It was unusual to have two professional parents at that time. I would imagine she was a very good third-grade teacher; her students often wrote her letters many years later. But you spend a lot of time around eight-year-olds and you have some difficulties in adjusting to people who *aren't* eight.

Zinos-Amaro: You didn't feel particularly close to her.

Silverberg: Not particularly. I didn't feel hostile toward her; she was not difficult for me to get along with. My father, on the other hand, was a rather intimidating, menacing presence. Of course, I was a tremendously challenging child, a great pain in the neck.

Zinos-Amaro: When you started writing non-fiction books, did your mom appreciate, being a teacher, that you were also helping to educate others? Some of those books were meant for younger readers.

Silverberg: I don't think she stipulated anything about the non-fiction books. I never heard anything about their reading *anything* I wrote.

Zinos-Amaro: Really?

Silverberg: Nor did I solicit it. I was never certain even that Barbara read anything I wrote, except the books she made the indexes for. But I've not been one to solicit opinions. "Did you like it? Did you like it?"

Zinos-Amaro: I wanted to come back to your writing for a moment. I was looking for passages where characters are reconciling themselves to their age, and I hit on this one in *Dying Inside*: "I make lists now of the things I once could do that I can no longer. Inventories of the shrinkage. Like a dying man confined to his bed, paralyzed but observant, watching his relatives pilfer his goods. This day the television set has gone, and this day the Thackeray first editions [...] and tomorrow it will be the pots and pans, the Venetian blinds, my neckties."

Silverberg: I was thirty-seven years old when I wrote that. I don't remember that passage at all, but it's nice. Of course, the book is called *Dying Inside*, and it's about diminution—or diminishment, as Lively says—and loss. As for the relatives pilfering, do you know an opera called *Gianni Schicchi* by Puccini?

Zinos-Amaro: No.

Silverberg: Well you should, because it's very funny, and you'd love it. In *Gianni Schicchi*, the rich Florentine merchant Buoso Donati has died, and his avaricious relatives are gathering around to see what's in his will, and by damn he's left everything to the monks. Devastated by this, they bring in the shrewd operator Gianni Schicchi, who says, "Don't worry about that. I'll dictate a new will." He gets into bed wearing a shroud and they bring in a notary. Masquerading as the not-quite-yet-dead Buoso Donati, Gianni Schicchi dictates a new will in which he leaves everything to his daughter, who's the fiancée of Donati's son. The relatives are standing around and have all made little deals with him, like "I want the mill" or "I want the donkey." He starts thwarting them and in a very funny scene they are exclaiming in anguish as he gives away the property that they have been anticipating. But he reminds them that in Florence fraudulating a will is punished by the amputation of the right hand and they are all accessories, because they have brought him in to dictate this will. So as he lies there in the bed, engulfed in shrouds, every now and then as they begin saying "What are you doing?" he will lift his hand and dangle it to remind them!

I knew that opera at that point and I knew about the relatives closing in. When my mother died in 1992 we got out to New York a day or so later and I found that my cousin had gathered up some of my mother's jewelry and had already selected what she was going to take.

Zinos-Amaro: Interesting. What did the will say?

Silverberg: Oh, the will made me sole executor. And the jewelry was mainly destined for Karen. Anyway, I wrote that passage more than half my life ago, but it shows that I was aware at thirty-seven of the obvious fact that you run down and lose things.

Zinos-Amaro: Do you make lists often in your personal life? Do you have an affinity for lists?

Silverberg: No, no, I make lists because I have to remember everything I'm supposed to be doing!

The lists in my fiction were there for matters of prose rhythm, as I mentioned in our first conversation.

Zinos-Amaro: Speaking of effects, I was reading an old interview with you where somebody asked which of your books you'd enjoy seeing turned into a film, and you said *Son of Man*!

Silverberg: [laughs] *Son of Man* would be one long special effect.

Zinos-Amaro: Has there ever been any interest in filming that book?

Silverberg: I don't think so. Practically everything I've written has been optioned at one time or another, but I don't think anyone's ever come around to that one. I just got a deal three days ago from people who want to make a miniseries out of *Born with the Dead*. All right, make a miniseries out of it. I don't understand how you would do it, but mine not to reason why.

Anyway, it won't happen, because none of these things ever happen, except occasionally some option money. The one that I think *would* make a terrific movie is *The Book of Skulls*. Many people have thought it would make a terrific movie: the option never got a chance to expire, because whenever it did someone else would jump in and pick it up. What happened there, unfortunately, is that the last man in the chain actually bought the rights and took them over to Twentieth Century Fox, I think. Fox said, "Yes, we will do the movie, and William Friedkin will direct it, and this and that and the other thing." Then everybody got fired, the movie never happened, and the rights remain with the guy who bought them, who occasionally makes some feeble attempt at negotiating a deal. The problem is that he wants his own screenplay to be attached to it, and that appears to discourage others. So there probably won't ever be a movie of *Book of Skulls*, but it's a filmable road movie.

Zinos-Amaro: Did you watch the recent miniseries adaptation of *Childhood's End?*

Silverberg: No. I almost never watch television and most science fiction movies make me uncomfortable. The only science fiction movie I've seen in perhaps the last five or ten years is *The Martian*, and that's barely science fiction; it's almost a documentary.

Zinos-Amaro: I remember you watched *Wall-E*. You liked it, didn't you?

Silverberg: Yes, but that's a cartoon.

Zinos-Amaro: It *is* science fiction.

Silverberg: Yeah, it is.

*

Zinos-Amaro: I wanted to conclude our conversations by asking you about some specific literary influences on your work. In connection with *A Time of Changes*, for example, you've mentioned Ayn Rand's *Anthem*.

Silverberg: Yes, *Anthem*. It's a minor work of hers. I've never read *The Fountainhead*, you know.

Zinos-Amaro: You've mentioned Henry Kuttner in relation to the "The Iron Chancellor."

Silverberg: Well, Henry Kuttner in relation to everything. We were talking yesterday about openings, and we looked at Graham Greene and Hemingway. Kuttner is the man I learned how to open a story from. Just about every story I've written has Kuttner underneath it somewhere; a sense of a chasm opening. You describe a situation, and somewhere in that paragraph there's that chasm, at least hinted at. That I learned from Kuttner—now a forgotten writer—and it's seemed to work.

Zinos-Amaro: You've mentioned Jack Vance in connection with "World of a Thousand Colors."

Silverberg: A very early story of mine. Vance is also connected with *Lord Valentine's Castle*; Vance's sense of color, his use of adjectives and his use of textures.

Zinos-Amaro: Jorge Luis Borges' "The Babylon Lottery" was an inspiration for your story "To See the Invisible Man."

Silverberg: Yes. Borges' character says it explicitly: "I was declared invisible for one year." I thought, "That's a good story, why didn't he write it?" But that's not what I would call a technical influence; more of a free-floating idea I grabbed and ran with.

Zinos-Amaro: Marcel Aymé's "Crossing Paris" and your "The Road to Nightfall."

Silverberg: Yes, Aymé, another forgotten writer. It's a novella that

266   Alvaro Zinos-Amaro

I read in college that involves wartime Paris and smuggling, I think, a bit of pig to a butcher across Paris; black market meat during the German occupation. When you begin the story it appears as though what they're doing is transporting a body. It's actually a comic story, but it begins very darkly. I read the Aymé around the time that I was beginning to conceive "The Road to Nightfall" and I thought, "What if it isn't pork? What if we're transporting, through an even darker place, an even darker meat product?" And that was where that story started. They made a very good movie of Ayme's story: *La Traversée de Paris*, with Jean Gabin.

Zinos-Amaro: Robert Coover's *The Babysitter* as an influence on "Many Mansions."

Silverberg: *The Babysitter* is a series of flash vignettes, a paragraph or two, depicting a situation I no longer remember, from a million different viewpoints. I thought, "I could tell a time travel story that way, because as you keep meddling with the past everything changes. Here's a different viewpoint in each situation." So I wrote "Many Mansions." It's a matter of the imitation of a specific structure. With Kuttner, and also Phil Dick and Sheckley, I learned ways of constructing stories that I generalized from and maintained throughout my career. *The Babysitter* is not so much an influence as a direct imitation.

Zinos-Amaro: I had noted Sheckley's name in connection with your story "The Silent Colony."

Silverberg: Yes. That was one of many. Sheckley and Dick descend from Kuttner. And all of three of them were very prolific writers, and very adept at constructing short stories.

Zinos-Amaro: When you say "descend from," was there an acknowledged influence that they talked about, or is it a literary genealogy that you're tracing?

Silverberg: I have no doubt that both Phil and Bob read a lot of Kuttner. It's inconceivable to me that they didn't. Whether I actually said, "Hey, did you set out to imitate Kuttner?" I don't remember. These guys have been dead for decades. But just as you can draw a thematic line from Joseph Conrad to Graham Greene to John le Carré, you've got Kuttner and then the three of us—who are roughly contemporary, however strange that seems now—as disciples of Kuttner.

Zinos-Amaro: Who are the disciples of you three? What's the next generation in that line?

Silverberg: Oh, I don't know. I hope somebody's been watching what we did because I thought it was pretty good.

Zinos-Amaro: Ian McDonald may be part of that next generation.

Silverberg: McDonald did do a version of "Born with the Dead," a brilliant reworking of it called *Necroville*. He certainly had my novella in mind; I did talk to him about that. There are also the writers who contributed homage stories to *The Book of Silverberg*. But let's get back to Kuttner and Dick and Sheckley.

Both Dick and Sheckley were well-established writers when I began my career. But it was only two or three years later. Sheckley began selling in '52; Dick also began selling in '52; I began in '55. They were both eight years older than me. Sheckley had been in the Army and in war; they'd lived different lives. But so far as our career history goes, we're virtually contemporaries. It's strange for me to think of it that way because I was looking at Sheckley as a god-like figure, but in fact he'd only been writing for three years when I began selling stories. And so though I think of them as ahead of me, they weren't by much. Then I got to know them, and observed them living through poverty and squalor; they each married five times; Dick died young. I admired their achievement at the beginning, but I certainly didn't want to have lived their lives.

Zinos-Amaro: Was there a specific technical influence of Dick in your short stories, or more Sheckley?

Silverberg: Both. And again, I think it all derived from Lewis Padgett, i.e. Kuttner: the way they would establish conflict right at the beginning. Sheckley was the more comic writer, and I have never been a particularly comic writer, though I can do it. Dick provided that chasm and then dropped you *deep* into it. I would read everything they wrote, the three of them. And I would internalize it. This is a different kind of influence from taking a sentence out of Borges or taking a method of assembling one particular story from Robert Coover. This was a profound, internal sense of what is a story, which I followed all through my life.

Zinos-Amaro: I know that "Call Me Titan" was a tribute to Roger Zelazny, but did his work ever influence yours in more general terms?

Silverberg: No. Zelazny was after me. That would have been a retroactive influence. "Call Me Titan" was written for a memorial volume. I was working in his tone.

Zinos-Amaro: We've talked about Faulkner. *As I Lay Dying* is connected to "The Songs of Summer."

Silverberg: Yes. However, "The Songs of Summer" is the work of a twenty or twenty-one year old writer, and *As I Lay Dying* is a masterpiece of world literature! But I did at least adapt his method.

Zinos-Amaro: Did you adapt other Faulkner techniques in other stories?

Silverberg: I tried not to. Faulkner is too individual; the great genius of American fiction. I didn't want to write like him. Also, I didn't have his material. Faulkner is a deep Southern writer. Start translating Faulkner into New York Jewish and it doesn't work well.

Zinos-Amaro: You've mentioned Faulkner and Greene as being significant for you. Are there any specific works of yours that tie back to something by Greene?

Silverberg: That connection is probably there, but nothing comes to mind. The works of my later period, like *Tom O'Bedlam*, *Hot Sky at Midnight*, the various Majipoor books; I couldn't assign any influence to them. By then the chief influence on me is me.

Zinos-Amaro: Now that you mention it, I think you quoted Graham Greene in *Kingdoms of the Wall*.

Silverberg: That may well be. I certainly read him with great admiration.

Zinos-Amaro: There is of course the well-documented connection between Conrad's *The Secret Sharer* and your own "Secret Sharer," as well as between his *Heart of Darkness* and your *Downward to the Earth*.

Silverberg: I had a funny *Downward to the Earth* experience about forty years ago. The Modern Languages Association was having its annual meeting in San Francisco and for some reason I went over there, perhaps to meet a friend. I walked into a seminar on me! They were discussing *Downward to the Earth*, and the academic looked up and said, "You know, it's not usual to have the writer present."

Zinos-Amaro: It certainly isn't!

In another interview you mentioned a period of great interest in the work of Donald Barthelme. I haven't heard you talk about him very much.

Silverberg: Well, I don't think about him very much. [chuckles] During the late '60s and early '70s, which was a time of great irreverence in our culture—the Vonnegut period, let's say—Barthelme was writing short stories that were made up of found materials and patches of this and that. I used those techniques; he gave me permission to do it. I would read his stories and think, "That's an interesting way to tell a story!" So I did some stories that reflected that kind of non-linear approach, whereas most of what I did before and after was extremely linear; the well-made story, with beginning, middle and end, and the Kuttner structure. But for a while there, in the early '70s, I would play around in the Barthelme lab.

Zinos-Amaro: The last writer I wanted to bring up was Anthony Burgess.

Silverberg: That's an interesting case, because about three days ago, someone on my chat group dug up Burgess reviewing *me*! In his collection *Selected Journalism* there's a piece on science fiction called "The Boredom of SF," in which he praises *Capricorn Games* and even quotes some of my prose.

Zinos-Amaro: That's pretty astonishing.

Silverberg: Gollancz had published a new edition of my book, along with a lot of other stuff, and mine was 30p more than the others. Burgess wanted to know why my book was more expensive, and he concluded that it was better written. [laughs]

Zinos-Amaro: [laughs] He was *not* a science fiction fan.

Silverberg: No. He hated the stuff. But he wrote some.

Zinos-Amaro: What is your history with his work?

Silverberg: I read most of his novels. He was a prolific writer. One of my favorites is a novel about Shakespeare called *Nothing Like the Sun.* Of course, there's *A Clockwork Orange*, which is somewhat repellent, but brilliant. There was a spy novel called *Tremor of Intent: An Eschatological Spy Novel*, shorter and less complex than le Carré, but very pleasing. There were five or six of his novels that impressed me with their prose and their narrative technique. *Nothing Like the Sun* is a stream-of-consciousness novel that probably was very unsuccessful commercially, but makes for exciting reading if you can get on the wavelength that he's projecting.

Zinos-Amaro: Do you think some of those works may have influenced you own?

Silverberg: I don't doubt it. There was a particular gloss to his prose that I looked at with admiration and some envy, in the spy novel in particular. And some of the stream-of-consciousness effect from *Nothing Like the Sun* crept into *The World Inside.*

Zinos-Amaro: Who are we missing in this overview?

Silverberg: Those are the right people. Though you haven't mentioned Homer.

Zinos-Amaro: [laughs] I suppose that's true. I also didn't bring up Sophocles' *Philoctetes* in connection with your novel *The Man in the Maze.*

Silverberg: Yes. But I wouldn't call it an influence when I simply borrow a plot from another writer.

Zinos-Amaro: That's a form of influence.

Silverberg: It's theft!

Zinos-Amaro: Fair enough! In this discussion on your work we've talked about your hackwork but also your more artistic work. You wrote about the process of your maturation as a writer in "The Making of a Science Fiction Writer," but I wonder if you can say anything more about how you went from a skilled hack to essentially an artist?

Silverberg: I was an artist first and deviated into hackery when I needed to make a living at it, because the artist that I was at eighteen and nineteen was competing with Sturgeon, Bradbury, Vance, Leiber, and that was tough, so I wrote what I could sell instead. And then later I went back to doing what I *really* wanted to do, which was to write good science fiction.

I don't think the writer who starts as a hack ever becomes anything more than a hack. I can't think of any examples of that. If you're writing thick-witted, crude action stories, and you're writing that because that's what you want to write and that's who you are and what you like, you'll continue writing that. You may not know you're a hack, and then you're certainly going to remain one.

There's a difference between a hack and a bad writer, though. Some writers become frustrated because they feel that their art isn't being recognized. They simply lack whatever magic it is that makes a good writer. The hack is somebody who deliberately limits his or her skills. There are many writers, poor bastards, who are doing the best they can, and it just isn't very good. Those aren't hacks. A hack is a craftsman who shapes his product to the demands of the market, and who scales down any abilities he may have that might *exceed* the demands of the market. You don't give the reader of Jacqueline Susann a Faulkner novel, because the odds are she won't understand it. Grace Metalious, who wrote *Peyton Place*, wasn't a hack; she was a woman of passionate intensity who told a story that meant a lot to her, and it meant a lot to twenty million other women. If you manage to write *Valley of the Dolls* or *Peyton Place* or, for a more recent example, *Fifty Shades of Grey*, you will reach a large audience that shares your sensibility. I don't have a large audience that shares my sensibility.

But I had enough of one.

AFTERWORD
Travels with Bob
by Karen Haber

Traveling with Bob is like having one's own portable database for a companion. Imagine Google with a goatee, a glass of Bordeaux in one hand and a fork in the other.

At times it can be more like vacationing with one's own investigative news team: within the first five minutes of arriving in, say, Guadalajara, he's taken in the air temperature, made a quick survey of the flora and fauna on the hotel grounds, speculated on the ground-speed velocity of an unladen peacock, scanned the hotel restaurant menu for *tortas ahogadas*, and mentioned in passing that the name Guadalajara, bestowed by the invading Spaniards, has Arabic roots, *Wadi Al Hajara*, meaning "river of stones." Enlightening, yes. Tiring, occasionally.

His travel prep is arduous, involving months of research, cross-referencing resources and friends' recommendations. In the time before computers, newspaper clippings and photocopies from guidebooks were sorted into heaps for each proposed trip. Now the computer holds the virtual heaps. Hard copy is still used, however. For every trip—and we make two big ones a year—a day chart is assembled, including museums, restaurants, and other activities. (This will go into the archives, post-trip.)

Did I mention how useful it is to have a traveling companion conversant in Latin and its later derivatives? (Italian, French, Spanish and in a pinch, Portuguese. He can even tease out bits of Catalan and Romanian.) His eidetic memory also comes in handy, especially in the realm of navigation. Within two days of arrival in a city, he generally knows his way around, whereas I've lived near San Francisco for thirty years and still have to use a map.

Bob's classical education and love of history don't hurt either. As we make our way through the great museums of the world, how wonderful to receive a tidbit from one's spouse about the burial habits of Etruscans or the non-naturalistic art of the Byzantines.

At the Hermitage museum in St. Petersburg, standing before a gilded display case holding Catherine The Great's cameo collection, he explained how the Cyrillic alphabet got its name—from Saint Cyril, a missionary from Byzantium.

The Early Cyrillic script was based on the Greek script with extra letters from the Glagolitic and Old Church Slavonic scripts for sounds not used in Greek. (Back at the hotel, over lunch, we debated the meaning of various Cyrillic neon signs in the plaza.)

In a coin room at the British Museum, studying a denarius from 44 BC showing Julius Caesar, Bob observed that the pleasure of antique coins is the opportunity to hold an actual piece of the ancient world in one's hand. He then went on to discuss how Augustus subverted the Roman Republic until he was emperor in all but name, and the republic became an empire.

Writers are fact packrats by nature. We like to pop info into mental pockets for pondering, amusement, or later use. Here are a few facts we've collected along our way. I know that Bob has made use of at least one of them in a story and/or novel.

—Dwarf elephants, no bigger than Great Danes, inhabited part of Sicily during the Neolithic. We saw their bones. (By the way, closer to home, the oxymoronic Pygmy Mammoths, unrelated, occupied the Channel Islands off California at the end of the Pleistocene.)

—A tri-clops inhabited a mosaic in a royal Roman villa in Piazza Amorina, a remarkable ancient villa in an unremarkable modern Sicilian town. If the imperial Romans saw how far their former colo-

nies had fallen, how disappointed they would be. (Hmm. And what
if they never fell? See Bob's *Roma Eterna* for more . . . .)

—Along the Upper Nile in southern Egypt near Aswan, Nu-
bians once believed in Sobek, the alligator god whose sweat filled the
Nile, and Khnum, the ram-headed god. Very amusing to see grinning
crocodiles in full hieroglyphic regalia standing in crook-armed relief
next to Anubis, Hathor, and the other Ancient Egyptian all-stars.
Some of these upright crocs made their way into *At Winter's End*.
Nowadays, the crocodiles get a lot less reverence from the Egyptians.
As for the khnums, we watched a flock of them herded across traffic
from the backseat of our taxi in Cairo. And I must admit that I prefer
that to a mess of crocodiles in the crosswalk outside the Nile Hilton.
Meanwhile, in Cairo, a city of 17 million people, families live in mau-
soleums in the cemeteries and their children skip happily around the
headstones.

It helps, when traveling, to combine endurance with curiosity.
While traveling through Sicily with our friends Saul and Arline Diskin, driving a splendid Alfa Romeo sedan, we stopped to visit the Roman ruins in Selinunte, site of a vast, ruined Acropolis. We admired
the remains of ancient temples and mosaics, and one splendid reconstructed temple that looks down upon romantic ruins backlit against
the Mediterranean. Then Bob took a hike there between temples—
through a field reputedly full of snakes, some poisonous. He lived to
tell the tale—maybe more than once.

Among his feats of endurance one must add eating. Bob is in-
defatigable. Have we just landed in Paris or London at dawn after a
long transatlantic flight and our hotel room is not ready? No problem!
Drop the bags and find a restaurant, preferably one that serves steak
tartare and onion soup, or, even better, blood sausage or kedgeree.
Bring on those curried haddocks, onions, and eggs. (Even now, the
thought of them makes me long for an aspirin and a dark quiet place
to weep.) Once, however, in Madrid, in a restaurant near the city hall
plaza, former site of many an auto-da-fe, I surprised Bob by order-
ing steamed barnacles—"devils' hooves" in the local parlance. These

turned out to be sinister-looking crustaceans with a sweet, mild flavor similar to steamed clams. Bob refused to try them. I made a note for him to check with his doctor.

One doesn't always have to travel far to locate a useful exotic fact: one night when we went out to dinner at a Cambodian restaurant in our hometown of Oakland, we were charmed by the exotic names of the dishes. These subsequently made an appearance as character names in *At Winter's End.*

So, yes, traveling with Bob is like having one's own private, grouchy wide-ranging database. Although he has grudgingly accepted the presence of backup information on my cellphone, I know whose version of data he prefers.

And when we're at home? Well, it's a lot like living with one's own private, grouchy investigative news team minus the kedgeree. At 6:45 sharp—except on Sundays, when I sleep in—Bob awakens me to deliver information he's gathered in the gap between his awakening at 5:30 and mine: air temperature, overnight disasters, reports on our three cats, speculations on possible dining options for the evening, and much, much more, until I make him stop. Life at home includes other certainties such as writing and taxes. We both work very hard to respect and protect one another's writing time. The only exception to this rule comes in March, when it's all hands on deck for tax time, followed by April, with its celebratory drinking and sobbing.

Thirty years of staying home and writing, mercifully interrupted by opera and other fine arts, the aforementioned epicurean pleasures, traveling, friends, and family. Exhilarating, yes. Tiring, occasionally. But the good kind of tired.

Karen Haber
Oakland, CA
March 2016

ABOUT ROBERT SILVERBERG

Robert Silverberg, widely known for his science fiction and fantasy stories, has been a professional writer since 1955. He is a many-time winner of the Hugo and Nebula awards, was named to the Science Fiction Hall of Fame in 1999, and in 2004 was designated as a Grand Master by the Science Fiction Writers of America. His books and stories have been translated into forty languages. Among his best known titles are *Nightwings*, *Dying Inside*, *The Book of Skulls*, and *Lord Valentine's Castle*. His collected short stories, covering nearly sixty years of work, have been published in nine volumes by Subterranean Press.

He and his wife Karen and an assorted population of cats live in the San Francisco Bay Area in a sprawling house surrounded by exotic plants.

ABOUT ALVARO ZINOS-AMARO

Alvaro grew up in Europe, mostly, and despite the advice of his betters earned a BS in Theoretical Physics at the Universidad Autonoma de Madrid (UAM). He is co-author, with Robert Silverberg, of *When the Blue Shift Comes*, and *Traveler of Worlds: Conversations with Robert Silverberg*. Alvaro's stories and poems have appeared in markets like *Analog*, *Apex*, *Galaxy's Edge*, *Nature*, *The Year's Best Science Fiction and Fantasy 2016* and anthologies such as *The Mammoth Book of the Adventures of Moriarty*, *The Mammoth Book of Jack the Ripper Stories* and *This Way to the End Times*. His essays, reviews and interviews have appeared in venues like *Asimov's*, *Clarkesworld*, *Strange Horizons* and *The Los Angeles Review of Books*.

OTHER TITLES FROM FAIRWOOD PRESS

Joel-Brock the Brave & the Valorous Smalls
by Michael Bishop
trade paper & ltd hardcover: $16.99/$35
ISBN: 978-1-933846-53-8
ISBN: 978-1-933846-59-0

Amaryllis
by Carrie Vaughn
trade paper: $17.99
ISBN: 978-1-933846-62-0

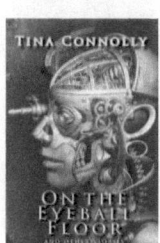

On the Eyeball Floor
by Tina Connolly
trade paper: $17.99
ISBN: 978-1-933846-56-9

Seven Wonders of a Once and Future World
by Caroline M. Yoachim
trade paper: $17.99
ISBN: 978-1-933846-55-2

The Ultra Big Sleep
by Patrick Swenson
hard cover / trade: $27.99 / 17.99
ISBN: 978-1-933846-60-6
ISBN: 978-1-933846-61-3

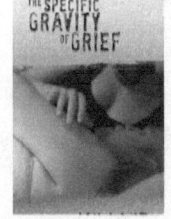

The Specific Gravity of Grief
by Jay Lake
small paperback: $8.99
ISBN: 978-1-933846-57-6

Cracking the Sky
by Brenda Cooper
trade paper: $17.99
ISBN: 978-1-933846-50-7

The Child Goddess
by Louise Marley
trade paper: $16.99
ISBN: 978-1-933846-52-1

www.fairwoodpress.com
21528 104th Street Court East;
Bonney Lake, WA   98391